# NIGHT

13 NEW TALES OF TERROR FROM THE AUTHOR OF DAY

## PATRICK KITSON

# CONTENTS

*In loving memory of*
Tim Darnley Sr.

*"I know writers who use subtext
and they're all cowards!"*

-Garth Merenghi

# KUDZU

Steven winces as the slow-moving automobile's headlight beams cast their yellowed glow into his eyes. Fifteen past eleven and this was the first customer since, well, whenever he started his shift, at least. Couple hours, maybe. Still, he adjusts the collar of his tacky orange polo shirt with the dopey green UFO logo as the black car comes to a stop outside his booth and the occupant gets out.

Whoever they are, they're covered top to bottom in a bright yellow rain slicker. Smart, what with the downpour as it is. Steven had been listening to the beating of raindrops on the corrugated metal roof of the small gas station for several hours now.

Tick, tick, tick on the rusty metal. It never seems to stop.

In his hometown of Mountain City, Georgia, the rain never seems to relent but for the odd fortuitous single day out of each week, when the clouds crack and light bolts blast the soaked land, briefly offering hot relief from the water-mire and gray skies overhead. Blue fills the sky and the birds sing, giving it just enough time—a day, maybe—for the soil to become dry to the touch before the clouds reseal and resume dropping buckets for days on end.

It's that time of year, and the entirety of the population—all 247 of them—have learned to live with it.

The invasive kudzu vines love the rain, wrapping their choking tendrils around anything they can: trees, power lines, old brick buildings, forgotten factories,dilapidated barns with peeling red paint, and condemned homes with rotting wood fences. The rains fuel the growth of the foreign flora in its race to consume the whole of the Georgia seaboard from nearby Clayton in the north all the way down to Saint George, just over the line.

It's not just Georgia, though. No siree-Bob. The brilliant idea during the Dust Bowl to use the subtropical Asian species to hinder soil erosion had not only not-particularly-worked, but had blossomed into a full-blown ecological disaster spanning over seven million acres of land between New York state and the Carolinas by the end of the century. Steven wrote a paper about it during his freshman year for *Intro to Bio 107*. Para-plagiarized most of it, but got an A, so all's well.

Lotta good the four-year degree from the nearby community college is doing for him now, working at the extraterrestrial-themed, unimaginatively-named *Saucer Stop*. Changing coffee pots for semi-conscious long-haul truckers and peddling windshield washer fluid to the sexy soccer moms of America in their tight little leggings.

This tall-ish figure walking up to the front entrance is surely no saucy soccer mom trying to sell her well-defined ass as gold, though. No. Too rigid in the walk. Not a loose-goose, shaking the ol' caboose strut, but rather a stuck-duck, stick-in-the-butt kinda thing.

*Bad back, maybe. Who knows.*

The bell above the door clangs as the rain slicker shuffles into the room. Rain boots squish on the linoleum as the figure walks up to the counter.

Steven runs his fingers over his thirty-two year old head, shooing the full side of hair on his left over to the not-so-full side. He watches as the rain slicker rolls its hood back and reveals a woman in her—

*Oh, shit.*

*Holy hopping shit! That's, um, what was it? Teresa, isn't it? Of course. No one else has that look of...*

*Oh, goddamn everloving Jesus, she's standing right goddamn here! Christ, does she—*

The woman with blonde hair and a narrow, almost gaunt face nods at Steven, but doesn't meet his gaze. He watches her eyes and, to his relief, realizes she's giving no hint of recognition.

She rifles through her coat pocket and hands him a fifty dollar bill. Her voice is low and hollow when she murmurs, "Fifty on one, I guess."

Steven turns and drops the bill into the till, then returns his gaze to her. "Need a receipt?" he asks in an equally hushed manner.

"No. I'm good."

"Cool."

"You know how much farther it is to Clayton from here?" she asks.

He eyes her suspiciously. In the bad, flickering lighting of the Saucer Stop her skin has an almost jaundiced hue to it.

"Not from around here?" he asks.

"Not anymore."

"Ah. Well it's, uh, just five more minutes south of here. On the same road you rolled in on."

"Thank you." She moves to leave, and as she does he notices that her hair also looks oddly aged.

*Is it just a trick of the light?*

She doesn't look back as she exits.

*Whatever, just as long as she's leaving. She didn't seem to recognize me. Then again, how would she? She never saw me sell her man those pills.*

*Deacon—that was his name. Regular townie D-bag. I didn't know they were cut with DXM. Bad batch, but what can you do? He was the real dope for not testing them, anyway. Another one of those party life tragedies.*

His supplier had apologized with a free half-boat of straight pills and that cleared up most of his clientele problems. So all's well.

*Thought she was flamed out too, but here she is topping up, so that's good, right? And she didn't recognize me. Thank God.*

Steven watches as Teresa stands by the car and opens the hatch to the gas tank, then starts filling up. She's void of expression.

Tick, tick, tick on the metal roof.

Not thirty seconds pass before another vehicle comes up the road and pulls in front of the Saucer Stop. A black, extended-cab truck with a silver rollbar and a massive deer-catcher grill.

An equally burly, hulking-shouldered young man in a maroon football jersey stumbles from the truck and drops to his knees. His red hair is wet and his blue jeans are filthy with fresh mud. He raises himself up using the door handle for balance. Steven laughs in spite of himself.

*Oddly busy for this time of night. And now I've gotta have one of*

*those awkward convos about calling a cab to ease my conscience in case
this dumbbell-dropping dickhead runs off the road two miles down and
the staties come a-hummin' for info 'bout it later. Best to offer the guy
some coffee.*

Steven watches as the football player walks to the back of the
truck and lifts up a bluish tarp, revealing a small red cooler. He
lifts the lid, pulls a fresh beer from it, and saunters toward the
Saucer Stop doors as he pops the top and takes a sip.

Teresa is still pumping gas, seeming completely oblivious to
the man in red.

*Great, still capping 'em back. I'll definitely have to offer him coffee
and hope he doesn't do a faceplant into a phone pole. Note the time, just
in case. What time is it anyway?*

His eyes move over to the clock, but his attention is tem-
porarily drawn toward the window to his left, just next to the
register. As he peers through the foggy old glass, he sees a crack
of lightning light up the grove of trees nearby. It looks like they
are almost writhing in the brief flash.

He squints and swears he can see the shadows of the vines
moving in the faint light of the neon signage out front. They look
like snakes in the dark, moving silently over each other. Outlines
of squiggles in the dim glow.

*Jesus, maybe I'm the one who needs the coffee. Eyes must be playing
tricks. What the actual fu—*

The chipped gold bell above the door chirps and the wet
linebacker moves through the store to the back, near the coolers.
Steven eyeballs him, but sits down on the stool behind the counter
and grabs a magazine from the stand beside him. He makes a show
of scanning through it while focusing on the footballer. The guy
is just standing, doing nothing in front of the beer cooler.

*Is he gonna try and swipe some wine coolers and jet? Wish I could just tell him that I'd gladly let him. Not like I could catch him anyway, but who actually cares? Not a hill I'm gonna die on. No siree, Bob.*

The young man is still standing, seemingly frozen in front of the booze case, when the woman out front puts away the pump handle and gets into her car. Just before she steps into the ride, she looks directly at Steven and gives him the coldest stare he's ever felt.

His spine shudders as his stomach hits the floor.

*She recognized me. I knew she had to. She was just hiding it before, but that look… Holy shit, that look was enough to send your blood running back up your veins like cockroaches scattering from the light.*

Her head disappears behind the car door and she kicks on the headlights. Just before she blasts off down the road, the headlights cast their gleam onto the nearby forest. Steven notes that it's now definitely moving around out there, like dark, wet interlacing fingers. Bigger than vines or snakes.

*Why does it look like that?*

Yet another set of lights come down the road toward the gas pumps.

*Another one? This is clearly the place to be tonight. It's never this busy.*

He's trying to recall the last time it was when the guy in the red jersey pulls open the cooler and yanks a bottle of wine from the second shelf. The quarterback tips back his head and slurps the rest of the beer down in three seconds, then belches forth a guttural boom of the paint-peeling variety.

Yuck.

Any humor Steven may have found in that is washed away instantly as the man turns and he is hit with a deeply sickening feeling of the worst kind of deja vu.

*It's Dave. It's fucking Dave! It can't be, but it fucking is.*

Dave tosses the empty can across the room toward a trash receptacle in the corner. It hits the wall and drops into the bin. The young man raises one fist in triumph. "He shoots, he scores! Putting three up on the board!"

*How can Dave be here? That's not possible.*

The last time Steven saw Dave was at the kegger up near Three Flows Lake, partying like the BMOC he was back then. Keg stands and rallying cheers to destroy the away team next week rang out among the firelight as half the senior class got toasted.

Then, as quickly as he rose up, he fell victim to his own stupid garishness. He drove drunk off a cliff on his way home from the party and left the football team utterly screwed for the rest of the year. After his funeral, they didn't win another game.

He was high that night too. Steven knows this because he sold Dave two grams of coke a few hours before that.

Sold a lot that night. Great place to offload wares.

Not that the two were related.

*Of course they weren't.*

Steven watches, horrified, as the man stumbles toward the counter, then pauses long enough to vomit all the beer he just chugged onto the linoleum flooring. It lands with a nasty splatting sound, puddles, and spreads out into the cracks between the flooring panels.

Steven feels queasy.

*Maybe I should ask if he needs me to call him a—*

"You can clean this up when you want to, bitch. Least you can do."

*Uh...*

Steven doesn't understand. He watches as the tight-end steps over his own cleari-ish bile and walks past the counter on his way out. The wine bottle top rips open easily in Dave's thick, hairy hands and he pours the purple liquid down his gullet for a moment. Swallowing, he mumbles, "Your goddamn fault anyway, punk-pusher motherfucker."

The door opens and the bell rings again as Dave struts out into the downpour and to his truck. The door slamming closed startles Steven slightly.

Just as Dave enters his truck, a new customer pulls up on the opposite side of the pumps, where Teresa pulled away not two minutes ago. A black jeep this time, with cans trailing by strings from the bumper.

Bolts of lightning hit the ground and thunder rumbles low. In the random flashes of light, it almost appears as though the vines are making their way across the street, wiggling like worms after a fresh rain, slithering this way and that along the cracked asphalt. And the rain is fresh, all right. All too fresh, all the damn time.

As Dave's truck revs up and speeds away into the night, Steven watches the third customer in as many minutes roll up their windows—*Why are they down in this weather?*—kick off their headlights and exit the vehicle.

And now things are getting creepy, because here comes the bride. All dressed in white, she struggles to fit her big wedding dress out of the door of the jeep, almost falling out of the vehicle. She eventually manages to step out, slamming the door and storming toward the entrance of the Saucer Stop.

A flash and the immediate, deafening crack of thunder.

*That one was close.*

The raven-haired woman in the white wedding gown makes the bell ring yet again, but unlike the others, she walks straight up to Steven and stares into his eyes. Her eyes are blood-shot and narrow as they pierce into Steven's like daggers.

"You're a real jerk, you know."

Steven knows why she's angry. He has never met her, but he can guess who she is without much effort. He gave a few pills to a friend of his sister who was planning to hand them out at a bachelorette party the following week. GHB. Gamma-hydroxy-buterate. Sometimes referred to as a "date rape" drug.

Not so dangerous if it's just you and your girls. And just so long as you don't take too many.

The bride had, though. One or two too many.

*I can't be responsible for every Tom, Dick, Harry, or Susie who can't drink responsibly, just as I can't be made to answer for all the sins of my dim-witted customers. It's that simple. I don't make anyone do anything. I don't own any of this bullshit.*

Steven glares back and leans forward as he speaks. "Look, honey. I'm sorry you went out like that, I really am. But if you think—"

"Shut your mouth! I don't have to give you anything more. *Nothing.* Not even my ears to hear your confession."

Steven smirks. "Confession?"

*What do I have to confess to? What is this broad on about? She's not even—*

An ugly idea pops into Steven's head and he tucks it back, right quick. Not that.

"I was ready to marry my man. Ready to have a life and so much more. Now I'll never be able to. Now I'll never have my chance. You took that from me, you shit," the bride seethes.

Between flashes of lightning, Steven notices the vines creeping closer and closer. He hears the thunder nearing every time it crashes. The rain is pouring harder and faster—tick, tick, tick on the roof as the wind makes the trees sway.

*Why is she saying this? What is this?*

The bride's rage-filled eyes pop like fire in their sockets against her pale skin as she says, "I'm going now, Steven."

She walks to the door of the Saucer Stop, then turns, glancing down at the shirt Steven is wearing with a sinister smile. "We are all going, Steven. Every one of us. But you…" She points her finger at his chest, directly at his heart, and hisses, "You and your stupid shirt can just stay right. Where. You. Are."

She turns and walks out of the building, but this time, the bell doesn't ring out. The door simply shuts with a loud crash.

Steven looks down at his shirt and touches the small saucer logo over his right pec. He begins to sweat, his heart pumping hot and hard.

He runs to the door and pulls hard at the handle, but it does not move. As his eyes cast down to his hands, he sees that a rope of green vine has effectively bolted the door closed from the outside. It doesn't move in the slightest as he pulls and pulls.

Kudzu, great for soil erosion and securing gas station entryways.

*How long have I been here? How many hours? How many days?*
*How many times have I tried to leave?*

Then a more stark thought enters his mind: *Does it even matter anymore? Pretty sure I know where I am and what this means. If it is what it is, then that's all it'll ever be, right?*

The wet, encroaching vines start to rattle the glass as the knotted tendrils writhe, wrapping around the small building. Thick ropes of kudzu snake around the four corners of the Saucer Stop as the lights start to dim.

The ground trembles and the room creaks with the stress of the open arms of the kudzu, snaking in spirals around the building as the wet leaves brush the metal roof with a sickening whoosh.

The lights overhead go out.

*How long have I been here?*

Too long, with no end in sight. No holy light. No pearly passage to gain entry to.

No rest.

Just the sinking feeling that this is what awaits every moment of eternity. The specters of those he has wronged, filling up their gas tanks as the vines hold him prisoner under the unrelenting torrent of the cold Georgia rains. So all's well.

*Tick, tick, tick.*

# FLANNEL

F lannel is a man's fabric, no two ways about it. Carded wool or worsted yarn woven to a fine American-hewn cloth. That's the stuff. The soft touch belies its true, rugged nature.

See, when a real man puts on his flannel, it's not unlike a knight donning his armor. It's what makes you solid and sturdy. It multiplies your gravitas. It's what gives you the gumption to say to the world, "Hey, world. Yeah, you. Go grab me a six-pack of Schlitz, and make it snappy."

Flannel is all Glen Givens ever wore, all day and damn near every night. He likely bought more of them than he really needed. Good thing, too, as the quality was slowly watering down over time. Like with all things, the real stuff was harder to come by these days as most modern flannel (or what the traders and tourists called flannel) was made from run-of-the-mill cotton or synthetic fibers. China-made hoopie-hoo. Cheap, cheap, cheap. And frankly, none too American, if we're being that way, and all.

Glen didn't ever think much about why he wore it. It was what great-great-gramps and great-gramps and gramps and pops and now he wore. Five generations of like-minded dressers, dressing as the like-minded do. *"By prepping for the day like a lumberjack, you've covered all angles,"* his pops used to say. Looked damn good doing it too.

And when it came to working a fire watchtower in the wintery wilderness, Glen knew that his flannel was as on-brand as scaly skin on a snake—right on brand.

From his view high upon the Colorado Rockies, he could see halfway to Wyoming, all the way to Nebraska, and a good way toward Utah. Snow-capped peaks and the green canyons between.

He has been a fire tower lookout for about a year now, and didn't think it could get any better. Hormel chili, SPAM, and stars for days to say nothing of gorgeous daybreaks, cleaner air than anywhere else in the state, and silence that was worth its weight in gold.

Of course, he could get games on his little TV, so he could keep up with the ups and downs of the Broncos season and watch Wheel every night at 6:30 p.m. The nearby stream gave him a fool's ransom in tasty fish and was great to read by.

It was really all he ever needed in a home, and he considered himself more lucky than he might've earned.

On Friday nights it was down to town for a heel kick-up at the Deaf Burro Bar and Grill. He and the eight-man, two-lady Fire-Spier Crew would rendezvous (if you'll allow the French for a moment) for Friday night after Friday night of dancin', drinkin', and doing what a working man does when he ain't working. Sometimes Glen would bring a sweet thing back to the loft for a toss, then give her marching orders come dawn's light. Always after a complimentary cup of java and an encore performance so she left with a smile. As a gentleman, who could do any less?

Yessir, every Friday night was the go of the week, alright. The sweet spot and a welcome respite for the rugged and weary alike. Come 5:00 p.m. on Friday, he'd shut the lights off on the lookout, then get down, turn around, go to town—boot, scoot, and boogie.

It was like a dream come true. A flannel dream come damn true.

And do the ladies love the flannel?

*You betcha, boy. They drip-a-drip drip for that shit.*

He stood inside the home he had fashioned for himself atop the tower over the last year. It wasn't much: Four walls filled with four big windows and one door to an outer walkway and the floor hatch which served as the front door. He'd added a couch (not so easy to carry up), a bit of tech and hobby-wares to keep the mind occupied (much easier to carry up), and plenty of food (the easiest, by far). A few strategically placed artworks, accents, rows of books, and odd statuettes from the local Hobby Lobby lightened the place up and added a whiff of nouveau interior decor-ism (he watched the Design Network sometimes). It was cozy as hell.

As the sun rolled down over the high hills, he could see the lights of town starting to pop up in the distance, the street lamp sensors beginning to glow. The road that led into town from the base of the tower wrapped down the ridge, a ten-minute drive from those lights and the denizens of the tiny township. When night fell, it began to be swallowed by the forest around it.

Glen rubbed his shoulder-length black hair against his scalp with one hand as he held a coffee mug in the other. He raised it up to his lips and blew on it. On the cup, a picture of a big chainsaw and the words, "MAN, FUCK TREES."

Sadly, this was no Friday night. Just another slow Tuesday,

and no games on the TV worth his time. He'd done about all he was gonna do on the watercolor of the eastern horizon that he was working on. It had sat on the easel in the corner of the room for a week now, maybe done—he couldn't decide.

His eyes scanned the room. On the coffee table was a tattered paperback copy of Cormic McCarthy's *Blood Meridian*. Lindy, one of the two ladies in the crew, suggested he read it a month ago. He had been at the Deaf Burro, nursing a cold MGD and discussing The Eagles' "Hotel California" with a drunk Graham Tillows (another crew firebug), when Lindy had approached and started explaining her take on the allegorical nature of the song. As the topic of the narrator's fate came up, she randomly mentioned that Glen should read *Blood Meridian*. When he asked why, she explained that, "It's an ugly and brutally honest meditation on the nature of man."

That was all Glen needed to hear.

Maybe tonight was the night to crack the Glen Livet in the icebox and pour a tumbler. Bring up the temp and settle in with a rugged book about men and their manly nature. Maybe this was the—

The radio on a wall shelf crackled to life and whizzed with static.

After a second, a woman's voice called out, "Fire Tower Three calling Fire Tower Seven. Come back, over."

Glen strutted to the radio. He already had his mind made up. *A novel idea,* he thought to himself, half-amused at his semi-lame turn of phrase. He picked up the handset on the CB and turned up the volume knob a little before clicking the button and responding, "Fire Tower Three, this is Fire Tower Seven. Reading you loud and clear. How goes the struggle, Sam? Over."

More crackling static, then, "Well, Glen, I got a damn weird thing that happened just now. Thought I might give you the skinny right quick. Over."

"Weirder than the time Danny sang 'Pretty Fly For a White Guy' during karaoke at the Burro? Over."

Static. "Well, I reckon yes. Weirder still. Over."

Glen chuckled and clicked the button again. "That would be damn weird, Sam, so I'm all ears. Over."

Sam was Samantha Iron-Feather. The other lady on the crew. Sexy-as-can-be Native American gal with a wicked-sharp mind and an even wicked-er sense of gallows humor. A damn good cook too, by all counts. She often made the group unbelievable grub that left the local vittles in the dust. Glen had considered it a few times (supposing she would even be interested), but when ya shit where ya eat, it rarely ends well. He had never made a move.

"It's going to sound … I dunno, pretty hard to square, Tower Seven. Over."

"I promise to keep an open mind, Tower Three. Over."

The line stayed silent for a moment and Glen took a sip from his mug, waiting.

Soon the hiss came back and Sam's voice called through the airwaves, "Just give me the benefit of the doubt here, is all I'm asking. So, yeah, there was a bright bit of light that came from Plato's Mine over here. Over."

Glen's brow furrowed. "Bright bit of light? Over."

"Yeah, like a flash of light that came from the mine. I couldn't see what it was at first. Then I saw it was a rapid succession of flashes. Very fast. Then they stopped. Over."

"The mine is still as shut down as it has been since '71, right? Over."

"Just as shut down, Tower Seven. Over."

Plato's Mine. An odd name, but a textbook tale. Abandoned for silver tailings in the late thirties. Then it was just an ore-haul hole for a few decades. In '71, a primary shaft collapsed and they closed it down, sans fatalities, which was uncommon. Since then, nothing. Until now.

"Okay, I'm biting. That is an odd turn of events. You sure you're not seeing some devil's fire or swamp gas? Over."

"That's the thing, Tower Seven. It wasn't just..." Sam paused. "I saw something else. Something I can't really reconcile, if I'm being honest. And if you hadn't noticed I'm trying as hard as I can to avoid having to explain it. Over."

This made Glen smile broadly. "Okay, well if this is the start of a really funny joke, you certainly have my interest piqued. You're likely to catch the trout you're fishing for with that line, so what's the hook here, Sam? Over."

"No joke, Tower Seven. And thanks for making me feel less silly. Honestly, I don't know how to succinctly explain what I saw, so maybe... I don't know. Over."

Glen's stomach gave a slight gurgle-turn and he realized that he hadn't fed himself in a good several hours now. He was mighty famished. The things he'd be willing to do for an order of the Deaf Burro's Hoppin' N' Heapin' Nacho Plate right about now were enough to make a nun blush.

"You're not just joshing me, Sam? Over."

"No, Glen. I think you need to know what's heading your direction. Over."

Now Glen considered himself all manner of different things: grateful, lucky, blessed, well-dressed, and getting better every day with the watercolor. But the kind of fella that folks in his hometown woulda referred to as a "yellow-skinned scaredy-cat" was not among them. Just the same, much like in one of those Dean Koontz novels he flicked through from time to time, he felt a disembodied cold breath lick up his neck and his hairs stand on end when Sam said this.

"Damn, Sam, what could all this possibly be coming around to? That's surely some spooky shit 'ya just spoke. Over."

"Look, Glen, I saw something come out of the mine just after the flashes stopped. It was hard to see but that one lamp that still flickers by the mouth of the mine gave me a couple of seconds to peer at it through my binoculars, and I'm telling you, I'm terrified of whatever that was. Over."

Glen also considered Samantha Iron-Feather all manner of different things: sweet but tough, a ruthless goddamn hold 'em player, a hard worker, someone you could trust, and probably just outside of Glen's league. One thing she definitely wasn't though, was a liar (outside of stiff poker bluffs), and she certainly wasn't prone to the type of unfunny comedy routines that this one was rapidly shaping up to be.

No, sir--he didn't like it one damn bit.

Glen walked right over to the wooden door of the nearby closet, between the lodgepole paneling he had put up on the walls to give it a cabin vibe, and yanked it open, pulling on the string to turn on the light. In front of him, shoulder line after shoulder line of real man's clothing. Real man's armor. True-grit woven, goddamn stainless-steel fabric only American looms and hands could create, by God.

He eyed the flannel ranks, snatched one particularly rugged piece, and slammed the rest of his coffee. Then he turned back to the radio as he pulled on his chosen armor. "Tower Three, you need to start getting real specific about what's going on. Over."

A new voice came through the CB. "This is Tower Six calling. Gotta say I'm pretty damn curious myself as to what the hell this is all about, Tower Three. Over."

"This is Tower Eight. Me too, over."

"Okay, yeah, I uh… This is why— Damn it. Okay. You know what? I'm just going to say it because soon enough you're all going to know I'm not full of shit."

The line went silent for a moment and no one interjected because, frankly, not one damn one of them had ever heard Samantha ever sound so rattled. This was a new thing, and it was giving everyone pause.

Sam continued, "Some sort of creature is heading your way and it may go right past you but when it shot out of the mine it looked like it was making a beeline south and you're directly south of us, so… Over."

Another moment of no one speaking, then Glen finally replied, "You said creature. Why'd you say that? Over."

Sam was the resident expert on local flora and fauna. Her not having a word to describe this thing was another odd bit lost on no one listening in.

"I don't know what it was. Over."

Glen could smell bullshit like a fart in a car and this one was surely stinkin'.

"Tower Three, all due respect, but I think you do. We're all family here, and no one thinks you're a fool, so just tell us what you saw. Over."

"Fine. You asked and I'm answering. It looked like a, uh… Fuck. Sorta maybe like a Kanton. Over."

"A Kanton? Not familiar with that one. Please explain. Over." Glen was mystified.

"This is Tower Six, what's that again? Over."

Sam quickly responded, "I'm just saying that's what it looked like. I can't describe it any other way. The full name is much longer and sort of tricky to pronounce unless you're fluent in Iroquois. Over."

"Tower Nine calling in now." Jim Kaiser was the old guard of the bunch. Though only fifty-eight, he was still the senior by decades and was about as close to an elder as they had. "I'm gonna ask this just one time, Sam, and I need you to shoot straight, though I suspect I already know the answer."

The radio was quiet for five long seconds as everyone waited. Finally, Jim finished, "You fuckin' with us? Over."

"Jim, I have a great movie I just started up that I'd much rather be focusing on than on the horn with you fine gents, sounding like I'm crying wolf over here. But I'm not and I'm worried about whatever the hell that was. Over."

Around the time that Sam was saying this, Glen could see, not a hundred yards away and due north, that there was a treetop shaking left and right. He watched for a good ten seconds before a thought struck him dead on. It was a little too damn early for the bears to be poking their noses out of their hidey holes just yet. Odder still that one would just randomly shake a tree like that.

Maybe it was a buck that caught its rack on a few branches and was trying to loose itself?

But that didn't really seem to square either considering that, as Sam kept talking and he kept watching, the tree stopped shaking and a tree just a bit closer began to shake. And not just a little bit.

At a glance he couldn't fathom what kind of creature would

be able to do that kind of shaking, save for a bear. And again, it just wasn't the season for that.

Glen got back on the horn and updated the rapt audience. "Uh, I do have some-sorta-something shaking trees due north of me. Perhaps that's our friend from the mine? Over."

Jim came back on and spoke rapidly. "Tower Seven, this is Tower Nine. Hopping on my four-wheel hog and making a trip to you with my thirty-aught. Get geared and latch up, I'm en route. Over."

Glen didn't waste time replying, "Roger, Tower Nine. Battening down and grabbin' my musket. I'll keep an eye out. Over."

"Tower Six calling, again. Uh, is this for real, guys? Over."

"Tower Six, this is Tower Eight, I don't think anyone here is pulling bullshit so you need to stay off this channel unless you're going to be helpful. I'm serious, Danny. Over."

"Okay, Graham. Damn. This just sounds cuckoo is all. Over."

"Heard, and I really couldn't agree more but let's keep the channel clear. Unless Tower Three wants to further explain what the hell a Kanton is. Over."

*Thank goodness Graham is asking the obvious question on everyone's mind,* Glen thought to himself, because he was focused on other things at the current moment. As tree after tree making its way toward Watchtower Seven began to shake in succession, Glen walked to the rack-shelf on the wall and pulled down his shotgun. He reached up and pulled a box of shells open and shoved several into his pocket, then started plugging one after another into the shotty.

Samantha answered, "It's one of the more unsettling legends in Iroquois culture. They're basically disembodied heads with eyes of fire and long tangled hair. These, uh, things would float through the air and hunt for humans to eat. And this looked a lot like that, except one thing was different."

Everyone waited.

Glen didn't. He pulled the panels on three of the four bay windows around him, save for the one facing north, latched them up, then snatched up his binoculars from the kitchenette counter, along with two sticks from his jerky jar. Then he locked the door to the outer walkway. He snuck up to the unobstructed window and peered through the north-facing window toward the failing light of the setting sun.

Sam finished, "It had what looked like a whole mess of eyes—spider-eyes—covering the head. I'm dying if I'm lying here, fellas. Over."

Glen plugged his mouth with one of the jerky sticks and shoved the other in his free pocket. He rolled the zoom knob on the binoculars and tried to focus on what was shaking the trees.

He didn't have to look for long.

Once, when he was just a punk kid, maybe eight at the time, he saw this movie at his gramps's house when he shouldn't have been up so late. It was color, but old-timey color. The rough stuff, somehow not as clear as black and white. It was this goofy yarn about a scientist who created a monster in his lab and loosed the thing on his enemies.

Damned if that multi-peepered creature wasn't the first thing Glen thought of when he first saw the ugly mugged-bastard. It was pasty white and looked like a head, but only sorta. That black stuff trailing it might have been hair, but the strands whipped around like appendages, flicking against the wind.

Mostly he saw those eyes Sam had mentioned. On this point,

she was as dead on the mark as Ol' Davey C. himself. The damn thing was almost entirely a big mess of eyes. Eyes and eyes upon eyes, surrounded by more eyes, each blooming with red and orange rings of fire from the iris's.

*Well there's something you sure don't see every day.*

The eyes seemed to notice Glen noticing them, as the pupils aimed toward where he was. Maybe the crazy thing had spotted the tower. Whatever the case, it was using its hair-stuff to wrap around branches with shocking speed, snagging random creatures and bits of shrubs and pulling it to the crest of its head. A hole opened on the top of the creature's skull, seemingly sucking stuff into it.

*That ain't right,* Glen thought.

Glen backed up slowly and grabbed the CB handset again. He held the chrome Remington pointing toward the thing, now maybe fifty yards away. His other hand clicked the button and he whispered, "Roger on the eyes, Sam. Lots of eyes. Over."

"Holy hell, Glen, is it near you? Over."

The creature was using its tendrils to shake the trees as it floated much faster now toward Glen's home in the hills. Watchtower Seven was about twenty seconds away from an uninvited visitor busting in. Glen pulled the pin and dropped the metal sliding plate that now secured all four big windows.

He had slightly miscalculated because it only took about ten seconds before a circular indentation punched a convex dome into the eastern metal panel. Glass crashed to the metal walkway outside. The thing smacked against the plate a couple more times, but less hard, as if it was checking it for weakness.

*Just like in Jurassic Park. Still, it should keep the little—*
*Shit! The hatch!*

The hatch on the floor of the watchtower shack that Glen had called home this last twelve months was not what you would call a marvel of modern technology. A couple hangers holding a thin steel plate in place with nothing but a half-inch iron bolt between whatever wanted to get in and whomever wanted to keep it out. That usually amounted to squirrels or the odd racoon. But that thing was no goddamn squirrel and it damn sure wasn't any gull-dern raccoon that Glen had ever seen the likes of. The plate may have been heavy, but with enough upward force applied, it gave like a damn French door.

"Tower Seven, this is Tower Eight. I'm coming too. Over."

"Jesus, this is a thing, right? Over." Danny sounded mighty shook up over in Tower Six.

"Tower Six, yes it is. Tower Three, get Terry and the other donut-snatchers up here on the double. Over."

Samantha responded, "Copy on the coppers, Graham. Over."

As it was going, Glen was probably as close to on edge as he'd ever been. This was the kinda thing that could make a man wonder about a whole wide world full of other career opportunities.

He dashed to the hatch, but before he could slam his foot on it, the bolt popped and the panel flew open. Pointing the shotgun barrel down, he was about to pull the trigger to say hello, when the creature opened its head-maw above the eyes, revealing circular rows of tiny, bloody teeth flicked with bits of branches, leaves, and fur. Its black tentacles sprouted from underneath and latched themselves to the opening of the hatch.

The air around Glen started to whoosh by and he realized the thing was sucking air into its open mouth. Damn strong breeze, too. Gale-force winds, like an HVAC hose on full, pulling Glen toward it.

He dropped the shotgun and it got stuck in the middle of the teeth, slowing the stiff suction around him. He stepped back and grabbed the hatch with both hands.

Like a saw, the rows of teeth started spinning and grinding the barrel as it kicked up sparks. Glen's eyes went wide.

Pushing the hatch door down, he struck the thing on its head as hard as his arms would allow. It dropped out of sight, but as the plate hit the floor, the squirmy arms became caught in it. One swift piece curled up and caught Glen's arm as he was pulling away. He quickly kicked the severed pieces to the side and sat down on the hatch plate. The thing screeched and smacked the hatch several times, but Glen's weight held it fast.

As Glen sat, he looked down at his slightly bloodied arm and discovered something more startling than that. His fingers touched the new hole near the elbow that had opened up. The screechy thing. It had done this.

*Fucker tore my flannel.*

You can touch all manner of things in this life. Hearts, minds, yourself. One thing you don't touch is a man's flannel, less you wanna get your mouth busted. And by God, Glen was ready to one-two this thing, but good.

He heard the radio sputter back to life. "Glen! Is everything okay? Are you okay? Over." Samantha sounded mighty shook.

He was close enough to the couch and figured he could grab it if he was careful. The thing screeched a high howl and began crashing into the four wall panels over the windows. His ears caught the shattering of the glass but the metal held fast. Probably American-made.

He used the moment to spring up and drag the couch over the hatch, then looked around. His gaze found purchase.

*Ah, yes. We got this covered, alright.*

He ran across the small room to the kitchenette and opened the cupboard underneath it.

*"A real man should know how to use propane."* That's what his great-gramps once said during a camping trip up to Lost Lake.

He looked beneath the counter and saw the tank. He'd just filled it up last week so it was ready to rock, should the occasion arise. And Glen figured it had risen, alright. He turned the knob on the tank to cut the flow and started to unplug it from the line.

The walls continued to shake and the tower seemed to sway just a pinch with each broadside strike. Glen knew he needed to do this fast.

*Just outside the door, the flare is on the wall and the rope line down to the ground.*

Having a bit of fun, Glen had fashioned himself a zip-line. Fortunately it was just outside, but—

*Shit, man. You don't have a handlebar. Graham is fixing it. Shitty shittin'-shit.*

*No trouble, just adapt.* Great-gramps had once said that during the Second World War, you always had to adapt to survive. Shoot down a German Focke-Wulf, crash your plane, escape the wreckage, cross enemy lines, hide some, run some, kill a guard with a boot knife, get back into allied countryside, and ride a friendly tank like goddamn Audie Murphy back to the barracks. Not the original plan, true, but you adapt. That's what you did, by-golly, and this moment was no different.

The creature had stopped smacking the northern side and was now hitting the building from the south. The iron supports creaked with the increasing metal stress.

*Not too long before the place ends up just like the Alamo.*

Glen picked up the cylindrical tank and turned the knob. Gas hissed out of the top as he rolled it across the room and heard the creature hitting the bottom hatch again. The hatch was striking the underside of the couch so hard it was shaking and shimmying like it was pole night at the Burro.

Glen unlocked the door, then kicked the couch hard as he could. The hatch popped open and the thing flew into the room, its fire eyes ablaze, burnin'-hot creepin' peepers focused on him.

He nodded at the creature with a smile and opened the door to the outside. Once on the walkway, he slid the wooden jam into place and turned to face the zip line.

Great-gramps also said it was just amazing how clear your mind can get when it's a life and death situation. You either fight or take flight, most say. Here and now, Glen opted for both.

His eyes traced the outer wall and landed on the flare gun dangling from its wall hanger. Caliber Four standard issue. He swiftly pulled the gun loose, tucked it in his waist and removed his flannel shirt. Multi-purpose armor.

He heard the thing crash into the door and crack the wood. Next hit was gonna be splintering or worse. Time to go if he was goin'.

He looped the flannel over the rope, tied two quick knots and held on as he zipped down the rope toward a nearby tree the line was anchored to. On the way down, he briefly noted sets of lights coming up the road toward his tower.

He dropped to the ground five feet short of the big trunk and landed on both feet. He spun on his heels just as the doorway broke from its hinges and the creature floated into the doorway and glared at him with hundreds of eyeballs. Glen glared back.

As the creature's hair-tendril arms flailed about wildly and an ocular sea of fiery circles bore down upon him, his own eyes ran down to his weapon.

There were four calibers available when it came to your average distress signal flares: Twelve-gauge, twenty-five millimeter, twenty-six and a half millimeter, and thirty-seven. Most people did fine with any one of the first three, but Glen had a big boy in his chamber. Thirty-seven millimeters of boom. The Fire-Spier Crew didn't fuck around, and this thing was about to find out.

*Am I really gonna shoot this ugly sum-bitch with a flare gun?*

Glen grinned.

*You betcha, boy.*

Taking aim like Crockett at the Alamo might've (who really knew, anyway?), Glen raised his hand and pointed the signal flare at the ugly, white-ish husk of eyes, whipping black tendrils and viscous fluids spurting from its head-mouth.

He gave the trigger a squeeze.

*Not a pull, a squeeze. Like Pops said to.*

The flare soared up in an arc and found purchase in the doorway of his soon-to-be-former abode. It hit just inside and started a small patch of fire next to the creature's head.

The creature shrieked one last time before it was engulfed by the explosive fireball that swallowed the watchtower. Flames belched out from the opening and blasted the shutters. Instead of flying with the flame outward, the thing howled, shook violently, and as the heat engulfed it, beady eyeball after beady eyeball burst open, releasing milky white plasma.

It dropped onto the metal grating encircling the tower with a clanging thud and stopped moving. Its black, slimy arms went limp and it burned just like the rest of the mess Glen had made.

*Must've been heavy. Not thirty-seven millimeters heavy, of course, but still.*

Glen reached up, whipped around the charred and nearly burned through flannel shirt, and undid the knots. It crumpled in his hands.

The headlamps of the two four-wheelers rushing up to him illuminated the area. The motors hummed for a second behind him, then died as Graham and Jim walked up to either side of Glen as he stared upward.

"Holy jumped-up Jesus in a manger! What the hell was that thing?" Graham shouted.

Glen pulled his armor back on over his shoulders and knelt down to tie his shoelace.

The radio on the back of Jim's four-wheeler hissed and Sam's voice came over the CB. "Did you find him? Is he okay? Over."

Jim walked over to the back of his four-wheel hog and clicked the transmitter. "He's here and he seems okay. Over." Jim looked at Glen. "You okay, pard'ner?"

As the others spoke, Glen could barely hear them. He watched as his home went up in flames, along with the dead thing who clearly didn't know who he was messing with. A flannel man.

For four generations before him, for Glen himself, and hopefully for untold generations to come, this truth would hold true: You don't mess with a man and his flannel. You just don't do it. Not if you got a brain in your noggin.

*Look what happens when you do.*

Yeah, there surely would be a bit of explaining to do once the red and blues showed up. Quite a bit. No trouble, though. Crew had his back.

He finished tying his boot, reached into his jeans, pulled out a jerky stick, and rubbed it against his sleeve. Then he stood up, plugged the bit of dried meat between his teeth like a Cuban cigar. and chewed on it, half-grinning.

*Yep, another damn fine day to be wearing the best fabric money can buy,* he thought. *Nice fire too. Warm.*

"I'm good, boys." Glen smiled, nodding at the burning structure. "He ain't."

# VAUNTED

Opulence was the cocktail of the hour as the dashing black tuxedos and ravishing white dresses passed by, limo after limo filled to the gills with the vaunted upper echelon in all its regalia.

*Vaunted* was an onomatopoetically fun word and Sarah enjoyed that. It meant to be praised or boasted about, especially in an excessive or undeserving way—which was likely why the word came to her mind as the procession of cars drove up to the small red-brick guardhouse of Starwood Estates, just outside of Aspen, Colorado. It was one of those crossword puzzle words you ultimately had to look up.

She couldn't see most of the occupants—it was night after all—but the clothing of the ones she spied positively screamed *sanctimonious fundraising dinner* or *self-congratulatory shareholder soiree.* The oft-vaunted at play.

*Nice.*

Setting a course that pierced straight through the heart of the gated community, a steady stream of the top crust, the cream, the (presumably) rich and infamous, rolled by with tinted glass windows and gleaming silver trim, up a single winding street nestled between two rows of wrought iron Victorian lamp posts.

Their drivers all looked the same, really. Same pale, gaunt faces, devoid of expression as they handed Sarah their gold-inlaid invitations. Her co-worker, Thomas, had said to put them in a pile because the lady at the top of the hill intended to come down and collect them later. Who knew why.

While most of the people in the neighborhood had cash to burn, this newest arrival in the community came from real money. Romanian royalty was the rumor. The lady in question was Marian Maurius, and she was matriarch of the new family on the block, as it were. Sarah hadn't had the pleasure yet, but the rumor was that Marian and her family moved here a month ago from Romania and into the palace at the top of the hill.

By all reports, the woman was utterly gorgeous. The night guys had said they'd seen her several times, and always spoke of her beauty. If pressed on specifics though, they had difficulty articulating any details about her appearance. They just said she was lovely. Oh so lovely.

And they all said it that way specifically. And they all repeated it. The four of them.

*Strange.*

When you took up residence in the biggest place on the tallest hill in the wealthiest subdivision of the Roaring Fork Valley, you were making a statement. The crown prince of Saudi Arabia had a comparatively modest place down the street and it wasn't half the size of the palace atop the Aspen tree-laden mound at the end of the drive.

On evenings when no one was in residence, Sarah had to do a neighborhood security check in her green and blue Starwood

Security-issued golf cart. Between the last owner and the Maurius', she had been there twice.

Once you approached the estate, the old metal street lamps on either side gave way to a switchback heading up. Five zig-zags and it rounded out at the top, opening to a large circular, cobblestone motor court. In the center of the court was a tri-basin marble fountain with purplish lighting illuminating the tiers and a to-scale marble replica of the Venus de Milo which stood centered atop the highest basin. Water ran down from the Venus's white stone head and the effect made the normally pale and placid figure appear to have rippling violet skin.

And the house, a lavish and extravagant love letter to late sixteenth-century Italian Renaissance architecture, had all the trappings of the wealth of those who called it home. Dark wood exterior with an arched mahogany double-door entry next to a multi-doored garage area. Among projecting eaves and imposing cornice structures it was vaguely asymmetrical, with parapets and balconies of stone and black wrought iron. The Venetian windows would normally allow for light to naturally filter through, provid-ing little need for electricity during the daytime hours. However, the blinds were always drawn on every last one of them.

*Curious.*

Sarah had been working at the guardhouse for several months--about as long as she had been in school at the local community college for her four-year vet tech program. She worked weekends, during the day mostly, and it was never this busy.

Limousines were uncommon, too. Sure, the vehicles that she had waived through during her tenure were ritzy, but this was on another level. Thomas had once told her that if they're driving Phantoms, they were the highest rolling of the high rollers. And every other one that passed her on that cold March evening was a Rolls Royce Phantom. Some black, some gunmetal gray with white trim, and all very, very luxe.

After about ten of them, Sarah knew what the massive motor court was for. She began to notice that nearly all of the limos were dark in the back. Most people would use a ride in a limo to take in the needless and overblown amenities available. To do that, though, you usually needed, ya know, *light*. The cars were mostly dark.

She would take an invitation, check the name off the list with her red pen, and push the knob to lift the yellow and white striped guard gate. Despite being tinted, against the guardhouse's bright lamps she could make out the figures of people through the glass and sometimes the reflections of shimmering dresses and jewelry. Still, the interior lights were usually dim or off.

After maybe fifteen or so of the posh Phantoms and one truly expensive vehicle that looked like a BMW hearse passed by, the line ended and the night was mostly dark once more.

As she watched the dark red eyes of the taillights wind up the hill, she briefly wondered what gala event could be the cause for such a gilded parade of wealth. Then she remembered she didn't give one solitary fuck about them or their cute shit and picked up her newspaper.

Sitting back in the leather chair, she flipped to the crossword and sudoku that she had been toggling back and forth between before the money circus had come to town. Her eyes occasionally shot over to the monitors in the corner showing images of the road leading up to and through the Starwood Estates, then back down to her puzzle.

Back to business. *An eleven letter word for something which is impossible to deny or disprove that ends with the letter E. Second letter is an R and the fourth letter—*

No need. She had it: Irrefutable.

*Which means that one down is … luminous.*

*Colors that change from angle to angle… Ah, easy. Iridescent. Booyah.*

It was like taking candy from a baby at a certain point. Her hand reached out and took hold of the Kiwiberry Ruckus Fruitopia she had resting on the wall shelf nearby and took a swig.

*Sweet.*

And this really, truly would've been a fine way to spend much of her evening, but then she saw that the parade apparently wasn't over just yet.

From her position on the mountainside, Sarah couldn't see much of the valley below. What she could usually make out were the high beams of the cars passing by on the highway as well as the lights on the gate pillars at the bottom of the road that led up to the neighborhood. It was two miles down to where it intersected with Highway 82, the main vein through the sixty-mile stretch of the Roaring Fork Valley.

At this moment, however, all the lights on the bottom key-coded gate were dark and five or six more sets of lights were past it and ascending in her direction.

She set down the newspaper and stood back up, then squinted to see more, however the reflection of the bright lights on the glass made it difficult. She could have gone out to see better, but she figured she'd have answers once the final members of the party reached her. And to that end, the first of the five new arrivals rounded the last switchback and came up to the guardhouse. Sarah saw it was a black panel van with no license plates.

*Huh.*

She would've had enough time to smash the silent alarm, had it occurred to her. But before she could fully move across the guard booth to where it lay, inverted, under the eave of the desk, the door to the van slid open and the muzzle of the gun pointing at her through the glass caused her to freeze.

*Nah, that can wait*, she figured. *No need to tempt the man with the full auto.*

He had a dark ski mask on, which seemed appropriately intimidating. But also a black microfleece vest, Doc Martens, and acid-wash Levi's which seemed inappropriately stylish, if we're being honest.

His eyes were cold and distant, if such a thing were possible, and Sarah lowered her own eyes to break from his gaze as she raised her hands up.

She could see other men getting out of the van. They all had the same basic clothing and frosty look as the first gunman. Three gunmen total.

The four vehicles behind the van had stopped and were idling with no one exiting. They looked to be larger shipment trucks.

The black van then pulled slowly to the right, onto the soft shoulder of the road. Once the engine stopped, a tall, broad shouldered, stupidly handsome man of mid-years with graying hair and chiseled features stepped out and started toward the shack.

Without slowing, he walked in through the door and stood before Sarah. No mask, a well-kempt yet ruggedly unshaven face, and a pair of eyes that could melt ice. A midnight-green duster jacket and blue jeans completed the fantasy euro-stranger look.

Sarah hoped to heaven that she wasn't blushing.

*Is that CK One he's wearing? Yowza. Shouldn't I be more worried here?*

But when he spoke, his voice was soft and soothing, like her Bio 103 professor, Mr. Maldry, who had a dulcimer tone which was better than valerian root for slumber.

"Hello. My name is Gregor and I am sorry about this but no harm vill be coming to you, I can assure you."

Uncertain why she believed him, she asked, "What's happening here?"

"Don't vorry, Sarah. This von't take but a little bit of your evening, and then you will be allowed to leave vith your life intact. Ve've no interest in you, as such."

*Right.*

Sarah wondered how he knew her name, and also what kind of uneven cross-continent accent he was rockin'. But she decided that asking too many questions might not be wise given her current position. Discretion being the better part of valor, and all that.

Gregor smiled and Sarah was even further disarmed. Straight white teeth. Soft lips. Probably had nice breath too.

*Christ, why does that matter, you twit?*

She watched as he pulled out a roll of duct tape--which was somehow not as alarming as it really should have been--from his jacket pocket .

Gregor eyed Sarah as he said, "I have to bind your hands, and legs, and mouth so you cannot summon any law enforcement. I know such things can be distressing, and I do apologize. I'm sorry."

Gregor moved toward her and she stood fast.

*Damn, he really smells good.*

She allowed him to tape her hands carefully in front of her, then he asked her to sit so he could tape her legs, and finally her mouth. His hands looked well-moisturized.

*Damn it!* she scolded herself. *Is that what you're gonna tell the police? That the culprit had soft hands and simply divine taste in upper-body wear? Grow up, Sarah. Focus. You might die, after all. But it doesn't really seem so, does it? I think dreamy eyes here is probably on the level. Probably. On the level and handsome. Oh so handsome.*

Just then, she heard the other engines rev outside.

Loudly.

The first two large vehicles that went past were white box trucks illustrated with the same picture of lamps and a smiling caricature of a big cartoon sun. Black cubed lettering on the sides read, "V.H. Illumination Supply Inc." with the slogan underneath reading, "Bringing the sun wherever we go!"

They rolled by without slowing and made a beeline for the palace at the road's end. Gregor nodded to the drivers as they flew past the guard shack.

Directly behind that one were two more long box trucks. These ones were green with yellow industrial lettering that said, "V.H. HVAC Inc.: Sucking up the soot and shit since time immemorial." Sarah thought it a mite bit on the nose.

They too went by in a flash and headed up the hill.

Gregor turned to Sarah. "I need you to remain here and just give us a few minutes to finish our operation. Then ve'll be gone."

*Sure, yeah, that sounds right.* If they were robbing the folks at the private gala event—and as far as she could tell, yeah, this was that—catching them unarmed and unawares would likely yield little to no party-goer resistance.

*It's possible they may even summon the cops themselves. They have a line out,* she thought.

*Maybe.*

As Gregor walked to the console and powered down the alarms, he wore a half-grin. This act would've notified the call center for the security company within thirty seconds normally. But then, she watched one of the men with guns shoulder his weapon and walk to the main telephone cut off for the area. He pulled down the switch on the side of the guardhouse and then returned.

Gregor walked to the door and then turned as he drew it closed behind him. He peered through the glass at Sarah on the floor. "This isn't going to last long. You have my vord. And please do not try to get out. It could get messy up there."

Gregor turned and walked back to the black van. The others with guns jumped in and they started up the road to the Marius's palace.

As she sat on the floor, she wondered how hard it would be to keep working on her crossword. She wondered what her parents would say when she told them that this job turned out to be a wee bit more perilous than one would imagine. And she also wondered if she was going to get a bonus for her trouble from the security company. It wouldn't kill them, and schoolbooks were damn costly nowadays.

The crossword was out of the question and the other two points were quite moot indeed. What none of those things had in common was the distinction of making a difference in her current predicament.

Her shoulder-length brown hair was half covering her face and she goofily blew on it to clear her eyes, then used the more practical method of brushing it aside with her bound hands.

*This sucks,* she thought. And not a little. If that hunky German-ish expat dude was to be believed, then this was a waiting game. Thing was, Sarah just wasn't very patient, if we're being real here.

Ostensibly for the safety and security of the residents and their property, an array of micro cameras had been installed at the end of the previous season after a black bear (Ursus americanus, if she remembered correctly) had found its way into a hot tub one evening with one particularly salty lady resident still inside. Bear didn't even get chance to take a swing at her before she fled the tub and ran into her house.

*Had he known her a little better, maybe he would've,* Sarah thought, then felt a little embarrassed for it.

But what mattered was that in this most crucial of junctions in the life of an awkward college kid from the sticks, she remembered she could kick on the displays showing what was happening at the estate up the hill, bound though she may be.

She slid on her butt toward the northern side of the shack and used her elbows on the wall to shimmy up to a standing position. Her legs limited her movement, but she slowly scooted over to the control board in the corner and the screens arranged vertically, two by four, above it. There were controls for all cameras located around the neighborhood. Nearly a hundred grouped into street cams and sets for the individual houses.

She lifted her duct-taped hands and used the tip of her right index finger to push a button and click over to the eight cameras covering the grounds of the Marius estate.

All the screens filled with madness. Chaos everywhere.

A feed on the top left showed the driveway. A handful of the gunmen from earlier were standing near the fountain, automatic guns at the ready. Several older gentlemen in tuxedos ran out the front door to the landing at the top of the stairs, then immediately turned and ran back inside. Yet, the men with guns did not open fire.

A feed on the middle right showed the side of the house. Sarah watched in horror as a woman with blonde hair in a red ball gown came crashing through a set of venetian stained glass doors and rolled out onto the grass lawn. The woman jumped to her feet with unnatural speed.

Sarah blinked.

One of the gunmen peered out of the open doorway and pointed a black, tube-like gun at the woman. However, instead of gunfire, a white bolt of light burst from the barrel, and as the woman was turning to face the doorway she'd just escaped from, she was gone in a flash of fire that engulfed her from head to toe in an instant. One second, if that, and she was replaced by a billow of dust that dropped onto the grass.

*Okay, what the hell was that shit?*

*Insane.*

On the top right screen, she could see the wide angle lens of the rear gate camera panning back and forth. It showed the back patio and yard area, replete with padded outdoor furniture and a long, narrow lap pool. The dark wood doors leading from the patio to the house rocketed open and several well-dressed men and women started to spill out and scatter.

Sarah could make out the shape of two men coming around either side of the house. Each seemed to fiddle with objects in their hands, then simultaneously tossed what looked like flash-bang grenades into the backyard area. She only knew what they were because she had watched her brother Tommy play video games for too many hours to count, and those things had a fairly distinct look and effect.

She knew she was right about them when they flashed with white light, causing the image to burn out for several seconds before it started to resolve itself. As the image clarified, she saw that the men were pointing their own tube-gun things at the rear exit.

The people in the backyard had all disappeared. Roughly ten piles of dust lay strewn about on the Italian marble tiles and grass of the backyard. A few others came out onto the patio, but each time they did, a white bolt erased them in an instant.

*Christ.*

Other screens had people running from windows and doorways and always being intercepted by masked men (and maybe some women too?). Each time, they disappeared. Only a flash, then dust. Again and again.

She let her eyes dart from screen to screen, but they were soon drawn back up to the top left view of the driveway. As Sarah watched, the front doors to the house blew open and a man's body, with what looked like an already broken neck, flopped out and down the staircase leading up to the doors.

The other men raised their guns at the woman who stepped forward into the camera's view.

There she was. The lady of the house. The mystic and matronly Mrs. Marius in all her majesty. Black gown and raven hair that ran down her back to the V-notch which ended just above her buttocks. Shimmering stones that looked to be diamonds graced her silvery necklace and matching earrings. Black high heels and timeless elegance.

*She really was lovely. Oh so lovely…*

The vampy lady with the stunning figure and long mane

of hair made from darkness stepped out onto the landing. She pointed at the men flanking the fountain and looked to be shouting something at them. They stood with their guns trained on her, but again, did not fire.

As fast as she had appeared, a long shard of purple wood erupted from her chest and she vanished in a flash of dust, leaving the studly figure of Gregor standing behind where she had been, retracting the wooden stake and shaking off the dust.

*Wow. Guy can handle evil things too. He's all man,* Sarah thought. All man. *So handsome, too.*

*Damn.*

As she watched the last of the gala attendees being reduced to atoms, it became clear what the HVAC trucks were for. Two teams of men in white Tyvek suits and hazmat face shields pulled out big, yellow, foot-wide vacuum hoses and started to suck up all the particulate remnants of the vapid, vaunted, and now vanished vampires.

Two of the gunmen picked up the body of their fallen comrade and carried him over to the black van, slid open the door, and deposited his body inside. It was a carefully choreographed dance of detritus disposal. She could hear the roar of the HVAC vehicles from inside her booth, further down the hill.

The people who came to clean up shop knew what they were doing as the beehive of activity only lasted what amounted to about ten minutes. Then the crews started packing up weapons and hoses with the calm that a clean-up crew in the aftermath of a wedding might.

*Just another day's work, by the looks of it.*

As nearly twenty people all started to exit the mansion and fill the vehicles, Gregor was the last one out the door. He turned and put what looked like a small piece of paper on the door, then jogged over to the black van. They left all the limos as they were, but started up their own rides.

As they began their rapid descent back down the hill, Sarah wasted no time in clicking the array back to that of the road grid, then plopping back down into the position that the manly monster marauder had left her in.

She waited nervously for a minute or two before the four big trucks rallied past without stopping at the guard shack. Behind them, the black van. It rolled up to the shack on the west side this time, and Gregor stepped out of the driver's side door. He walked around the shack to the door and entered. Two men with ski masks followed and started to move to the camera monitoring system in the corner.

Gregor stood before her, then gently set a black briefcase on its side next to Sarah. She wondered for all of one second what might be in it, before Gregor broke the suspense.

"This has 100,000 American dollars inside, unmarked and non-sequential. Nothing that has happened tonight can be traced back to you. Ve are switching the tapes vith properly time-coded replacements. Vithout realizing it, by having aided us tonight, you have unvittingly helped to spare the lives of untold scores of potential victims, Sarah. Thousands, maybe more. Together, ve have beaten back the darkness once more. The money is for your silence. Hide it. Do not deposit it into a bank and spend it slowly. No one will know. All you have to do, Sarah, is tell no one."

Gregor knelt down next to Sarah and looked into her eyes. Brows furrowed and scowling as much as one really can when their mouth is duct-taped shut, she mumbled. His hands moved to her mouth and she recoiled slightly. He peeled the tape off in one smooth motion.

"Here, give me your hands."

She raised her bound wrists and he flashed a small blade which cut through the duct tape like butter. He then sliced open her leg tape and folded the knife back together as he stood up slowly. His dark green duster jacket looked expensive and soft up close.

He held out his arm to her and she clasped onto it to steady herself. It felt as though it was made from stone, it was so firm and unmoving.

"This vas a better outcome Sarah, I assure you. It's likely you vould not have been allowed to survive the night."

"How do you know my name?" She really was curious by now.

"Ve do our research, Sarah. Ve have unfettered access to all manner of globally-networked operational intelligence."

Sarah's eyebrow cocked up. "Seriously?"

He smiled. "Not really, no." Gregor tapped on his right breast and Sarah looked down at her own chest. Her ID badge. Mystery solved.

*Crazy.*

"Ve are vith a small yet committed group vich shall remain nameless. But, it goes to say that our goal is to deal out the extermination of a particular denizen of the darkness that you could call a vampire."

"Uh-kay, that's pretty crazy. *Could call?*"

"Could call, vould call. Ve call them by this name, naturally, but its title is ultimately of little matter. You know vat they are and vat they can do, I suppose?"

"No, but yeah sorta, I think." Sarah rubbed her wrists. They would be totally red for days after this. Her study group would think she had been getting hella kinky with some unknown suitor in her spare time. The questions and cocked eyebrows on Monday would be just super-duper fun.

She wondered what she might tell them, then figured she could just be honest and say a gorgeous Deutschlander with a charming voice, and haunting eyes had bound her by the wrists and she'd simply done everything he'd asked her to after that. It just might shut them right on up, too. Worth trying, anyway.

"Ve're going now. I hope you keep this to yourself, Sarah." Gregor stood up and moved to the door again. The others had finished switching the tapes in the recorders and had started to load up the vehicle with their claim.

Gregor stopped short of the door and turned again to face Sarah. "And I *vaunted* to thank you. So, thank you."

Gregor held out his hand. Sarah looked down at it, then back up into his cold, gray eyes. Her hand met his and limply shook it as she wincd.

*Funny.*

# P38

ttendees and vendors of the 1989 SHOT show in Dallas, Texas were greeted at the door by two bubbly, buxom blondes in tight-white, tit-poppin', pre-shredded tank-tops, holding Kalashnikovs in one hand and putting commemorative tenth anniversary lanyards on the attendees' necks with the other.

The Shooting Hunting and Outdoor Trade show had been the preeminent gun expo in the continental US since the early 1980s and had pulled out all the stops for the big double digit anniversary. The two big-bosom blondies at the front were both models for *Playboy* during the 1988 season and had every ticket holder happy they'd come just as soon as they walked in.

Teddy smiled in his tight red, "Have a Coke and Smile!" T-shirt as he entered the main hall, and the scantily-clad bunny on the right slipped his badge over his neck. He thought it was a nice touch, and frankly felt he wouldn't mind touching them either. He winked at her, but her gaze went straight past Teddy, toward the next man who stood behind him, informing him he could go now.

Patriots of all stars and stripes as well as the bullet bimbettes, NRA members, avid big game hunters, doomsday preppers, gun whackos, God-fearing Second Amendment advocates, steely-eyed Japanese businessmen, and German arms manufacturers in Armani suits were all present and accounted for. The vibrant red, white, and blue color schemes were legion.

During that cool January night in the Dallas Convention Center, flags hung everywhere. The room was heavy with the aroma of burnt popcorn oil. Hats floated through the crowd that read, "Don't tread on me," while flashy booths with neon signage advertised the latest in explosive tipped ballistic rounds of all calibers.

Extension mags were big that year, and every other booth offered up their own contribution to the trend. *Sports Illustrated* was on site with a camera crew, filming a segment on the so-called "Air gun renaissance." It was also the first time anyone had their hands on a Remington Model SP-10 auto-shotty or a Bazalt RPG-29 "Vampir" rocket-propelled grenade launcher the commies were usin' these days to shoot at, well, Afghans and whatnot.

It seemed like every other attendant wanted to be the John Rambo of their respective neighborhood, or at least get their picture taken with one. There were more than a few life-size cardboard stand-ups of the titular character to be found at the expo, some for sale, as well as one red bandana-ed Stallone looka-like who would charge you five bucks for a ripply-muscled photo with the family.

*Smile and say, "Hey-yo!"*

Teddy first walked the full length of the expo, taking in all the lovely sights and sounds the noisy convention hall and its oc-cupants offered up. More gorgeous women modeling concealable sidearms. Kids popping caps as they rushed past wearing *Howdy Doody* cowboy hats. Gun belts and bullets and camo, oh my!

Hot dog carts could be found every fifty feet, filling the air with their cheap meaty scent. After just two hundred yards, Teddy couldn't take it anymore and stopped to get a fully-loaded dog topped with relish, sauerkraut, onions, and hot liquid cheese. He stuffed it into his gob and devoured it before he got to the next set of carts. Then he rushed up to the Bud Light vendor and overpaid for ten ounces of racoon piss in a red solo cup, which he swallowed in one gulp.

Wiping the beer from his mustache-lined lips with his jean-jacketed sleeve, he scratched his fire-red hair and looked around. The Dallas Convention Center was big and open and impressive. Stylish early-eighties updates to the decor were starting to feel a smidge out of time, yet it retained a professional sheen.

Despite it being seven in the evening, the place still had a good crowd, though not nearly as much as during the daylight hours. Things ran until ten so it wasn't surprising. Probably would start to die down once the bars got into full swing in the next hour or so, Teddy figured.

He tossed the empty cup in a nearby receptacle and decided to see who was pumping out the music he heard from the other end of the hall.

As he passed by booths for Heckler & Koch and Taurus, he saw a super-tall Uncle Sam on stilts handing out bright green flyers for an upcoming monster truck rally the following weekend. He walked up and took one from the hands of the bearded man.

*Might be a good time,* he thought as he folded it up and slipped it into his back jean pocket.

He wasn't here for any flyers though. He needed a good side-arm. Something simple and reliable. He had given his .357 Sig Sauer to his older brother as a wedding gift about six months back and now, as small arms were concerned, only had a .22 Glock and an old, damn-near antique Colt .45 he'd inherited from grandma in his armory.

Two pistols weren't enough. What if you need a back-up piece? You gonna trust an old Colt? Not when it mattered, you weren't.

So here he was.

He walked past a big display from Lockheed Martin showing off the newest laser-guided missile systems that they were already outfitting the next gen of US Air Force fighters with. Huge back-drop images featuring scenes that looked as though they'd been pulled straight from Top Gun. Carriers and sunsets and close-ups of firing missiles trailed by white smoke streams.

He nodded at the cute girl with freckles who was giving a demo to a group of ten businessmen types. Projected on a screen next to her was a profile of the missile's inner workings. She was using a laser pointer to draw attention to various functions and she smiled back as he strode along.

He stopped briefly at the big double-tabled setup for Smith & Wesson. It was pristine, immaculate, and damn near holy in its gleaming grandeur. Shining chrome rows of all the new pistols and shotguns. Designer ammo boxes and tactical gear hung up, ready to shoulder and try on.

*Look no further,* he thought.

Handsome people in tailored suits and afterparty-ready dresses crowded around a short man with a bullish look and bald head. He spoke in a distinctly New York accent about slides and reloaders while intermittently straightening his tacky purple tie, giving a demo to those assembled.

Teddy looked at the guns and leaned in to get a gander at the price tags. *Yikes.* Brand new wares had that brand spanking new price, too.

He figured it was time to get realistic about his budgetary constraints and consider a smaller, private vendor. He knew there were plenty to peruse. Could use another beer, though. His eyes searched and found another beer cart.

As he reached the back of the hall a few minutes later, fresh Bud in hand, he saw that a raised up stage had a really nice kick-up going on in front of it. A ten-man, two-lady band filled up the stage, and their music— plucking guitars and rocking drums— had everyone on their feet. Men with cowboy hats squared off with their long-dressed dates, swinging them to and fro. It was quite the little party in the back now, wasn't it?

On his way back through the expo hall, he grabbed another beer and made short work of it. He then stopped briefly at the Beretta booth, where he scored a complimentary neon-pink beer cozy that had Robert Blake's face on the side. Pretty funny. The prices were still a bit too high though, so he continued to wander.

He passed by a giant foam bullet expo mascot that was taking pictures with people, just like the John Rambo from earlier. He briefly tried to hit on one of the scantily clad Mossberg girls who was holding the newest pump action auto-shotguns, but to no avail.

As he floated along, he realized this was the kind of place he felt the most comfortable in. Around good, decent folks cut from the same cloth.

It was right about then that he noticed that there were other, narrower hallways that branched out and that were clearly the domain of the smaller, cottage industry-type arms dealers. The sort of cats who just barely got their vendor status approved, and only because there would be an uproar if they were all denied.

Still, they were relegated to the out-of-the-way spaces and narrow hallways that permeated the outer reaches of the Dallas Convention Center. Outta sight, outta mind.

Teddy noticed that to his right was one particularly badly-illuminated smaller hallway that went back about seventy-five yards to a wall with a fire exit set into it. There were only a handful of guys in small booths at the mouth of the hallway, then way in the back there was some tiny little spot that Teddy could barely see.

His curiosity was strangely piqued by this mundane sight, and he investigated, walking into the area.

He passed the first two vendors who were prepper dudes with lots of camo-patterned everything on their tables. If you needed a camouflage sniper-scope, these guys had it for you. But Teddy pushed past and continued toward the rear wall.

Teddy walked up to the booth near the fire exit. It was a small and modest spread of sidearms as well as various edges and blades laid neatly up on a long sheet of shiny black fabric. Each had a holster and carrying case neatly placed alongside them.

The man who sat on a small white and yellow lawn chair next to the table looked to be in his sixties, at least. Shoulder-length gray hair and alabaster skin with veins starting to color his forehead and cheeks. He wore a flannel button-up covering a T-shirt that read, "The mistakes of the past are but the lessons of the present, granted us to prevent the tragedies of the future."

The booth didn't have any company association plaques or any distinct markings on any signage. Or any signage at all, for that matter. But the man had every item looped up with a dangling price tag and had a few stickers on his table's ammo box, including an NRA logo and circle of multi-colored dancing Grateful Dead bears.

"You like the old stuff?" the old man mused without looking up from his magazine—a tattered vintage copy of *Guns and Ammo* from the seventies.

Woo-doggie, Teddy suspected he knew what the guy was getting at. It figured, too. The guy was probably a come-lately, white pride kinda fella. Too white pride for Teddy's liking anyway. War did that to some fellas. His grandpa had served and fought against the Japs and Nazis, so it really wasn't like Teddy to cotton to that sort of anti-American horseshit. Guy was probably trying to offload some dark market china plates from the Third Reich or some such malarkey.

"You serve?" Teddy asked.

"Yes, sir. Second World War. Captain David McDaniels, 104th division, US army, at your service."

Teddy was mildly surprised but quickly said, "Well shit, thank you kindly for your service, sir."

Dave paused for a moment and studied Teddy's face before he responded, "Uh, yeah. Well, no problem, son. It was my honor to serve my nation."

As Teddy looked over the blades, which were a wide variety of military-style boot knives and tactical edges, he noticed one item was set apart. The gun at the table's end was spaced a good foot away from the others and had no holster or case with it, yet it had the same tag as the rest. Oddly, though, it was encased under a glass cube. It looked to Teddy to be an old Walther with a brown handle, ribbed grip. A forties model, maybe?

"What's that one there?" Teddy pointed at the small gun.

"Well, something I haven't been able to sell, tried though I have for years. You didn't answer my query from a moment ago. Do you like the old stuff?"

"If you mean some swastika-stamped, ugly-shit relics of dead German fucks who tried to kill my grandpappy, then I suppose you could say I don't, no. That what yer askin', fella?"

"Sure is, son. Sure is. Glad to hear that that ain't your cup of tea, neither." Dave's weary eyes looked Teddy up and down. He cracked a tiny grin. "That thing wouldn't be of much interest to you in that case. I'd rather be rid of it myself. It was never my kinda thing either."

"What type of Walther is it?"

Dave cleared his throat. "It's a P38. Directly issued to the Wehrmacht as a replacement for the Luger P08. Nasty little chunk of an even uglier part of history."

"Why do you keep it then? Why not just throw it out?"

"I figured I need to give the next owner a heads up before I saddle them with that particular mustang. I throw it into a lake or trash can, and then what? I can't worry about some kid finding it and disappearing without a trace or something."

This piqued Teddy's interest. What the hell did disappearing without a trace mean to this cowboy?

"Come again? What disappears?" he asked.

"It's got a problem, or rather a manufacturing defect. No, that's … that's not really being honest. It's more of a… Well, let's just say it, uh…" Dave trailed off mid-sentence. He eyed Teddy and then rolled his eyes as they returned to his issue of *Guns and*

*Ammo* magazine. He quickly answered, "I mean, what it does is it teleports you to Nazi Germany."

Teddy laughed from the depths of his belly and it echoed off the yellowed walls of the narrow hallway. "What the hell is that supposed to mean, fella?"

"Just what I said, sonny. I'm being quite literal." Dave flipped a page in his magazine.

"Where to, exactly?" Teddy asked.

"A side street, somewhere near Castle Wewelsburg."

Teddy chortled loudly. "Aw, come the fuck on now!"

"I'm not playing at anything and I have little patience for malarkey, friend-o."

"Now, what's a man supposed to think when he hears another man roll one off the assembly line that rattles and creaks like that bullshit right there?"

"I don't much worry about that kinda thing, if we're bein' honest. And you know I am."

"Ah." Teddy rolled his eyes and walked right on up to where the gun lay. It was in fine condition if the age the man was claiming was genuine. "You a big sci-fi fan when you're not being a real American hero?"

"I was never a hero, and it does precisely what I said."

"So now it's a Walther that warps you around the world?" Teddy asked with a smirk.

Dave looked Teddy square in his eye and muttered, "Yep. Lift up the glass box and find out."

Teddy smiled a mile-wide smile and was quick to call the guy's bluff as he carefully lifted the glass enclosure which was heavier than he would've expected. Setting it aside, he looked at the gun.

Teddy reached down to take a hold of the Walther and raised it up as he gripped the handle in his fist. "You're honestly sayin' that—"

Feeling the inlaid wood ridges curved against his palm, his vision began to rapidly blur. The room spun like a tilt-a-whirl as a kaleidoscope of rushing colors wrapped up his eyes in a vivid and disorienting menagerie of rods and cones.

Before he could rub his eyes to stop the rapid visions, the spinning stopped and the eye-burning halogen panel lighting of the convention hall was replaced by a black field of stars with cool moonlight casting down onto a long cobblestone corridor between several buildings that looked out of time.

He was outside, at night, standing in a place he could barely describe.

Teddy took a breath. The air was cold and crisp. He gazed up and saw the full moon hanging in its heavenly throne. Then his eyes peered down the blue-stone walkway between the buildings.

He cautiously took a few steps forward. The alleyway was dimly lit but he could see that the street it opened onto was alive with the sounds of celebratory chatter and nightlife. He walked along the bumpy stone road until he exited from between the white and gray buildings and saw revelries in full swing.

Teddy surely wasn't exactly what the average citizen of the Earth would describe as "worldly," but in his modest estimation, the buildings he saw on all sides resembled things he'd seen in school textbooks and in period piece films about various wars and historical people. The ornate and frankly cutesy-looking façades of the buildings looked European and distinctly pre-war in their design and architecture.

*Almost looks the same as those houses they have in* The Sound of Music, he thought.

Green iron lighting posts lined the street and violin music filled the air, emanating from the open window of a nearby pub. Every so often, a burst of laughter from a group of people cut through the frosty night. He spied several groups of jovial and jabbering folks in old-timey duds meandering along the wide street that had no lane markings or street signage that he could see.

Tables were set outside cafes. One had a group of men playing cards and smoking cigarettes. Nearby, an older gentleman with a bushy white beard was sitting on a stool at an easel where he used a brush to divine his creations onto canvas. The artist paused, noticing the odd-looking man coming out of the alleyway. Teddy didn't notice on account of eyeballing the filigree patterns on the floral dresses the ladies in the street were wearing.

The artist stood up, adjusted his spectacles and called out to Teddy, "*Hallo, du! Was machst du da hinten?*"

*Shit. Is this really…?*

His eyes looked past the man shouting, and for the first time, he noted that hanging every fifty feet from the roofs of the buildings, just over the facades, were long, blood-red flags with thick black swastikas in white circles emblazoned upon them. Seeing how many there were now, he was mighty surprised he hadn't noticed them sooner.

Holy hell, it really was.

Teddy was in Nazi Germany like the crazy old fucker—well, maybe not so crazy actually—had said. He decided to see if this was the real deal Holyfield.

"Hey buddy!" he called out to the man. "Should I have taken a left turn at Albuquerque, or what?"

The old man's neutral look of curiosity rapidly disintegrated and his lips curled into a malicious sneer as he shouted much louder this time, *"Amerikanisches Schwein!"* The wannabe Picasso pointed the tip of his brush at Teddy in an accusatory manner, then turned and hollered out, "Hey, hey, *hier ist ein Amerikaner!*". He repeated it.

Teddy certainly weren't no linguist either, but he got the gist of that one, alright. The feeble ol' Kraut-doggie had sold him out, but good.

Voices around him largely went quiet and the violin music suddenly stopped. His eyes went wide as several of the people spread around the street immediately set their eyes upon him, some standing up from tables and others shouting variations of what the first German had. Folks were peering out of second and third floor windows, and not far to his right, two men in Nazi uniform were storming in his direction.

Teddy was suddenly aware he was still gripping the Walther tightly in his right hand. They must've seen it, because the soldier on the left made for the buttoned strap on his side holster.

Teddy figured it was as good a time as any to drop the gun and try to explain what he could to the bee's nest he'd just accidentally kicked. His hand released the Walther.

As the pistol slipped from his grasp, a tunnel of light and rapidly passing colors spun around him. Just as he felt he might pass out, his vision came back. The harsh light of the halogen bulbs hit him again and he focused his eyes.

He was still in the convention center, standing before the table just as he had been, and the P38 was lying in the same spot it had before he had picked it up. Dave was still flipping through his copy of *Guns and Ammo* and smiled as Teddy trembled slightly.

His head was dizzy with the rush of it all. Teddy's eyes lowered to meet Dave's.

"Holy fucking shit! The goddamn k-k-kickin' hell was that?" Teddy stammered.

"Uh  Büren in '41, if I'm correct. Gotta hand it to those Germans, they were a squirrelly and crafty bunch durin' those years, but they knew how to party."

"I can't believe that just happened!"

"No one ever can, son." Dave flipped to the next page.

"How does it do that, ya think?"

Dave shifted in his chair and used one hand to scratch at his graying chin stubble. "Must have been the experiments they were doing on all that weird stuff like teleportation that made such a thing possible."

"The hell, you say."

"Right hand to God." Dave held up his right palm.

Teddy stared, dumbfounded. Never in a million years would he have ever believed such a thing could happen. But, by golly, it just had. And now Teddy wanted to know more.

"Whe-where did you get it?"

"I found it on a German SS high-officer in that same town called Büren in '45. My guys and I had been reclaiming areas north of Frankfurt and we had to clear the land around Castle Wewelsburg. If that doesn't sound too familiar, that's where Himmler had his experiments. Nazi occult stuff, ya know?"

"You feedin' me a line, sir?"

"No, son. When we arrived, orders were to search and destroy any technology we found, which was a might bit odd, 'cause usually they wanted to hang onto that kinda stuff. But orders is orders. We took apart a bunch of big metal machines with crowbars, smashed up labs, torched documents, and made a real clear message of the place. Didn't fully take the place down, but everything was gutted and later burned by our boys.

"We found this guy in one of the labs, and he had the gun on him. I touched it and it did what it does to me for the first time. I didn't know what to do, so naturally, I panicked and got right out by letting go of it. Once I realized what had happened, well, I luckily had some leather gloves with me and used 'em to get it in my bag. Then I brought it back home with me in a hollowed out King James."

"You don't think you shouldn't let people touch it?"

"Well, son, not everyone is so handsy, ya see. But nobody ever gets hurt. They grab it, see what I mean, then return and just walk away, changed somehow. Like now they know how shaky the reality around them really is. Truth is, you're one of the rare people who wants to chit chat about it afterwards. Most amscray, post haste."

"You don't reckon this is a bad thing you're doing to unsuspecting folks?"

Dave stopped reading and looked at Teddy. For the first time he flashed something like intimidation in his dark eyes. "Son, after what I've seen, I know bad things don't always happen to bad people, but what I do know is that if something bad does happen to a bad person, the world is only better for it. And you can cash that check, haus."

Teddy scoffed. "That don't quite square, ya know?"

"Neither does that gun, nor the shaky world around ya, so go figure." Dave leaned back, raised his copy of *Guns and Ammo* back up, and resumed reading. "Anyway, I warn everyone who grabs it. They make their own choice." Then he chuckled. "Bad thing. Ha! Like you've ever seen a bad thing, sonny."

Teddy didn't know what to say in response. What could you say, really? The man hadn't actually lied. Teddy had been warned, and now here he was, still safe albeit possibly irreversibly affected in unknowable ways by this moment.

And he was sick to his stomach. In some deep recess that he could not articulate, he sensed a frozen darkness entering his heart that he knew would never leave, and he suddenly felt very sad.

He looked at Dave, and without saying another word, started back down the narrow, badly-lit hallway.

As Teddy disappeared around the corner, Dave chuckled a bit more to himself and leafed through his magazine.

It must've been a good hour later, when the white noise of the expo echoing off the walls of his shitty location was dying out and the other booths were breaking down, that the tall, lanky man he'd likely been waiting for marched down the hall. His shaved head and green button-up jacket told Dave all he really needed to know. This guy *was* looking for something off the menu.

Clevold L. Kreigshauser was nearly goose-steppin' as he strode up to Dave and looked around. Classic skinhead get-up right down to the dumb OD green bomber jacket and tight-laced black jackboots. His eyes scanned the assemblage of weaponry and eventually Dave himself. He sneezed into his hand and wiped it on his skinny black Levi's.

"You like the old stuff?" Dave mused without looking up from his magazine. He wryly smirked, nearly imperceptibly.

Clevold misread the micro-expression and figured he had finally found someone else in this classless heathen pool who had the real goods. "I'll say that I've got time-honored views and my blood is pure. Some people these days just don't like to hear the truth. Most people, actually. But I'm thinking a vendor of your discerning tastes may just have more than the rest of these silly gerbils might."

Dave thought the guy was about as subtle as the gull-dern Air Force jet that flew overhead earlier in the day and had set off all the car alarms in the parking lot. Which was to say, not very subtle at all. Still, this was his guy alright.

*The fly had caught a spider and it was time to kick him outta the web.*

"This puppy on the end here might be up your alley." Dave pointed to the Walther P38 which still lay where Teddy had dropped it against the silky black cloth on the tabletop.

Clevold's eyes lit up when he saw the tiny, barely visible but unmistakable swastika etched into the barrel along with the P38 stamp.

"Was this one—" Clevold's slender, tattoo wrapped, heavily-ringed fingers reached out to the gun.

"Hey, whoa! Hold up a minute there, pardner!" Dave stood up and walked over to where the gun lay. He pulled a pair of leather gloves from his back pocket and slipped them on. He then lifted up the gun with the left hand and used the index finger of the right to click the safety into the *off* position.

"Is that Wehrmacht issued?" the bald neo-fascist excitedly demanded like a jubilant child might.

"Yes, sir, it is. Good eye on ya'. Found on an SS soldier and smuggled into the US by Bible. I just gotta make sure you know what that gun there is capable of."

"Capable of? Other than ending unnecessary lives?" Clevold smiled and rubbed his hands together before him in anticipation of snatching the gun from off the table.

"It sends you to Nazi Germany."

Clevold laughed a deep, guttural boom, slapped at his

kneecaps, and spun around in a circle. That wasn't one he'd heard before.

"Hahahaha! My man, my man! Lemme hear you correct— you say this thing can take me to Nazi Germany? I mean, uh-heh, what does that even mean?" Clevold was positively tickled by the novelty of this man's brand of psychosis.

"I mean exactly what I said, *my man*. Small village near Castle Wewelsburg, during some sort of festival."

The man in the jackboots began to rub his hairless scalp. "You mean where Himmler had his whole thing? So this is, what, one of his experiments? That's a pretty fanciful claim, my man."

"Yet truer than you wanna know."

Clevold laughed again. "You're fucking crazy, buddy. Certifiable."

"So you really don't want a little part of the Reich's history to call your own?" Dave's eyes gleamed wickedly, his lips curled maliciously.

"Well, ya know, I might could want that, sure, but only if the price was right."

"Then pick up the gun, son. Just be sure to send the mustachioed midget my warmest regards and it's yours to keep, no money needed."

"Right, man." Clevold wondered briefly what exactly the gent with the odd manner could be meaning to say, when he took the plunge and snatched up the gun.

He was about to take it in his other hand to aim down the sights when a rainbow of lights and flashing colors engulfed his vision. He felt spinning for the briefest of moments before his eyes stopped whirling in multi-hued patterns and focused on the open alleyway before him.

The bluish cobblestone lit by the full moon and the white mid-thirties German deco-walls of the imposing buildings flanked him on each side. He looked down and the brown-handled P38 in his hand, then gazed up at the sky. The stars were bright, and as he lowered his eyes, he could hear music and see light from the street.

Clevold Kreigshauser strutted up the alleyway, lifted the back of the bomber jacket and tucked the gun into his belt. The metal felt cold against his skin.

He reached the mouth of the alley, and when he carefully looked out, he saw the lively people, the red banners, and the bushy bearded man at the easel. His eyes were wide and he watched as German men, women, and children walked along, oblivious to his presence, on the wide, mostly signless street.

Clevold squinted, and across the street, partially masked by shadows, were the figures of two German SS officers. To him they appeared stylish and sturdy, but he knew they posed a threat, nonetheless. His hand moved back to where he had nestled the barrel between his waistband and back, and he tried to remove the Walther. However his fumbling digits caused the gun to slip from his grasp.

Though he expected it to hit the ground with a clang, the sound never came. The gun had completely disappeared.

He didn't know what to do. There was no way this could be real, but he certainly understood what Germany in the late thirties and early forties looked like. This was, if nothing else, the most historically accurate, culturally insensitive theme park on the planet that he'd been randomly shot to. Somehow though, he knew that this was the real thing.

He heard footsteps coming up the alleyway behind him. From a street further back, a man and woman, the man in army garb and the woman in a large yellow floral dress, clung to each other for balance as they stumbled toward him, laughing all the way. Clevold wasn't exactly sure what his best chance might be, so he leaned against the wall and pretended to be fiddling with something in his hands as the couple walked past.

As the two moved along the alley, though their voices lowered and they cast suspicious glances Clevold's way as they murmured in German to one another. Clevold could understand roughly every other word and they were definitely using words like *frem-der*, which he knew meant stranger, and *verdächtig*, which meant suspicious. He didn't look up because he figured his eyes might betray him.

The couple moved out into the street and walked directly toward the two officers across the way. The man turned and pointed at the open alleyway where Clevold stood and started saying something to the soldiers in German.

Nearby, the bushy bearded man at the easel stopped stroking the canvas with his brush and looked up from his stool.

The two men in Wehrmacht uniforms walked in step with the third soldier toward Clevold's position, leaving the woman behind briefly.

In this exact moment, he figured that running was only going to get him gunned down from the back. His best bet, risky though it may be, would be to try to explain to someone what had happened. Despite the fact that he had no fucking clue what that actually was.

The men had nearly reached him when the third broke off to run down the street, possibly to summon others.

Clevold turned to face them and unzipped his jacket. He had a cheap white tank top on underneath and as the soldiers got to within a few feet, he pulled up the shirt, revealing a huge black bar swastika tattoo that filled most of his muscular stomach.

The soldiers stopped and seemed both surprised and suspicious. They looked at each other, then one spoke quietly to the other in German. Then they walked up to him and grabbed him from both sides. Using his own weight against him, they buckled his knees and dropped him to his chest on the ground.

He felt the freezing stone against his body and wrestled to gain leverage, though none came. One of the men buried a knee in his back and his cheek pressed against the ground. He stopped struggling.

From his face-down vantage point, Clevold could see a small, rapidly approaching vehicle. It was a boxy open-top military jeep-like thing. He wasn't sure he'd ever seen one quite like it. The four men who rode in it wore the same uniforms as the bastards who held his arms behind his back and were calling out to the others in the jeep.

*"Wir haben hier einen Amerikaner! Er hat versucht, uns mit falschen Markierungen des Reiches zu täuschen!"* yelled the one to his left.

As the jeep stopped before them and the two soldiers lifted Clevold up, his eyes blinked in the light of the bright headlamps.

The man in the passenger seat stepped out. He had more emblems on his sleeves and seemed to be the highest ranking officer amongst them. He pulled off his black officer's hat with the skull logo dead center on the front as he came around to the front of the jeep. He was young looking, with blue eyes, slicked back blonde hair, and a clean-shaven face.

Without looking at the captive, he softly asked of the two men holding Clevold, *"Wo kommt er her?"*

One of the men holding his hands spoke while pointing at the alleyway, *"Die gasse."*

The other soldier in gray fatigues laughed at this. The senior officer smirked in a cold manner that gave him no comfort.

The German moved directly in front of Clevold and shocked him by saying, "You are pretending to be a loyal German, American?"

The other German citizens had gone quiet. The violin had stopped and everyone was gazing out open doorways and windows.

The officer took out a flat silver tin with the SS logo on it and pulled a cigarette free from it. He started to tap the filter on his wrist without breaking eye contact with Clevold. He placed it in his mouth and flicked a small lighter on, lighting the thin white smoke. His eyes were calm and direct, more curious than threatening. He clapped the lighter closed and pocketed it.

As he exhaled his first puff into the cool moonlit air, he asked, "Why put this mark on yourself, American? Why do this to fool us, but no uniform to do the same? Why be so easy for us to discover, yet do this?" His finger pointed toward Clevold's chest.

Not knowing what to do, Clevold shook in the cold night air and quickly slid his right arm loose from his captors grasp. He shot it up into the air, palm flat at an angle and shouted, "Heil Hitler!"

Not one of the fifty onlookers made a sound. The street was almost perfectly quiet.

The officer looked long and hard at the skinhead before him, while the men holding him laughed.

"And why do you say that? What would make an Amerikaner worthy to serve the Führer?" The officer's eyes remained cool and calm.

"Because I am from a future where you have lost the war, and only men like myself bear allegiance to the glory of the Reich."

The officer eyed him and his features softened ever so slightly. "Okay, Amerikaner, any way to prove this story?"

Clevold remembered his wallet. "I have identification on me. In my back pocket."

The officer nodded to the two soldiers holding him and he felt a hand reach into his back pocket, then draw forth his wallet. The same hands reached around and tossed the wallet into the hands of the officer.

He drew a long pull from his smoke as his fingers flipped through the wallet and he pulled out Clevold's state-issued Texas ID. His eyes scanned the card and after a moment, he said, "Kreigshauser, that's a nice touch." Then, stifling a laugh he asked, "Who is the US president in the future Mr. Kreigshauser?"

"The new one is a guy named George Bush."

A small smile briefly crossed the blonde German's lips.

The guard behind him on the right asked the officer, "*Was heibt das?*"

The blonde officer grinned and replied, "*Er sagt, er kommt aus der Zukunft!*"

Everyone within earshot started to laugh. Clevold felt very alone in that moment.

The officer continued, "This document is strange, American future man. I'll admit that. And, looking at these other items inside of your wallet, they all seem to corroborate the first. So I think, why would you create false documents for such an improbable story? I do not know, but I know that I have a few questions. First, you say we lost the war. How is that?"

Clevold realized he may still have a chance here. He swallowed, cleared his throat, and calmly answered, "The Führer makes a series of factually incorrect assumptions and even larger tactically unsound military decisions as a result. He greatly underestimates Allied preparedness and overestimates Germany's, which lead to his forces being mis-utilized and dispersed in such a way that he cannot survive the final Allied push. Japan and Italy will recede from the war effort. The Allies and the Russians return with improbable numbers which overwhelm Germany and lead to the fall of Berlin. With no hope of victory, Hitler commits suicide in the Führerbunker with Eva Braun on April thirtieth 1945 using a Walther PPK."

The blonde officer asked, "Eva Braun?" Then he smiled, taking another contemplative drag, exhaling slowly. "And what about Germany? What becomes of the motherland?"

"In the immediate aftermath, everyone is tried and many are executed for war crimes. The Reich falls, the high command dies, Germans are globally treated as second class citizens long after the war ends. For decades, in fact. Jokes are made about the Führer. Comedy films will eventually depict you as dim-witted devils. A new generation of liberal German rats outlaw the swastika in the motherland. The truth is hidden from our eyes, the glory of the Reich is lost. And only a handful of us still believe in the words and goals of the largely forgotten empire. That is what happens."

The officer stood before Clevold and then eyed the two men holding him. They loosened their hold and he pulled his arms around and slid the shirt back down over his stomach.

The SS G-man before him handed him his wallet and took another pull of his smoke. He exhaled into the crisp air then dropped the cig on the ground and stomped it out with the heel of his jackboot before asking, "Okay, and why do you still believe?

If what you say is true, why would they allow you to support dead men and lost ideas?"

Clevold didn't hesitate to reply, "I am of German descent, and patriots of pure blood like myself and others still live, despite constant persecution. We still believe in the future of the master race, sir. Hitler was—*is*—a prophet, however he is but one integral part of the larger idea that I would only humbly ask to serve."

The two men stood silent, along with everyone else within a two block radius, for several seconds. Finally, the man in the Wehrmacht uniform smiled and said, "Well that isn't a terrible answer, Amerikaner, and I can see that you believe you aren't lying. My final question: How did you arrive here from 1989, if that's actually what occurred, Herr Kreigshauser?"

"I was looking to purchase relics of the Reich at a weapons exhibition in America. A man showed me an old gun he vaguely implied had been experimented on by Heinrich Himmler at Castle Wewelsburg. When I picked it up I was teleported to this alleyway. And then you found me."

One of the guards interrupted and Clevold understood him to be asking what he was saying. In response, the officer shouted, "*Scheiß drauf!*"

Clevold smiled. He knew that essentially meant, "Shut the fuck up."

The guard quickly retracted his small as the tall man in the SS garb held out his hand to shake Clevold's. "Reinhard Heydrich."

Clevold smiled and shook his hand. "I know who you are, sir, and it's a great honor to be meeting you. Director of the Gestapo, hand selected by Himmler, am I right?"

For the first time, the German officer registered something

like a flash of surprise on his face, then smiled. He patted the man on the shoulder and said, "Yes. It is good to meet you too, Mr. Kreigshauser. I hope we may assist each other. Come with us. There are others who will want to ask you questions."

"I would be honored to answer. But first, may I have one of those cigarettes?"

The blonde German, who would later be known in infamy by such monikers as the "Blonde Beast", the "Butcher of Prague", and by the führer himself as the "Man With the Iron Heart," grinned a warm, friendly grin and tapped out another smoke for his new acquaintance, then lit the cigarette for him.

All around, people were whispering to one another, but also turning away. The music had restarted and some of the street revelers had decided that the whole thing was of flagging interest, returning to their cards and dancing.

"Follow me. Himmler himself will want to speak with you immediately."

"After you."

Clevold followed him over to the open-top vehicle and Reinhardt waved the driver toward the back, then stepped into the driver's seat. He put his black SS officers hat back on and started up the engine.

Shooting a look to Clevold, then to the front passenger seat, the other three men who had arrived with the officer said nothing but quietly squeezed into the back together.

Clevold slid into the passenger seat and realized that he may be able to help the cause in a way he had never dreamed. And he would never be able to thank the crazy old man for this good fortune.

The jeep started down the street toward Castle Wewelsburg

as the dark night refilled with the sounds of jovial German voices and violin music.

Back in 1989, the gun reappeared in midair over the table, then dropped a few inches back onto the soft black felt. Dave gave a frosty smile as he slipped on his gloves and popped the safety back into the *on* position, then placed the glass cube back over the gun as he started to break down the booth.

He was sometimes curious about what happened to the ones he sent back, not that he cared much. But he wondered what that ol' bomber jacket–wearing, jackboot–kicking guy was doing now.

*Probably already gone the way of the Führer,* he thought to himself with a satisfied smile.

# CHOOSE



*Quod ad placandum malum serpentem deo sacrificium faciendum sit. Maledicat me et perficiat fabulam circulus…*

### *<u>WARNING!</u>*

Do not read this book directly from front to back! The following novel is a chance for you to take control of your destiny. Your choices are what will decide how the story unfolds before you. They might bring you good fortune, or may, in fact, seal your doom. You are responsible, because it's your choices that move you through the story.

You'll be given multiple paths to continue down, and after you choose, follow the instructions to see what's next. As you proceed through the pages that lie ahead, take your time to choose the right path.

Don't rush. Don't worry. Don't ask who Lothalimoc is, why the Kindred have chosen you, or why you didn't see this coming.

Above all, we are *ad maledicendum tibi nunc!* So, *futue te Ipsum!*

The snow gently falls through the darkness outside of Sounds Easy video rental and CD shop in the snowy mountain town of Carbondale, Colorado. It's a cold, crisp, and beautiful Friday night in early December 1992.

It's 9:59 p.m., almost closing time, and you have been lounging back in the black leather recliner behind the counter. With only a few customers in the last hour, you've been intermittently straightening up and passively watching a screener copy of the oddball new independent horror film *Dead Alive*, directed by the crackpot Kiwi who also helmed *Meet the Feebles*. You have it playing on an eleven-inch television hooked up to an early eighties Magnavox VHS recorder.

As you turn off the lights and quickly return copies of *A Few Good Men*, *Batman Returns*, and *Wayne's World* to the neon-colored racks which hold the VHS tapes, there is a soft tapping on the front door.

You straighten the collar of your blue golf tee with the *Sounds Easy* VHS cassette logo on it, anticipating a late customer, but it's your crazy—albeit terribly amusing—metalhead friend, Niklas, holding up his Slayer shirt while he presses his bare chest against the glass. He's making gross, lurid faces at you. The tapping was the metal studs of his pierced nipples hitting the glass.

You laugh and come around the counter to lock the door and tell him you'll be out shortly. After counting out the drawers and putting the deposit in the safe, you head outside into the snowy air at about ten minutes after ten.

You are greeted by all your college friends gathered in various vehicles and standing about in trendy black attire, smoking clove cigarettes. A couple trucks, Nik's black Jeep and your reliable old '84 Volkswagen Jetta are in the lot and you hear electronic beats piping from one of them.

Your crew wants you to go with them and drop some LSD up Ol' Thompson Creek Road, not far from the abandoned silver mine. Niklas scored a couple of ten-strips of Purple Pyramid acid and figures tonight's the night to go get nutty in the woods.

If you think that heading up into the forested hills with your kooky homeboys and taking the Diamond train to Lucy-Ville is a great idea, turn to page 4.

If you decide you want to go smoke a joint at your place and pass out while eating Funyuns and watching MTV, turn to page 5.

You and your homies make a pit stop at the 7-11 for orange juice, gum, and more cigarettes. Then you head up the back road out of Carbondale. You left your vehicle back at the video store so ride with several others in the back of your friend Adam's brand new red and white Ford F-150.

You smoke a bowl from a glass pipe on the way up and the snow stops falling. The trippy, electronic beats of the Prodigy's "Out of Space" pump out from the truck's cab.

After ten minutes, past where the road plateaus and branches off into four-wheeler trails, you arrive at a small, dusty turnoff spot. It's the perfect place for a bonfire, just a five minute walk up the rocky old road from the mine.

Your friend Adam stacks some wood and sparks the fire. You take a shot of vodka from Niklas's flask and chase it with orange juice. Metal, hip-hop, and techno music saturates the night air with raw energy and the ever-enjoyable promise of adventure.

After you grab your acid from Nik, you drop it onto your tongue and join your friends around the small but bright fire. Everyone laughs and dances.

After a few minutes, a green flash of eldritch light pulses out from the mine just down the road from your impromptu revelry, along with an accompanying green fog. Everyone sees it and some of your friends ask if you'd like to come investigate with them.

If you'd rather stay with your saner friends and not risk getting your damn neck broken by a rotting wooden support-beam, turn to page 10.

If you feel as though you're young, full of promise, that nothing can ever do you any harm, and you wanna test that theory by going to the clearly perilous mine, turn to page 8.

Owing to your sad, deep-seated need to be accepted by others, you stupidly go with three of your less cautious friends (Nik, Tina, and Jenny) down the rocky, dark mountain road to the mine. Nik has brought a big black Maglite which illuminates the path.

When you arrive, a faint glow still emanates from the mouth of the cavern. There is a broken, rusted metal sign out front that reads, "Property of Roaring Fork Silver Co. Closed for public safety, 11/21/78." It also says to stay out because the mine is condemned.

Your friends pull away the creaky, brittle boards keeping trespassers out and you all enter the mine. The air is oddly damp and sour inside, and cobwebs continuously block your path which must be pulled down and away so you may proceed.

You see tracks working their way down into the darkness, and after a while you pass by an old minecart. You continue on and come to a split in the mine shaft where you notice that the light is coming from further down the right-hand path.

If you don't value your life and feel compelled to investigate the spectral glow further, turn to page 16.

If you suddenly grow a brain and decide that the juice ain't worth the squeeze on this whole dangerous enterprise and want to leave immediately, turn to page 13.

Shoving aside any goddamn sense of propriety or self-preservation, you and your rag-tag constituency of ne'er-do-well dunces take the right-hand path and continue toward the eerie glow illuminating the earthen walls of the mine shaft.

As the four of you walk along the dilapidated metal tracks, the green glow grows brighter and brighter.

You enter a larger chamber which is well lit by the light coming from a small stone altar against the far wall. There are dripping stalactites hanging from the ceiling creating rippling puddles below.

Upon the altar, creating the light, is a vaguely egg-shaped, jagged-edged shard of what looks like an iridescent emerald, twinkling with its own internal glow. Nik says it looks like something out of Superman's cave, hands you the Maglite, walks right up to it, and picks up the stone.

As he touches it, the color coming from the stone changes rapidly from a warm green to an eye-straining red that makes the wet-walled cavern appear to be covered in blood. Tina and Jenny say this is too spooky and they want to leave.

Niklas asks if you think that the acid is kicking in or if this is really real. You aren't sure, but notice that under where the stone is on the altar is an old, withered book coated in a thick layer of grimy dust.

Tina notices it as well, and snatches it off the altar, saying that she thinks you all have maybe ten minutes before this shit starts to hit you like Hunter Thompson in the Nevada desert, so you should go if you're going.

Jenny agrees, saying she really, really wants to leave now.

Suddenly, the stone flashes black, then red again, and Niklas starts to chant in an unknown tongue.

*"Maledicam mihi, o monstrum tenebrosum. Eripe animam meam a me! Lothalimoc, manducare me!"*

His eyes roll back in his head and go jet black as his mouth hangs open. A dark, oily substance oozes through his teeth and dribbles down his chin and onto his red Slayer shirt.

Jenny pulls at her long brown hair and screams. The echoing sound reverberates off the stony ceiling and hurts your ears.

Tina starts to shake her head furiously left to right as she clinches the book tightly in her hands.

Nik holds out the stone before him and rushes toward you and the girls with it.

~~If you want to just stand there, get done in, and allow the story to mercifully end long before the curse is fulfilled, turn to page 43.~~

If you choose to follow Jenny and Tina, who are already running for their goddamn lives out of the chamber and back toward the mouth of the mine, turn to page 32.

As you run along the mine with your dead-eyed, black sludge vomiting, erstwhile best buddy chasing you and the vacuous, shrieking twits that flank you on each side, you wonder what the hell is happening.

Niklas howls like a madman and swings the rock wildly as he follows you. You start to create distance between yourself and Niklas and see the minecart ahead. You tell Jenny and Tina to run ahead and to just trust you.

They keep on as you duck behind the minecart and wait for your possessed friend to scream by. When he does, you kick out your foot and trip him.

He flails as he stumbles forward, crashes down, and lets loose the stone, which flies through the air. His head hits the rock floor with a hard *THUD* and you know from both the sound as well as from the thin stream of blood spurting from his scalp that he is very much dead now.

Tina and Jenny stop and turn your direction. They ask if you're okay and you say you think so. They are heading toward you when Jenny slows down to look closely at the still glowing red shard of doom lying on the floor.

If you decide to feebly stand by and watch as Jenny picks up the stone, turn to page 64.

If you would rather shout at Jenny's stupid ass to keep her grubby little mitts off the rock if she values her life, then go fuck yourself, Chuckles, cause you're mine now.

You know that things are escalating rapidly when Jenny grabs the stone from the floor and starts to run her pink tongue against the jagged amber edges of the rock. She laps at it wantonly and begins to passionately suck on the rough tip, causing her lips to start bleeding.

You think to yourself that she is starting to look like a deadite, when Tina shouts for you to follow her. You snap out of your daze and make toward Tina.

As you pass by, Jenny takes a swing at you, trying to bludgeon your skull with the red stone. You twirl-flip the Maglite in your hands like a badass and swipe at her cheek. Several teeth go flying from her mouth and she briefly falls to the ground.

Tina grabs your hand with her free one and you haul ass out of the mine.

You burst from the opening to the cavern out into the dark night and crash into the grass. You waste no time getting up and running as fast as you can up the hill toward the party. You can still hear your probably very dead and possessed friend Jenny shrieking and shouting from inside the mine behind you.

As you crest the hill, you see that many, if not all, of your friends are lying motionless on the ground. A group of eight or so black-hooded figures are standing in a circle around the fire, holding hands and chanting in another language. Their voices join to form a bewitching hum that is similar to a siren's rapturous call, wiggling and slipping itself into your narrow ear holes like a slithering multi-armed arthropod, penetrating your cerebrum with an orgiastic cacophony of whispered horrors.

If you'd like to cover your ears, run to the nearest vehicle, and make a beeline for the familiar lights of your nearby hometown to hopefully summon, I don't know, the goddamn army or something, then that's completely understandable.

If we've left you no choice but to walk up to the sound of the humming and chanting, turn to page 128.

Nothing seems real as your brain presses against the walls of its cranial prison with undulating terror and fear. Your eyes are starting to register the initial visuals of the LSD and a barely perceptible, surrealist splash of vibrancy starts to make all the light around you twinkle.

You've got to get out of here now or you are wildly fucked.

The shrouded figures cease their unsettling chanting and turn all their heads toward you and Tina at once. She holds the old tome in her shaking hands. You both stand there as the people in black beckon you to join them by the flickering firelight.

Tina starts to walk toward them and you hold out your hand to stop her. She slams the book against your chest and rips free from your grasp. She starts to hiss and mumbles in tongues as she meets the dark congregation next to the bonfire.

She lays her head back and falls backward into the arms of one of the hidden persons. The other seven start to pull at her clothing with what look like sharp claws, ripping into the fabric. The hands pull and prod at her clothes until they are in pieces on the ground and she is naked, her young, nubile flesh aglow with firelight.

Your eyes go wide and you're just thinking this may be both the worst and last trip you're likely to take, when you hear a loud, crackling, thunderous voice calling out from the sky above you:

"My kindred will take off your flesh just as my kindred have taken off the flesh of these putrid vermin. I will wash my eyes in the bile and blood of your youth. You will feed me."

If that all sounds great to you and you figure, *Hey, I've had a few good years, made a few good memories, and when you think about it, everyone's gotta die eventually. Plus, there's something to be said about choosing your own demise rather than having it dealt out to you by the harrowing roulette wheel of dumb fucking luck,* then you need to have your head checked, you crooked little nut.

If that doesn't sound okay at all, and you want to ask the disembodied voice in the sky just what the hell is going on, then turn to page 187.

You put the dusty old book between your knees and cup your hands over your mouth as Tina starts to twirl naked in the twilight-twinged, orange glow of the fire. Her black hair fans out as her body spins, and hands with hairy claws and pointed nails reach out to her.

You hear Jenny come screeching out of the mine, sounding like a rabid animal. A few minutes and her crazed ass will reach you.

You shout skyward, "Yeah, I mean, if there is some way for me to avoid, if you please, becoming sustenance for your voracious appetite or getting brainwashed by that ugly little stone, please let me know!"

The dead bodies of all your friends start to rattle and shake upon the cold earth, gurgling black oil from their eyes, noses, and mouths. A sickening stench of putrefaction and decay assaults your nose and you dry heave into the dirt at your feet.

The loud, thunder-clap voice booms against your ears again, "Open the tome you possess and fulfill the prophecy of my Kindred."

You ask how to do that, exactly, and it clarifies, "Turn to the fifth tale inside the tome and read the opening line. Then my Kindred shall begin to rend your flesh from your bones so we may feed it to the Ancient Serpent, Lothalimoc!"

You make it clear that you're not into all that shit right there and will smack a bitch in the head with a goddamn Maglite if it comes to that, but the booming voice insists.

On the ground, the wriggling bodies of your doomed college pals start to glow with the same eerie green light you saw coming from the mine, mixing with the orange flashes coming from the raging bonfire next to all the shrouded figures.

Everything is getting hard to focus on; that dose of Purple Pyramid is really kicking now.

You watch helplessly as the shrouded figures raise Tina above their heads. Her naked flesh reflects the moonlight, the firelight, and the green light.

Tina rubs her own nipples hard and fast, then uses her nails to rip them completely off, spurting and dripping blood over the curve of her breasts and down her sides as the hooded people turn and face the fire.

They toss Tina into the fire and she writhes in what appears to be something akin to divine ecstasy as her pale skin melts and the muscles and bone underneath are exposed. She doesn't scream, but rather moans and groans and begins to have rapid, squirting orgasms as her life is taken by the fire.

Her body stops shaking and starts to curl inward as the sub-dermal deposits filled with cooked human fat erupt outward and her hair flames up as she blends into the embers.

You swing the Maglite at the skull of the nearest cunt in a shroud and they fall to the ground. The others rush up to grab you from both sides and you try to shake them off, but are pow-erless. They shove you to the ground and toss the book into the dirt by your head.

You lift yourself up and pick up the book. The title is *Night,* and it's by some hack who will never make it. The front cover has Mt. Sopris on it and the back jacket is filled with untrue ad-ulations about the fuckwit author and his middling literary skills. Still, you flip it open to the fifth story.

The loud voice says, "Read the opening line!"

After all you've now seen and heard, after all the death and agony, do you really think it's the best idea to read the first line of the dumb story and turn to page 666?

If you still need to remember why this would be a terrible idea, turn back to page 2.

I'll tell ya this, reader: You've gotta be some kind of whacko with a death wish to have made all the terrible decisions to lead you to this point. I mean, you had so many outs.

Nevertheless, you pick up the book like a fool, and with Tina's charred corpse not too far away, Jenny howling like a goddamn banshee nearby, Nik long dead, and you currently lying prone like a douchebag in the dirt, you read the first line aloud.

Say it with me, everyone:

**_Quod ad placandum malum serpentem deo sacrificium faciendum sit. Maledicat me et perficiat fabulam circulus…_**

Reading it aloud, much to your chagrin, seals the ancient markers, fills the moon with blood, and opens the long-dormant hellmouth inside the mines. It releases the ghoulish specters of vengeful tommyknockers from the 1800s, old-world native American demons from around 5000 BC, and a particularly nasty subterranean stone serpent deity from time immemorial. All freed from their entrapment in the Terra Firma.

You've really gone and kicked the bee's nest now, you twat. Why exactly did you have to let the demons out? Why fuck with ghost miners? What did they ever do to you?

And most of all, why bring forth Lothalimoc in all his slithery badness? That was a bridge too far, my friend.

Demons with seething fury and slathering maws lumber out from the mine's mouth, along with the dead souls of men and women who died in the mine.

Lastly, a big stone serpent the size of a school bus slithers up the road toward you, the corpses, and the hooded crackpots. It comes to a stop before you and raises its hood, showing you the gray and black folds and hypnotic rippling gold waves. It somehow makes you feel safe.

It opens its mouth and a huge pile of glowing green apples come spilling out onto the ground before you. Jenny runs up and starts rabidly gobbling big juicy apples from the pile.

The fanged beast with the rippling scales says you need to eat one of them, then you may rest.

Flipping through the first few pages of the story and frowning, you ask, "What's all this other stuff in the book under the Latin about me being at the video store earlier this evening?"

The voice says, "Shut up, mortal, and eat!"

If you trust what the big snake is telling you, and wish to snarf down one of the apples, then turn to page 5150.

I don't know why I even bother with you. Turn to page 5150.

You reach down and pick up one apple, then take a big bite. A swirl of nausea-inducing blackness engulfs your vision and before you can vomit, you fall to the ground, unconscious.

You awaken inside a padded room. You look around and there is nothing except for a small similarly padded door and tiny barred window in the ceiling, allowing you nothing to look at. That is, save for a massive, deeply unnerving mural of unimaginable horrors that you've apparently scrawled into the wall. You must've used your blood and waste over the last God knows how long to depict the last scene you saw before you arrived.

Your smeared, dried, and caked blood has been used to draw dead naked bodies, bearded phantom miners, and ugly hulking beasts with horns and claws. Your filthy, stinky, surprisingly-chunky feces has been used to form the rock snake in its true form. It's disgusting, really, and you should be ashamed of yourself.

(Seriously, pal, you got problems and you need help.)

But you'll get it here, no doubt. Or not. Really, who's to say what comes now? Here at the sanitarium, where you might've always been, but where you'll surely now always be.

And now you, unwise reader, by way of your foolhardy decisions and by simply reading the accursed passage, have thus rend a hex unto thine self. A curse growing inside of you. The moment you lay your head on your pillow tonight and fall asleep, it will loose itself upon your unsuspecting psyche, tearing it asunder to the point of madness.

Isn't that nice?

You really should clean that off the wall.

**The End**

# UGATS

Vinnie Carbone squints at the windshield as he snubs out his Vantage cigarette in the Oldsmobile's squeaky pull-out ashtray and grumbles, "Kick on the wipers, why don'tcha? I can't see *ugats* through this glass!"

The man driving the car, Vito Corpisi, laughs as the warm night air of the Nevada desert whistles by. Rocks and gravel spin away as the tires make a line through the barren back road that Vinnie knows to be all too convenient for such sojourns.

*Another gunny sack full of problems to go to the boonies and solve.*

And there were advantages to this particular back road. Namely, it was more remote than other drops of the like, but also had some geographic features that made it perfect for Vinnie's brand of disposal.

See, when you leave a body in the ground, there's any number of ways that it can be found. You could get tailed to or spotted at the drop, coyotes might dig it up, and every so often, something truly stupid and unlucky happens. Like last year when a hiker burying his own shit accidentally unearthed what was left of Mickey "Marbles" Maccirone.

Guy got the nickname on account of when the coppers found his crime scenes, they'd usually say that, "Whoever done this clearly must've lost his GD marbles." So there weren't any tears shed when one day he just up and disappeared.

But when hippie shit boy made his discovery, the resulting investigation led to two solid guys from the Provozo family getting pinched. They were now serving fifteen to twenty in High Desert Correctional on that and a smaller RICO beef.

So you don't just bury the body a few feet down, like you wanna get caught. No, no, no. What you gotta do is go and get you a nice, deep, and extremely narrow ravine you can drop 'em into. Basically impossible to recover a body from, and the carrion and beetles will quickly take care of any issues you might otherwise have long before anyone gets wise.

Sure, it might be a good hour or so north of Vegas, but when you have some JW Blue Label to sip on and Sinatra crooning through the speakers of your now-vintage, classic sky-blue 1977 Delta 88 Royale, you can make the time in no time at all (the V8 455 engine with its 225 horses under the hood doesn't hurt, neither, if we're bein' honest over here.)

Vito asks, "The hell is there even to see in this dark? There ain't no deer out there."

"I dunno, just wanna see what's ahead, is all." Vinnie uses his hands to brush back his hair. He, almost exactly like Vito, has a black hand-tailored Armani suit, suspenders, a white button-up shirt, and a slicked-back wave of oily black hair. Vito has a goatee going though, and Vinnie is clean shaven. They also wear different ties, and Vito is nearly a foot taller.

Vito shoots back, "Ain't nothing to see, 'cept the same ol' dark and lonesome road, my friend."

"So maybe I like lookin' at the stars and whatnot. What's it to ya? And what're you, Gene Autry over here with the poetry?"

"More like Frankie Valli," Vito says, using his hand to click the wipers. But instead of making the view any clearer, they mostly smear the bugs that have been accumulating on the windshield. He taps the button to squirt as much washer fluid as he can on the glass, but some nasty little things are positively fused to it. Turning off the wipers, he lights up a cigarette, then crank-rolls down the window and feels the warm desert air rush into the car.

"We don't always gotta come all the way out here, ya know," Vito muses between puffs.

"You seen what happens when you leave these things to chance. Plus the short time on site makes up for the long trip. We drop, roll out, then we can bust out the coke and start the weekend right." Vinnie sniffs twice, unconsciously.

"Why not now? It would only make this Johnny Walker go down smoother." Vito flicks his smoke and takes a pull off of it.

Vinnie replies, "We ought probably wait till we get this done, then we can head back and still catch the midnight review. Sandra's on tonight. Gotta make an appearance."

"Gotta get ya some 'cooz more like, but I'm here for that. She got a fellow dancer who knows how to work this pole over here?"

"They all do, naturally. And they got them pure pursed lips. The best. We'll get you set, no worries."

Puffing his smoke, Vito says, "Got fifteen on the game tomorrow. You?"

"Nah. But you reminded me I gotta go and do my pickups on Monday and make sure the guys at Caesars are re-stocked. They got that, uh, big convention coming next week. The pool and spa thing."

Vito flicks his smoke out the window and crank rolls it up. "Yeah, gonna be a hoot." He squirms in his seat. "Yeesh, fucking coke is burning a hole in my pocket."

Vinnie's reply is swift, "You can go nuts on the way back. I'll drive."

Vito grins. "The last time I let you drive Baby Blue you damn near wrapped it around that telephone pole near Hollywood and Vine, *marone!* I'm driving."

Vinnie smirks at this. "Yeah. Could've used some of that fine Colombian flake that night. Why didn't you just toss some bumps under my schnoz?"

"Would've been tough. You were barely making sense by then. I shouldn't have let you drive anyway. Woulda had to drag your face across the mirror, so to speak. But yeah, some snort couldn't have hurt. Wouldn't hurt then, probably wouldn't hurt now." Vito shoots a guilty look at Vinnie.

"Whatever, fine. We're almost there anyway. So go for it, I guess."

Vinnie watches as Vito excitedly steadies the wheel with his knee, then pulls out a small black vial of cocaine and unscrews the top. He taps a bit of it onto the spot between his thumb and forefinger and draws in a long breath, inhaling the large bump. Then he uses a miniature spoon affixed to the underside of the cap to scoop some of the white dust and holds it out toward Vinnie.

Vinnie leans in and uses his left hand to close his left nostril and snorts deeply. Vito gives him two more in rapid succession then does a few more himself, still expertly balancing the wheel with his leg.

Vinnie sniffs hard and says, "Watch for the turn here in a minute. There's that sign."

"I know, I know. I got it, my man," Vito muses cooly as he slips the vial back into his pocket. He picks up the Johnny Walker and undoes the top, taking a long pull and passing it to Vinnie.

Vinnie takes it in his free hand and sinks a good pull with a slight twitch of his right eye. Handing it back to Vito, he says, "You know that, uh, military place up further down the road?"

Vito nods. "You mean the military base?"

"Yeah, you know what I mean."

Vito nods again. "The one we haven't ever seen on account of the big fence?"

Vinnie clears his nose with another snort of air, then whistles, "Sweet Mary and Joseph! Who needs foil to cook that up when you got that kind of bounce for the ounce? Hoo-rah! And yeah, uh, that one."

"What about it?" Vito asks.

"We don't wanna end up near it. Heard that Gino came up to drop a package a couple months back, just before he took ill. When he got out to the fence, he saw some big fucking lights in the sky."

"Why was he at the fence?"

"Who knows? Cause he was a fucking momo?"

"Yeah? So what?" Vito cocks an eyebrow.

"So he said he couldn't remember what happened but he was out, and when he woke up, the package wasn't nowhere to be found. And he didn't recall how he got back in the car. That was just a few weeks before he passed away, God rest his soul."

Vinnie pulls out a smoke from a pack on the dash and quickly lights it up, then cranks down the window just a bit.

"Gino was always full of shit. Probably just sampling too much of his own wares and got spooky-kooky. Could even be what caused the cancer, poor bastard." Vito hoots up another bump of chino.

Vinnie's head shakes back and forth. "H don't cause cancer. It'll make you allergic to money, family, and friends, but it don't cause no cancer."

"What am I, a fucking doctor over here?" Vito asks, sniffing at the air.

"You self-medicate like one!" Vinnie chuckles.

"I'm takin' that as a compliment." Vito snorts another bump.

"Nah, man, I'm sayin' they probably got nuclear tests up there and he got too close and the radiation ballooned up his gut and killed him."

"That's how radiation works? You just gotta get close?" Vito asks, genuinely curious.

Vinnie nods solemnly.

"Sheesh. Okay then. Maybe we stay clear, then."

"Supposing we do," Vinnie agrees.

"So the lights were what? Radiation lights?"

Vinnie scrunches his nose, "I dunno, I never seen one before. What do radiation lights look like anyway?"

"You tell me! Ain't like I ever seen one." Vito laughs, then leans forward and squints through the windshield again. "This is it."

Clicking the turn signal, he cranks the big wheel to the right. The massive boat of a car kicks up dust as it drags its heavy ass around ninety degrees, then speeds down a much less paved road. There are intermittent spots with disused asphalt all broken up, but after a mile or so, it's pure dirt. They drive for about two more minutes and when they spy the crest of a ridge to the south, they pull over and kick off the lights to the Oldsmobile.

Vito rubs his hands together and sniffs. "Some good shit! Good shit! Yes! Let's get this done!"

"Amen!" Vinnie agrees.

They exit the car and casually walk around to the trunk, both shooting glances around them. Vito uses the key to turn the lock and raise up the door. Inside, a long dark green duffel bag.

Vinnie nods to Vito and they both snatch up one end of the large sack. Vinnie says, "On three. One, two, three!" and they pull the duffel out of the trunk.

They hold it suspended between them, while Vito declares, "I'll go first." But he doesn't move. "Wait, we need the uh, the flashlight!"

Vinnie nods in agreement, then both men drop the bag at once. It hits the dusty ground with a dull *THUMP*. Vito walks to the driver's side and yanks open the door. A moment later he reappears and clicks on the small black flashlight. Sticking it into his back pocket, he walks back over to the bag. The two men reach down and hoist it up again as they start toward the ridge in the semi-darkness.

Slowly walking past rocks and wiry desert bushes, they grunt and groan.

Vito sighs. "Heavy bastard."

"Should've eaten more diet cannolis, God rest his soul."

"Philly didn't say what happened?" Vito asks.

"Just that he had made his last mistake. I'm thinking it's the whole Frankie Bones thing."

"Well, it was bound to be something." Vito tosses a glance ahead of them and says, "Edge is coming up. Let's get him outta the bag."

"Yeah," Vinnie replies, exhaling loudly. They lower the duffel more gently this time and Vinnie starts pulling down the zipper. They are both so focused on the sack that they don't notice as it begins to gradually get brighter around them.

It takes a moment before either realizes that the light is casting down from above. They look at one another, silhouetted in light. Staring up, neither catches a clear sight of what hovers above before their vision is filled with white and they disappear into darkness.

***Initial prompt. Quantity measurements. Inventory of human tissues. Ten nanosectors. Laterally moving up by four degrees. Subdermal extraction would be recommended—***

As Vinnie opens his eyes, they are blurry and unfocused. He can just make out a fuzzy circle in the distance. Shutting his eyelids, he rubs, then reopens them.

Still cloudy, much like the windshield from earlier.

He can sense that he is lying down. His mouth is desert dry and his nose feels clogged. He snorts hard, hacks some phlegm and shoots a big chunk of cocaine down his sinuses and into his throat. It instantly goes numb and his vision rapidly clears right up.

He is lying down and staring up at a silvery, metallic, but impossibly smooth and seamless ceiling that has a white ring in the center, like a dim halo illuminating the area.

Vinnie sits up and surveys his surroundings. He's inside a small, circular room that has two stool-like pads floating a foot above the metal floor in front of some sort of display. Vinnie squints and vaguely makes out that it is filled with a faint red-grid pattern that seems to show the landscape outside of the room. It appears to be a semi-aerial view of the desert.

He realizes he's sitting on a table that is also just a long metal plate floating above the floor. *Like a doc's examination table,* he thinks.

Next to him, on another table, faintly grumbling through his little goatee, lies Vito, his eyes closed as he fidgets about on the metal plank.

As Vinnie's head turns to survey the whole room, he sees another panel of an odd, unnatural shape, black with small glowing dots all over it that continuously rearranges into unfamiliar shapes. Before this screen stands two tall, slender figures.

As they turn, Vinnie spots big eyes, gray skin, and huge heads. The creatures stare at Vinnie for a moment, then one of them turns its head almost imperceptibly.

At once, a sound like rushing water and a chorus of whispers calls out, sounding like many different voices speaking at once. He cannot hear the sound, so much as sense it in his head.

### *One of them has awakened.*

Vinnie stares wide-eyed at the two extraterrestrials. "W-what? Did you guys say that? Your lips ain't movin', so I—"

### *He can hear us.*

"Course I can. You're saying it loud enough! But again, them lips ain't moving so how are you managing that?"

### *Yes, to put it as you would understand, we are reaching out without speaking. You should not be able to hear us.*

"And yet I do." He looks the two figures up and down then rubs his eyes again. "Holy shit! You know, the movies and shows and shit got you guys pegged, alright. Right down to the skinny arms and huge-ass eyes!" Vinnie chuckles as he rubs his eyes again.

The two aliens gaze down at their arms, slowly at one another, then up to meet each other's eyes before returning their gaze back to Vinnie.

"Yeah, you look just like every other fucking saucer flyin' momo I seen in those science fiction flicks. You got a ray gun and all that?"

*We have no need for weapons.*

"And you speak English? Odds on that have gotta be long, eh?" Vinnie asks.

The many-voiced whispered sounds come again.

*Our mental projections have the ability to accomplish communication regardless of the lifeform, language, or communication medium. Sometimes we have a hard time communicating with Psychlos, but that's because they have no brain to speak of.*

Vinnie stretches his arms. "Yeah, yeah, whatever a fuckin' Psychlo is, pal. Hey-ya, do me a favor and wake up my friend over here!" Vinnie points over at the still mumbling and unconscious Vito.

*You should remain lying down.*

"Ugats with your two cents on the winks, Kimo Sabe! I ain't lyin' back down and my man over here ain't, neither. You know, when he gets up and all." He looks around the room again, then says, "Where are we? What the hell is going on?"

Vinnie rolls his feet over the edge and drops down onto the smooth, shiny surface. Despite having heels on his black shoes, it makes no sound when he lands. He curiously taps his heel again to make sure.

*Yep—no sound,* he realizes. "That's funny."

The aliens share a glance.

Vinnie walks over to Vito and slaps him lightly on the cheek. "Hey, buddy! Hey! Needin' you to come around about now."

He waits a second, then when nothing happens, slaps Vito harder this time. Still, his friend just mumbles and flickers his eyelids as if in REM sleep.

Vinnie pulls out his own small black vial from a side pocket of his jacket and undoes the metal screw top while the aliens watch. Then he pulls out the tiny coke spoon and gives himself a little bump. He sniffs hard and feels more collected nasal blockage loose itself and hit his throat. He hacks hard, pinching his nose, then snorts again.

"Oh yeah, that's good! That's what Daddy needs—that's my fucking ride!" He looks at the two gray otherworldly figures and holds out the spoon. "You want a toot?"

**What compound is that?**

"It's yay-o. Pure, uncut Colombian mist, no footprints here," Vinnie says as he takes another spoonful in the other nostril and snorts hard. "And like the man says, you can't fly on just one wing!"

**What does it do for you?**

"Keeps your wits about ya. Makes you tougher and sharper."

*The chemical must be why he isn't staying under.*

"Hey! You gonna wake my buddy up or do I gotta do it? He's a heavy sleeper, lemme tell you.'"

**Please lie back down.**

"No, we're all done with the table thing. If yous momos ain't gonna do it, I'll take care of it."

Vinnie takes his pinky and ring finger on his left hand and shoves each into the vial, coating them in white dust. Then he takes his fingers and slips them just into Vito's nostrils.

Vito twitches, coughs, hacks, and takes a big whooping breath as his eyes spring open. Shooting straight up, he looks at Vinnie. "Uh, the fuck was that?"

Across his upper lip, a white mustache. Vinnie smiles.

"Had to drag your face across the mirror, buddy. Here, take another whiff and meet our two new friends."

Vito snatches the vial whilst suddenly registering the large elephant in the room—rather, the two small gray ones. Making a suspicious face, he scoops a little spoonful of cocaine and plugs one nostril, snorting hard. He pinches the bridge of his nose and then clears his nostrils as a small rock of blow smacks his throat. Nearly coughing, his eyes go wide and he rubs his goatee, clearing away the powder.

Vito slides off the table and stands up next to Vinnie, facing the aliens. He glances at his Armani-suited chohort, then back to the gray figures and asks, "How we supposed to talk to 'em?"

"They talk. Like spooky little whispers in your head," Vinnie muses. "Hey! We want you to beam us back down! We ain't going with you to the mothership, got it? We got places to be."

*It would be inadvisable to immediately return you.*

"Says you, but why?" Vinnie asks.

*Because we are not yet finished.*

Vinnie chuckles. "Oh, nah, you're definitely finished, buddy. You're gonna be more than fuckin' finished if you don't turn this bucket of bolts around and put us back where we belong—on the ground."

*That would be inadvisable.*

"Yeah, you already said that." Vito slips his hand between his shirt and jacket and smoothly draws forth a large silver and gold Magnum Research Inc. Desert Eagle in all its clunky glory. Stroking his goatee with his free hand, Vito grins. "So how's about I shove the barrel of this fucking Desert Eagle here into that puckerin' little gob of yours, then maybe you'll be wanting to fuckin' take down this plane?"

"Ain't no kinda plane I ever seen before—" Vinnie begins, but is interrupted by his friend.

"Whatever, Vin! Flyin' saucer, then. Who gives a rat fuck? Ain't no carnival ride I paid a ticket for." Vito keeps his eyes steadfastly locked on the two extraterrestrials.

"And what did I say about that goofy-ass Desert Eagle, Vito? Shit's impractical!" Vinnie mumbles.

"No, man. It's practical alright. It's practically gonna liquify E.T.'s ugly, wrinkled fucking head over here, is what it's going to do. And maybe a little later with the sidearm advice?" Vito steps toward the tall extraterrestrial that is closest to him and points the gun straight at the thing's face. "You hearin' me, you chunky fuckin' pumpkin head?"

*We understand you. There is no need to fear us.*

Vito scoffs, his gaze remaining cold and fixed on the one standing before him. "Who the fuck said we were scared? You scared of these ugly mugs, Vin?"

"You know they ain't scaring me none," Vinnie says as he crosses his arms and reaches into both of his shoulder holsters, returning with both hands full of gleaming gun—one barrel pointed at each of the bug-eyed bastards.

Vito continues, "Yeah, you got it twisted around, see. It's you two War-of-the-Worlds-lookin' marks who should be fearing us, ya' heard?" He cocks back the hammer on the massive hand cannon.

"I'm thinking we're serious now," Vinnie begins. "Take us the fuck back down and I think I can speak for both of us when I say we'll go ahead and call this one bygones. We just want to finish what we were doing. Capeesh?"

*Burying the body of the other human?*

Vito grimaces. "What'd you say, cheeky fuck? Don't tell me I got snatched up by a couple of freaky fuckin' aliens so that I could get a moral lesson from guys who like to fiddle around in buttholes!"

*We don't do that.*

"Hah! Not what I heard, my friend. Way I heard it, you dig around in that shit all day. How about you, Vin? What'd you hear?"

Vinnie smiles, keeping his guns trained on the two grays. "I heard about the butt thing. You guys are famous for the butt thing."

*Butt thing?*
*Don't encourage them—*

"Hey! You two can do that shit as ya please; we ain't judgin'. But unless you want your bloated skull to have a close encounter widda bullet, you let us go now."

*Can't we just let them go? They are making me nervous.*
*No, we need to extract the glands and then terminate them.*

"*Marone!* We can hear you two brainiacs!" Vito shouts.

*They aren't going to hurt us unless we hurt them.*

Vito grins widely. "You two are what we would call a couple of dippy, small-time dumbfucks here on Earth. Couple of dipshits, alright, despite all your high tech bullshit. I used to pimp out simple bitches like you back in the clink."

*Clink?*

"This fucking guy! *Marone.* I'm done with all this bullshit right here!" Vito watches as the one on the right starts to walk toward a small outcropping in the spherical room's walls. Pointing, Vito demands, "Hey! What're you doin'?"

The alien continues moving toward the smooth dome on the wall.

*We are doing nothing.*

"But I sees you doing something! You tellin' me to ignore what I'm seeing with my own eyes?"

*Everything is going to be okay.*

The two men watch the alien pull some sort of tool from the wall and turn to face Vito.

Vito hadn't survived this long on account of his good looks, so he quickly pulls the trigger and lets loose a fat round that obliterates the alien on the right's head in one shot.

Its slender body crumples to the ground as the disfigured stump where its round head used to be oozes a black tar-like substance.

Vinnie doesn't hesitate to squeeze off a round and hit the second alien square between his eyes. A drip of blackish fluid runs down into its face as it too falls onto the floor without making a sound.

The room around them begins to shudder slightly and they reach out to grab each other's arms for stability. Their startled eyes meet as they feel the sensation of lowering down, but keep their footing.

Vito slips his gun back into his shoulder holster. "Are we crashing?"

"Uh, maybe?" Vinnie lets go of Vito and starts to put the guns back into his holsters.

The movement suddenly stops. Then nothing.

They both look around. The two screens are still glowing and Vinnie walks over to the one with the landscape image. It seems to show that they are close to the ground. The other screen is still making random patterns with the white dots.

Vito whispers, "You think we're stuck?"

"Why are you whisperin'?" Vinnie whispers back.

Vito scowls. "Cause, I dunno. That was nuts, no?"

"Oh yeah."

"This thing got a door, or what?"

At that moment, the screen with the white dots goes black and the halo-shaped light from above goes dark.

"Oh great. That's great," Vito groans.

The black screen lights back up with a series of bright green dashes and oddly-shaped characters in a repeating sequence. Vinnie hears a distant chirp, then nearly hits the deck as they both hear a loud *whoosh*, and air begins to rush through the room from an unknown source.

Vinnie shouts over the noise, "I'm not sure this was a very—"

White light engulfs their vision, followed by black. Not solid black, as before, though. As their eyes adjust to the darkness, they see that they are on the ground, staring out at the night. While they slowly realize what happened, they look at each other, still standing just a few feet apart.

They both gaze up and see a faint ring of lights on the underside of the craft, floating just a few feet above their heads. It silently ascends skyward as they watch, transfixed. Seeming to speed up, it simply blinks out of their view.

Both continue to watch for a few seconds, as if it will reappear. When it does not, they look at one another.

Speaking first, Vinnie asks, "You okay?" He notices that he's still clutching his guns tightly. Thumbs click safeties as he returns the guns back to their respective holsters inside his jacket. He runs one hand over his smooth, black hair.

Vito looks at him and nods. "Yeah. Yeah, I'm good. Did we, uh, just get beamed?"

Vinnie brushes off his sleeves. "It weren't no freight elevator, that's for sure."

"That mean we're technically astronauts now, Vin?"

Vinnie laughs and finishes patting his sleeves. "I dunno. Think there's a test you gotta pass first. But maybe."

"Cool. But jumping Christ! What do you think that was all about?"

"No idea." Vinnie lowers his eyes to the ground ahead of them and sees the partly unzipped duffel bag still lying where it had been before. "Come on."

They walk over to the bag, unzip it, and each grab one end of the body inside.

"Let's get this prick in the hole so we can get the fuck outta this place and never come back," Vinnie says.

"Good thing we didn't wait on the chino, eh Vin?" Vito asks, smiling broadly.

"Yeah, good thing, alright. Certainly not the worst idea you've ever had." Vinnie grins as he kneels next to the dead body. "Tell ya this though: I'll never doubt the power of cocaine again. Never. Now grab his fucking legs."

# LOBO

Back in the mid 1980s, when Gene Schilling first started his job at the police department in Carbondale, Colorado, the town was little more than a one-stoplight gas station pass through on the way to the quasi-greener pastures of the Aspen/ Snowmass resort community.

Carbondale was smaller then, comprised of a single grocery store (City Market), a 7-11, two competing video rental stores (Sounds Easy and Crystal River Video), four parks (Sopris, Miners, Staircase, and Bert N' Ernie), and a handful of tiny neighborhoods and eateries tucked into a narrow valley, flanked by farmlands, abandoned mines, and mountain trails.

Absolutely rife with all the niceties of small town life and situated spectacularly at the base of Mt. Sopris, the most picturesque peak in all of the Rockies, as far as the locals were concerned.

As years rolled off the calendar and the town grew, so did Gene's status among those in the department. He was regarded as the warmest and most genial of the members of the small force numbering about fifteen at the time.

"You're popular because you're so damn kindhearted, Gene,"

was what Joann Dodea, the department's only female officer at the time, had once said. She'd noted his natural calming effect on those with whom he was working, as well as those he was duty bound to arrest.

This was interesting to some because unlike some of the taller, more athletic members of the department, he was also the shortest at just five foot, six inches, with an unassuming ring of brown hair round his head. He also lacked the staunch, hard-nosed demeanor too-often associated with those in his profession.

Most of the police in the small town shop had been yelled at too many times by perps or suspects or even, on occasion, one another. But not Gene. Nah, he greeted all with a broad smile that disarmed and endeared him to just about everyone.

Naturally this sometimes made him the butt of the odd good-natured and/or affectionate joke, largely on account of his casual attire being what some might be so bold as to describe as dated. If you ran into him off-duty at the local city market, you'd likely see him in high water pants, suspenders, a white collared shirt and a pocket protector in his right breast pocket, always replete with several pens darting out—a custom silver Mont Blanc among them.

At the Mountain Fair—the local music, food, and arts festival that occurred every year at the end of July—he would try to get into the spirit of the festival by wearing a tie-dye shirt under his police vest. He was a big Grateful Dead fan, and being of the Boomer generation as he was, it seemed appropriate, if a little playful, to wear a nod to the counterculture progenitors upon which the spirit of the fair had largely been based.

To others, he seemed, at best, a bit goofy. At worst, a total nerd-o. Kids snickered and other officers would laugh and say, "If you're lookin' for Gene, ya really can't miss him in that getup!"

It was no surprise then that he kept rising through the ranks. The guy was positively unflappable under stress.

When a few nameless kids broke into the local middle school one evening and left the place utterly trashed, windows smashed, classrooms ransacked, and absent a small fortune in quarters from looted vending machines in the teachers' lounge, he'd simply quipped, "Well no one got hurt, and that's good. Good enough for me."

And so the case was essentially dropped. Small towns, ya know?

"Walk softly and carry a big stick," some say. Or in Gene's case, a big heart—dopey though it may sound to a cynic's ear. That's the way the whole town saw him.

And so it was that he was likely up for the big chair of the department in the next few months when the spring of 1996 rolled around.

He had expected to be in the running, but another officer was eyeing the office at the end of the hall as well. Deputy Mark Littell, also known as the blind cop on account of his low arrest numbers, despite his decade long tenure with the office. As the moniker would imply, he was also a nice guy and often looked the other way with small indiscretions. Ergo, Gene had the better chance, but he would've been lying if he'd said he thought had the promotion on lock.

Partly because it was as he had done for years prior, and partly because he could use the boost of support from the locals, he had been giving up his time as of late to do some volunteering for the local charities and schools. This usually meant giving a disinterested group of little rubber people a good talking to about the dangers of drugs and alcohol.

The DARE (Drug Abuse Resistance Education) program had been created in 1983 and by '96, was in nearly every school from coast to coast. As the local DARE ambassador, it was Gene's dubious charge to be the go-to authority where the scourge of chemical abuse was concerned in his own little town.

Like another valley resident, famed gonzo journalist Hunter Thompson, he carried with him a little briefcase full of drugs of all different types. But unlike Thompson, his was full of quite convincing mockups thereof that were housed inside impenetrable little glass bubbles that lined the walls of the case.

The drugs were to show the kids what moral decay looked like up-close. The bubbles were so that any clever kids didn't risk absconding with anything that even looked like the real stuff. Not that they never tried, the little buggers.

Kids would be kids, Gene knew that.

Around April, the middle school offered its seventh graders the chance to spend a full week away from their parents and go on one of several so-called mini courses. Essentially off campus vacations with a sprinkling of educational value, they included things like going on tours of old hotels, camping and hiking excursions, and the like.

When Mr. Jennings, the seventh grade science center teacher and a long-time acquaintance (almost everyone in town was by this point in his career), offered him the chance to drive the bus for a group of boys on a mini course for a week, he agreed because he relished the opportunity to get out of town for a few days and help another member of the community enrich the minds of the towns youths.

It had all sounded good on paper.

The mini course that he'd agreed to be the bus driver for was called "Down the Colorado" and involved hauling twenty or so puberty-cresting, foul-mouthed, middle-class spawn who didn't shave yet across Utah and Colorado whilst following along the path of the eponymous river. All the while, Mr. Jennings would use the colorful scenery and visits to various places of interest to hopefully impart as much knowledge and information about the Colorado River as this particular group of hormonal know-it-alls was willing to absorb.

For the kids themselves, it was a chance to test the limits of what they could get away with in a setting wholly absent of parental figures for an entire week. Like going to Vegas, but for a kid.

The morning of the trip, the rabble of kids stood—vapid, drooling, and largely disinterested in the world around them—in front of the Carbondale Middle School administration office, waiting to fill the bus with adolescent chirping and merciless white noise for days on end.

Gene showed up fifteen minutes early and helped the kids load their suitcases and duffel bags into the bus's undercarriage compartments. Then off they set.

Seven days ahead of driving and carriage-ing kids from scholastically relevant stop to intellectually stimulating point of interest. They stopped in Grand Junction to have dinner at a restaurant, the last such endeavor of the trip. The food for the next seven days would be hot dogs and scrambled eggs on white paper plates with plastic utensils.

As they drove the yellow student transport across state lines into Utah, the kids asked if they could use the bus's PA system to pump out some of their new-fangled musical interests.

Mr. Jennings was napping near the front, and Gene wasn't trying to be the square of the two adults. He was happy enough to play the part of the hip uncle figure who would let you get away with what your parents wouldn't, within reason. So they played hard rock music from Alice In Chains and Soundgarden and particularly (in Gene's humble estimation) a violence-oriented hip-hop album called *E. 1999 Eternal* from a group called Bone Thugs-N-Harmony. Gene would be lying if he said he'd loved the stuff, but he tolerated it just the same. The kids were surprised and delighted.

They stopped and put up in a small motel for the evening, then headed back out at dawn's first light. Trekking across Utah, they stopped at a dinosaur museum (to see how dino bones were great indicators of the movements of ancient water systems), a natural history museum (to understand how the ebb and flow of the river had affected the development of the American West during the manifest destiny era between 1812 and 1867, and the boom-time decades that followed), and a beach on the side of a particularly calm spot of river (to set up camp for the night).

A few stern but run-of-the-mill talkings-to was all he and Mr. Jennings had had to deal out, and the kids largely kept their unrelenting chit-chat to a dull roar and their hijinks hidden from view.

Fast forward to the evening that would change Gene's life in incalculable ways. The third night. The night the entire world would become aware of what kind of a man Officer Shilling of the CPD was.

Goblin Valley, Utah was where they had ended up in the afternoon of the third day. Set upon the orange dusted remnants of a prehistoric riverbed, it drew its name from the large numbers of hoodoos in the area.

These spire-like structures made up of softer sedimentary layers like sandstone, topped with a capstone of harder erosion-resistant rock that protected the column beneath, were also called "goblins," and dotted the landscape like gargoyles watching over a place of worship.

Anticipating something much more aligned with the region's ominous-sounding name, the kids happily voiced their crass disapproval at how "not scary" the figures ended up being.

You just can't impress kids these days. Gene knew that.

Following a stomach-bracing dinner of Bar-S hot dogs, generic off-brand potato chips, Big K soda and assorted veggies that no one touched save for Mr. Jennings and himself, Gene set about to make sure all the young men knew exactly what problem they would be creating for themselves should they deign to make too much of a ruckus once the two chaperones hit the hay.

The first two nights had been largely uneventful in that the boys had only needed to be scolded for being loud and obnoxious three or four times before they seemingly got the memo and reverted to a dull roar.

He went tent by tent and asked quite politely of all the occupants that since he'd be staying on the bus that evening, that they collectively try and spare their science teacher an unrelenting series of trips into the dark to demand they keep it down.

Most agreed. Some got cute. All knew he was serious, though. Because the simple fact was that when a teacher told your parents you fell woefully out of line, it was one thing. An inconvenient bump along the road of life. When a cop told them, it was a whole other enchilada. He knew that, and they knew that he knew this as well. The armistice was tenuous and strained at best, but should hold, in Gene's humble estimation.

He waited a few extra minutes for Mr. Jennings to settle into his tent before he set a bucket of water next to the smoldering fire, flicked on his pocket-sized, black Maglite, and beat a dusty path to the now decade-old yellow school bus standing a good fifty yards away. It was located halfway around a large boulder that he'd parked next to, and the flashlight's beam ran over the words "Roaring Fork School District" on the side of the vehicle as he approached.

He walked to the front, used his fingers to wrench open the door on its squeaky hinges, and boarded the bus. Gene closed the door behind him with the swiveling door latch, and out of habit more than concern, clicked the locking mechanism into place.

Knowing full well that the kids would be up before he was in all likelihood, he figured it good to skip reading for the night. He was accustomed to knocking out a chapter or two before he went lids down in the evenings. Tonight, he'd likely skip the former and make haste for the latter.

The narrow aisle between the rows of cracking, faux-leather seats provided little space in which to maneuver if you weren't a broad-shouldered stock of a man that usually slept on a king size Posturepedic mattress every night, let alone if you were. Gene was.

Rolling out a three-inch thick pad of body contouring foam along the hard-floored aisle, he lay down his sleeping bag and pulled off his glasses, setting them down on a seat near his head. He balled up the top of the bag and used it as his pillow.

As usual, he was out almost immediately. But he didn't sleep deeply. The windows to the bus were cracked, and some un-known amount of time later, he awoke to the sounds of a noisy ruckus happening somewhere out in the dark evening.

As he opened his eyes and fumbled about the unresolved darkness, he located and put on his glasses. They did not help much.

As he found and started to pull on his pants, he could, through the cracked open bus windows, hear muffled screams and harrowing roars that sounded, at least in Gene's humble estimation, like that of a lion. Goblin Valley was in Utah, not Africa. So it was more likely to be a bear. But bears weren't exactly native to dusty rock piles either, so what the—

Suddenly, he could hear voices in the dark coming closer to the bus with such speed that he instinctively snatched his gun from the holster and held it at his side. He left the safety on.

After another moment he heard footsteps in the dark and the vehicle shifted in place from someone pushing on it from the outside.

"Let us in! Let us in! Let us in!" shouted one of the young men shaking the school bus.

As Gene dashed toward the front door, he saw that it was four of the boys standing outside of the yellow folding door, smacking their palms against the glass. Paul, Cody, Josh, and Nelson.

He had already heard their names several times as they were part of a small clique that had secured the area at the back of the bus when they had embarked on their journey, and had been scolded several times by Mr. Jennings. They were also the wannabe white boy twerps who had requested he play Bone Thugs several days earlier.

He disengaged the lock, slammed his hand against the door release, and it popped open, folding the door to one side.

Cody McCallister, a shorter young man, sprinted in first and ducked under the first seat he saw near the bus's front, just two rows back. He panted deeply as he slowly rasped out, "Fuck. fuck! Jesus jumping fuck, that was crazy. And fuck, fuck—"

Paul Kerling and Nelson Crawford rushed past the off-duty policeman and huddled down near the last few seats of the bus's rear section. They looked absolutely terrified in Gene's estimation.

Lastly, the somewhat less alarmed, yet still fear-filled face of Joshua Larin came from the darkness as he leaped into the bus, grabbed onto Gene's hands, and before the cop could do it himself, fiercely yanked at the lever and slammed the door closed.

Josh, also panting hard, then asked, "Is there a way to lock this door, dude?"

Gene slipped the lock into place and pulled his hands away. "What is happening out there, boys? Where is everyone else?"

From the back, Paul stood up and spoke evenly, though his eyes were serious and cold. "Dead. Everyone near the camp is dead, I think. We were on the ridge overlooking it and came here when we saw that thing start to—"

"Whoa," Gene said, putting his hands up. "Who's dead?"

Josh began to walk down the aisle of the bus as he said, "All of us if we go out there, dude. We need to leave now or we are going to die. Like, probably right away, too."

"Yeah, get the keys! Let's go!" Cody called out.

Gene looked into the eyes of the young men and he was suddenly filled with a sick feeling, because none of them seemed to disbelieve what they were saying.

"You saw something attacking everyone? Like an animal? If you're being straight with me, then I need to go out there."

Cody suddenly materialized from the shadows, quickly rushed over, and wrapped his hands tightly around the door's control mechanism. "No one is unlocking this door! Not even you, Gene.

Fuck that! It will kill us! It was chewing Alex's goddamn leg off! It might have seen us!"

Gene was having a hard time buying all this, so he calmly asked, "What were you guys doing that far away from the camp?"

He snapped the safety off the pistol and peered through the side windows of the bus.

Cody hollered back, "Gee, Gene, I guess we were busy, uh, fucking–uh, fucking not being torn to fucking pieces by some evil wolf-lookin' mother fucker, mother fucker! Fuck!"

"Shhh!" Paul stood, scolding him as he walked over to where the off-duty cop stood near the center of the bus. "While that was admittedly a dumb question, yelling isn't gonna help us stay hidden, jackass."

He stopped a few feet shy of the adult holding the gun and looked out the windows as if trying to see what the officer was seeing. Which was nothing.

"Fuck you!" Cody whispered back at him.

At least he was being quieter, Gene thought. "You should watch your mouth, son."

Cody glared and said, "Say any damn thing I want to right now."

Nelson called from the back of the bus, "He's a cop, Cody. Grow a brain."

Cody replied, "Like that shit really matters right now? We were just lucky we weren't in our damn tent. We'd be absolutely dead. So very dead."

Gene softly repeated his earlier query, "You didn't answer my question. Why were you guys out of your tents?"

Josh spoke quietly as he stood next to the others, "Cards on the table, we were smoking weed, dude."

Gene smiled and looked at the young man with a cocked eyebrow. "Pretty forthcoming. Didn't know you boys were growing up so fast."

Josh flatly replied, "Well, I'm pretty sure we're all fucking dead up in this tin can so I give negative shits about what you know right about now, no offense. Unless one of the things you know is how to kill a werewolf."

"Oh come on, guys. What the hell is this now?" Gene truly felt as though he had nearly reached the end of his willingness to play along with whatever this was. He lowered his gun and relaxed his stance as he asked, "Was it a wolf that attacked the camp? It wasn't a coyote or—"

"No, it was a werewolf! Fucking serious, man!" Cody hissed quietly.

Gene snapped back, "Werewolves don't exist! So stop it! And I gotta tell you that if you boys are making all this up, you are well and truly setting yourself up for a whole world of shit."

A nerve-rattling scream of agony pierced their ears from outside the bus. The darkness carried with it guttural roars and sickening cries from those still in the throes of the attack.

Cody dove under the seats again, scuttling like a crab between the rows, unseen. Everyone else on the bus went silent and kept their eyes fixed toward the direction of the camp, around the other side of the massive boulder. The orange glow of the fire around the boulder edge was occasionally broken up by a large shadow.

Paul whispered, "Yeah, no, for real though, hundred percent a werewolf. I know werewolves and that is very much one of 'em, yes."

Gene didn't know what to think. Something was wrong. This

wasn't a joke. Still, it was too much to believe what the young men were saying.

Nelson crassly retorted, "You know werewolves now?"

Paul glared at Nelson and hissed, "Was that or wasn't that a fucking werewolf we saw earlier?"

Nelson looked down and sheepishly conceded, "Yeah, it was werewolfy, alright."

"Then shut the fuck up!" Paul said.

The noises from outside stopped and the bus occupants froze in place, intuitively fearful of giving up their position to the beast. The orange glow around the boulder was clear and unobstructed. No shadows broke up the light.

No one breathed. Not one single, solitary muscle flexed.

Gene slowly clicked the safety off on his sidearm, just for good measure, and leaned toward the nearest pane of glass to peer through. The boys backed up slowly toward the back of the bus, staying huddled in a group.

Gene's eyes were clear and focused on the boulder when he heard a squishy sound from outside for all of one second before the severed gray-haired head of Mr. Jennings blasted through the glass to the left of Gene's head, just missing him and rolling to the floor.

He stumbled back and had to catch himself on the rows of seats, then straightened up and aimed down sights through the hole in the window.

Beyond the jagged shards of glass framing the open hole and silhouetted against the fire's ember glow was a seven-foot-tall, hairy, bi-pedal figure, maybe fifty yards away. It might've looked like a bigfoot, but for the fact that it was much denser and more muscular than the images of sasquatches he was familiar with.

And despite its tall height, it was still in a semi crouched stance, as if ready to vault forward on all fours at a moment's notice.

One thing was nauseatingly clear, though.

*It's seen we're here. It is watching us. And mocking us. The hairy knob-job.*

Gene didn't ever get into any metaphorical dick-measuring contests with the other officers on the force, and sure wasn't about to do any different with some supernatural beast in the desert. He fired two rounds in quick succession.

Both struck the wolf in the head.

The first hit the wolf's right eye, and a line of blood raced down the thing's fuzzy cheek. Yet it did not move, and the blood stopped as soon as it started.

The boys in the back moved to the side of the bus facing the beast and looked through the windows. They saw the creature breathing deeply and staring in their direction, letting out large gusts of steam into the cool night air. The young men hastily withdrew and looked at Gene.

Cody the crab called out from somewhere under the seats, "What was that? Is it dead?"

Paul whispered as he continued to recede from the windows, "Not dead. Probably pissed."

The wolf dropped down and began to use all four huge hairy limbs to propel itself with stunning speed at the side of the bus. Several more rounds flew from his gun barrel that, in Gene's humble estimation, hit their mark true, but did nothing to slow the pace of the lumbering wolf-figure.

Before he could turn to tell the others to get down, the side of the bus was hit with enough force to cause everyone to grab hold of anything they could to steady themselves. The bus rocked hard to one side as if to tip, but came back down with a hard THUD, sending everyone sprawling.

The three boys crouched down and Gene fell into one of the seats. He pulled himself up and moved toward the boys, keeping his gun ready and trained for any movement.

He whispered to the three terrified young men, "Where is it?"

None answered, but instead looked up as they felt the impact of the creature landing on top of the bus and stomping across it to the white square hatch in the roof that was normally used to provide better circulation whilst the bus was in motion.

All four sets of eyes stared at the opening.

The bus shook violently and the plastic hatch was swiftly ripped free from its moorings and tossed aside as the snout of the fanged beast slipped into the bus's innards and sniffed vigorously. Its muzzle twisted and contorted as the kids and single adult backed away from the area beneath the hatch and toward the bar-braced back of the transport.

Slobber and blood hit the aisle floor in drippy drips and just as Gene raised his gun to fire one last round at the furry proboscis snapping its teeth in hard clicks through the hole in the ceiling. It retracted, and a spine-wrangling, gut-piercing howl burst from the wolf atop the yellow school bus.

Paul's eyes darted left and right, looking for any type of weapon he might take up in defense, but there was nothing. To Gene he whispered, "Fuck, are we gonna do, dude?"

They all had reached the back of the bus and were huddled together, save for the human crustacean, somewhere under the seats.

Gene flicked his head and kept the gun trained on the open hole. "I'm gonna use this last bullet and hope that the one that does the trick."

     ❧ PATRICK KITSON ❧

Paul was snuggly nestled between the officer and the back door as he whispered, "The shit isn't working! You need to—"

Paul's words abruptly stopped as the claws of the wicked hairball shoved into the hole and started to slash at the air below the opening. All eyes went wide and the four pushed against the rear door. Gene stood between the boys and the clawing limb jutting from the ceiling.

The arm retracted into the hole, then both claws re-entered and clamped either side of the opening. With more force than any of them believed, the werewolf began to tear the hole wider, crunching and screeching sheeted metal and creating a much larger, warped and tangled hole with sharp, jagged edges.

A moment later, it dropped through the hole onto all fours.

Gene spoke rapidly, "Need to what, Mr. Kerling?"

Josh replied instead, "He's talking about the fuckin' legends and shit. Like we have some silver bullets lying around."

"Something silver! In *The Sandlot* that one gypsy chick says it can basically be anything that's silver!" Paul yelled over the roars of the rising wolf-figure.

Josh pointed the big Maglite at the wolf.

"There aren't any werewolves in *The Sandlot*, man!" Nelson murmured, frozen in abject horror at the blood-soaked werewolf standing before them.

Cody crawled somewhere unseen along the floor of the bus and yelled out, "He's right about the silver thing. It's in *The Sandlot*."

Gene's mind flashed over every possible scenario in a blink. His *ah-ha* moment came in a jolt and his hand reached into his breast pocket, pulling out his Montblanc Meisterstück 163 Full Silver ballpoint pen.

Gene knew that he could always buy another pen, and besides, you know, he was probably about to die, and all. So he tossed the gun limply with his left hand at the creature's head. A dense hairy branch of an arm swatted it out of midair and it clanked against a seat back, then hit the floor.

Gene's right thumb flicked off the pen's cap and he nodded at the werewolf. Blood and mucus dripped in viscous vines from the thing's sneering, needle-dotted mouth below reflective eyes that were mirrors against the black flashlight's harsh beam. It breathed fast and hard, sucking all the air out of the ten feet between them.

Hairy muscles rippled and flexed with the pre-movement of an impending attack and Gene knew that he needed to act or die. He snatched the Maglite from Josh's hands—eliciting a, "Dude!" from the startled young man—and barreled down the aisle toward the wolf.

He swung out the black metal tube, and the wolf caught the Maglite in mid-swing. Just as he had planned. With his free hand, he buried the tip of the pen into the bicep of the creature, ripping through flesh and sinew, eliciting another ear-shattering howl that caused all the boys to drop down, covering their ears.

The werewolf, stunned by this, looked at Gene with eyes which were suddenly filled with what looked like grief mixed with gratitude as it held the flashlight with the arm that the pen protruded from.

Gene ripped the Montblanc from the thing's arm meat and re-buried it square in the elliptical iris of the wolf's right eye.

It didn't hesitate to recoil back and flailed violently for only a moment or two before dropping like a gunny sack onto the flooring in a dense pile of hairy arms and legs.

The boys remained huddled in the back of the bus and it

wasn't until he opened them back up that Gene realized he had shut his own eyes tightly as he jabbed at the beast's eye. Now one lid opened cautiously, glancing down before the other eye joined in.

He stood before the heap of wolf, waiting for something—anything—to happen. A growl, a twitch, a slash … something. But slowly he realized that, against all odds, the haphazard play had actually worked.

It was dead.

The three boys standing just behind Gene slowly rose from their crouched positions and walked up to peer over the cop's trembling shoulders at the dead creature.

From somewhere beneath a seat, Cody cautiously asked, "I-is that it? Is it still alive?"

Paul replied, "Nah, man, it was struck dead by your bravery in the face of danger, ya douche."

Nelson smiled and clapped the officer on the shoulder. "Fucking A, man! That was sick!"

"Dude," Josh opined as he too gave the cop's shoulder a soft bump with his fist. "You just greased a wolf. Like a fucking *were-wolf*, wolf! That's heavy shit! Not just heavy shit, but like, *seriously heavy shit*, Officer Shilling. You saved our lives, dude."

The otherwise composed boy started to tear up as he spoke, and without warning gave the officer a hug, then quickly withdrew.

"Yeah. Thanks for, uh, killing it, Gene. You're a goddamn badass," Paul managed to say, despite the fact that the young man was shaking terribly.

Nelson agreed, "Yeah, man. Thank you. Jesus Christ, I'm glad you did that." He paused to consider. "How did you do it, anyway?"

Gene looked down and observed that the thing was clearly dead. He knelt down next to it and cocked his head as he looked at its long, drool-flecked snout and dark face. He reached out and slowly withdrew the silver Meisterstück 163 ballpoint from the lycanthrope's crusted crimson eye socket with an audible slurp, then rubbed it clean on his leg.

He stood up and turned toward the boys, rotating the pen around in his fingers. "They say that the pen is mightier than the sword, gentlemen. And I hope that tonight has taught you all that if nothing else, they, who'ere they be, remain correct in this regard."

He slipped the blood-stained pen into his front pocket and smiled warmly at the young men. He may as well have been the goddamn Terminator for how cool he seemed to them in that moment.

Cody called out from under the seats, "You're kind of a badass, bro. Thanks for being our bus driver!"

Once the police, state troopers, feds, medics, coroners, media, and hysterical families arrived the following morning, the effect of the news was seismic. It was the world's top story for months.

Lending credence to Gene and the boy's story was the fact that the creature hadn't changed from its lycanthropic form, so anyone who had a working set of peepers simply had to concede that it appeared to be some sort of human-wolf hybrid they had on their hands.

Even crazier still was when they discovered a few tattoos on the arms of the beast, including one in black and red block lettering, etched forever onto the flesh that read, "LOBO." They matched those of a recently missing Goblin Valley park ranger named Christopher Reginald Demeter.

He'd been on the job for several years, but at thirty was still just a young man. Man-wolf, wolf-man, whatever the nomenclature, his curse was the cause of the destruction in the park as well as the deaths of fifteen young men and a science teacher.

In time, other mysterious deaths in the park were attributed to him as well. The suspected number of victims reached into the dozens, if not higher. And so, there was essentially zero public outcry when the decision was made to use his body as a tool for further research into the lycanthropic condition.

Controversially, the president allocated to the families of the dead teenagers one million dollars each to ease their financial burden during their time of grief. Not all took it. Most did.

The world went absolutely wolf-crazy with the revelation that lycanthropes did indeed exist and they now had irrefutable proof of it. Just as would happen a few years later in 2001, when fishermen caught a giant squid off the coast of Japan and the world was forced to admit that Jules Verne's speculation about sea monsters wasn't so crazy after all.

The fantastic had become real. Myth made manifest.

Werewolf literature and media experienced a massive renaissance. *The Wolf Man* was re-released into theaters and became the fourth highest grossing film that year.

On television and college campuses across the country, biologists, evolutionists, and historians debated the plausibility of the existence of other mythic creatures with renewed scientific rigor. Respected scholars of all stripes claimed that they had personally always secretly suspected there was something more to the werewolf myth.

Montblanc began to advertise itself as the definitive writing supplier for wolf-slayers worldwide, despite the fact that no one knew if any others existed. They also gifted Gene a check for $100,000 which he promptly donated in full to the local middle school to provide counseling to the many (like, everybody) who were affected by the tragedy.

Gene was faxed, emailed, and sent hundreds of offers to join various law enforcement agencies, to appear on television programs, in magazines, and as a regular on the lecture circuit.

All the talk shows wanted an exclusive. Jay Leno's people had offered him a pretty penny to appear the same night as Cameron Diaz and the guy who brought wild reptiles onto the show, but he'd turned them all down. To him, it just didn't seem right to make money or gain notoriety off the whole affair.

It only added to the myth of him.

To the people of Carbondale, he was a living legend. He couldn't get a local restaurant to take his money. There was a line a mile long to buy the guy a beer. To the world, he was a funny and charming enigma.

Hollywood continues to fight over the film rights to his biopic to this day.

Eventually, thankfully, the world continued on to be just as awful, wonderful, beautiful, and crazy as it ever had been and the shiny new object of global werewolf obsession was casually tossed aside like a discarded toy to make way for new stuff in the new millennium.

Like shootings and smartphones and social media.

That shit.

It wasn't long after the fanfare and national news lost interest (about four months) that the town elected a new chief. There was no other possible nominee and the so-called blind cop wouldn't cut it. They wanted the best, so they got the best.

Gene accepted the appointment graciously, but was a little embarrassed by the full-on parade they threw in his honor. They wouldn't let him stop it, so he tried to be a good sport.

Finally agreeing to grant a single interview to the local paper, the *Post Independent*, he was bluntly asked by the young reporter, "So, Chief Gene Schilling, you've saved four young men from certain death and become known to the entire world. Your name is now forever etched into the history books. You've also killed, consequently confirmed the existence of and possibly contributed to the extinction of werewolves as a species. What are you going to do next?"

His reply was swift: "I'm going to the Mountain Fair, baby!"

And he did just that. A few weeks after that interview, the annual fair started up and just as he had done every year previous, he made sure to wear his über-groovy tie-dyed shirt. The same one he'd spent years getting chucks n' yucks and being oft-ribbed about.

But that year things were different, you see. That year, in a unified sign of solidarity, as well as recognition of the deep respect they all held for their commanding officer, the whole damn department showed up in full multicolored hippie regalia of their own. Every last officer sported their own tie-dyed shirts, pants, and bandanas, delighting all the fair attendees and creating a long-standing tradition that has endured ever since. For nearly thirty years as of this telling.

So, nowadays, if you just happen to find yourself in Carbondale near the end of July, and you happen to swing by the annual Mountain Fair, and while enjoying the festivities—perhaps sipping an ice-cold lemonade or gnawing on a tasty gyro—you just so happen to see a policeman or police woman wearing an item of tie-dyed clothing, smiling with pride and maybe a dash of self-effacing humor, remember this:

It isn't an affectionate homage to some foundational hippies dropping acid and listening to *Sgt. Pepper* in the 1960s. It isn't a love letter to the brazen, bygone 24/7 drug-fueled party that was the Roaring Fork Valley in the seventies and eighties. It isn't necessarily about the liberal artistry that has been a fixture in the zeitgeist of Carbondale's denizens since its inception. It isn't to be ironic and it certainly isn't because a bunch of culturally-exhausted Boomers of the seventies, discontent Gen Xers of the nineties or apathetic Gen-Zers of the now couldn't find something original to do with their clothes in the last half century.

Though those are surely all good guesses.

Nope, the real reason they proudly adorn the tie-dye to this day is because, in 1996, soon-to-be Police Chief Gene Schilling humbly, selflessly, calmly, bravely and deftly secured his near-mythic status among the citizens of Carbondale and the world at large by saving four young, irresponsible dope-smokin' ne'er-do-wells from certain doom, whilst single handedly killing one nasty piece of moon-lovin' werewolf after stabbing it in the fuckin' eyeball with a silver Mont Blanc pen, of all things.

True story. Just ask somebody.

# METEOR

Cholla Eaton had been jockeying for the weather woman position at Station KTOP, the local network affiliate out of Denver for UBC (the United Broadcast Company), for about six months before she finally got the call.

She was actually at her favorite coffee shop, Peak Grounds, enjoying a double-shot caramel macchiato while reading a book by Clive Cussler (*Inca Gold*, specifically) when she got the text from the station manager telling her to come by the downtown building in the morning and dress sharp. She knew she had it then.

*It's in the bag, baby. We got this and then some.*

Unconsciously straightening her blonde hair, she laughed at her own nervous energy and then immediately sent out texts to her roommate and mom. They both replied with long text strings filled with congrats and emojis aplenty.

Naturally, Mom had to put a little cold water on it, as loving moms are always cautiously wont to do. But Cholla politely responded by saying that they wouldn't bring her in to tell her she didn't get it. They'd send an email or just ring her up. That bit had set her mother straight.

This was the break, alright. This was the dream of a six year old girl who drew clouds and lightning bolts on her school notebooks, and later a sixteen-year-old obsessed with the movie *Twister*, finally coming true. It was all happening—and fast.

Four years at Cornell's prestigious metrology program and a year-long part-time internship at KTOP in Denver had finally paid the dividends she had so sought after for so long. She had, after all, only accepted her admission to attend Cornell over Brown because it was a better school for such a career pursuit.

And *pursuit* was an appropriate way to describe it, because it was actually not so easy to break into the mainstream. Because of that, her mom thought she was cracked at the time, also due to being an alum of Brown herself.

But now the doubts were over in one fell swoop. Now she had gotten somewhere. A start, at least. And that was the best feeling she'd had in years.

She spent a semi-blissful morning doing some clothes shopping, getting a manicure, and made a hair appointment for the following day. She made the moves to up her game. Meet the occasion head on, as it were.

Also, the station mostly employed men, and she knew that modern career advancement was a delicate balance of persuasion and boundaries. The name of the game was to charm and disarm.

The afternoon brought with it the sickening feeling of having to let her current employer know that she would have to immediately quit once they offered her the position officially. She'd only been working at the Tattered Cover bookstore for a few months, but she was well liked by her co-workers and the managers alike, and she was bummed to have to tell them. They'd be totally amazing about it, of course. So her regret was borne primarily from the fact that it was the job that she had enjoyed the most up to that point.

She arrived at two in the afternoon and dropped her stuff off in the cozy little break room of the large multi-level bookstore. The top level was adult and contemporary, the middle floor was for special interests and oddities, and the bottom tier was for children's books of any and every stripe.

Before starting her shift, she walked below the high-arched ceiling, past the richly stained wood bookshelves, and back to where the other Clive Cussler novels were lined up on the top level. She thumbed around until she decided that *Dragon* might be the next adventure she would endeavor to take with the dashing undersea protagonist, Dirk Pitt. Her hands slipped it from between the other books and she made a beeline for the front desk. She'd purchase it after her shift.

She walked up and stood behind the counter, setting the book on the back rack to hold it until she finished her shift and could snap it up.

Her co-worker, Terry, sat on a stool behind the big desk with the registers. She was rocking your basic Hot Topic, nü-goth revival garb, as per usual. Bug-eyed glasses, onyx hair, too much eyeshadow, and stockings like the wicked witch of the west. You know the type.

Terry twirled her black and white striped legs around on the swiveling seat and then came to a stop, leaning in to whisper conspiratorially to Cholla, "*Cussler?* Bit domestic for your refined palate, isn't it?"

"It may not be Pynchon, Wallace, or DeLillo, but I'll tell ya, I'm secretly a girl of simple tastes. Cussler novels are a lot of fun, and I'm also increasingly a smidge burnt out on the semi-self-congratulatory intellectual exercises that come with the post-modernists. It's like, we get it, no one is cutting the grass, and even if you do, it grows back. Big whoop. Here's a suggestion for those guys: Grab a lawnmower and cut the shit, so to speak, or do please cease the flapping of thine jaws. Whereas, with Cussler, you get simple escapist fun minus the aforementioned self-aggrandizing intellectual masturbation. Just like nineties action movies. You can't say that about most literary dreck these days."

"Sure, agreed. Just seems like basic AF, James Patterson-level self-insertion wish fulfillment fluff," Terry mused in response.

"Ever read one?" Cholla asked.

"No, I can't say I have," Terry conceded.

Cholla nodded knowingly. "You might like 'em. I know I like my characters with agency and a preternatural need to survive dire circumstances rather than pontificating upon their respective existential crises, ad nauseam. Theory about action is great and all. Theory put in action is more interesting, no?"

"Sure, sure. If you say so. On the topic of surviving dire circumstances, you got any plans for the end of the world?" Terry's black-orbed, big-lashed eyes blinked wildly and she grinned like a madwoman.

Cholla wondered if she knew how crazy she looked right then, so she just went ahead and asked, "Do you know how crazy that look in your eyes is right now?" Cholla smiled politely as she asked, naturally.

"Ha! Nah! This is going to be the wack-tackiest apocalyp-ta-loopiest fun for the whole nuclear family in eons, baby! And it's happening tonight. We finna get blizzy until the EMP kills the lights! You should come by and party like it's 1999."

"1999?" Cholla mused as she pulled her employee ID lanyard over her head.

"You know, 'cause of the whole Y2K thing, am I right? Prince was totally psychic, you know?"

"Not at all, but I do take your meaning. And I do agree, this could be bad." Cholla started scanning book after book into the system with a small scan-gun, stacking them up next to her on the desk. "This guy I went to school with who shifted his major sophomore year to astronomical engineering emailed me two weeks back and said I should be stocking up on water, batteries, canned goods, and shotgun shells. I didn't think he was serious until he sent me a link of him and several other scientists at some symposium last month where they discussed the effect the meteor would have. They were painting a much less rosy picture than the news has been for the last two months."

Terry's pierced septum twitched and her mouth drooped slightly. "You don't actually think it's gonna be really bad or anything, do you? Like from a scientific perspective, or whatever?"

She genuinely looked nervous and Cholla figured, if nothing else, it would be gracious to take it easy on the poor girl's nerves.

"I'm sure he was overreacting a bit. He was always a little too serious."

This was half true. Cholla and Max had briefly dated in junior year but he was just that—way too serious and much more career-oriented than even she. No small feat, to be sure. So they'd opted to avoid the distaste of hostility to the passive simmering of a platonic relationship. He kept her up on the latest haps regarding astrophysics and astronomy with comedic flair that was at odds with his oft-stoic demeanor. In return, she provided sage guidance in his aimless and largely unsuccessful love life, post-her.

However, the thing about Max was that he was, above all else, serious about being serious. And when he was being serious, you could bet that it was serious. So when he said that the readings they'd been taking of the meteor for the last several months showed unbelievable levels of a specific type of gamma radiation and indicated that it had the theoretical capability of knocking modern tech back into the stone age, she believed him.

The news has been more speculative about the whole affair, projecting possible scattered outages comparable to the effects of a bad solar flare.

Still, the average person didn't want to even begin to go there mentally, so Cholla finished, "Bet it's gonna be the party of the century, if nothing else."

Terry smiled, seeming appeased.

Several hours later, Cholla was waiting behind the store in the tiny parking lot when Colette drove up in her silver mid-nineties Volkswagen Jetta. As Cholla pulled open the car door, she wasn't even a little surprised to hear, blasting from the speakers, the opening lines of the most excruciatingly typical song to play when the end drew nigh:

*"That's great, it starts with an earthquake, birds and snakes and aeroplanes. And Lenny Bruce is not afraid…"*

"With the R.E.M. already?" Cholla quipped as she got in the car. "Figured you'd wait till we cracked open a wine bottle and cheese spread to watch the horrors unfold below, dahhhling."

Colette smiled. "Gotta get while the gettin' can be got. Who knows what's gonna happen tonight? It's probably gonna be the same wet fart Y2K was, but if it isn't, we should try to enjoy the fireworks, no? So we bang out with the appropriate soundtrack, for starters. The Molotov cocktails come later."

"I'll stick to wine."

"We'll see." Colette Armstrong brushed her long brown hair out of face and put the car into drive, speeding off.

They'd been roommates for about a year, and the two got along so swimmingly that they had just re-signed another one-year lease renewal. Also a smart play considering how prices were skyrocketing in the mountain market. Everywhere, really. And they were essentially each other's best friends these days.

"Might've spooked the natives, myself. Mentioned to Terry what Max was on about last week and she seemed worried."

"So do you," Colette confirmed with a wink. "He thinks he's an extra in a Roland Emmerich film with his whole doomsayers schtick, and I guess the news doesn't have access to the same data he does, right?"

"Or they just don't know how to frame how scary the prospect is. I think that maybe they harbor the false belief that an ounce of cure is worth a pound of prevention. It's deeply troubling if you play the whole scenario out and think about how bad things may get—and how fast. But yeah, perhaps he's gone round the bend, as it were. Academia is nothing if not filled with Icarus figures, so it's certainly possible."

But she knew he wasn't the type and he always triple checked his data fields, so…

They drove home to the Spire, one of the nicer apartment locales in LoDo. Built in the mid to late aughts, it was great for the up and coming business class wannabes. The forty-two floors of posh condos, pools (yes, plural), a gym, a spa, and a top floor lounge where you could get a late nightcap (their Manhattan was absolutely to die for), made it preferable to much of the other housing offerings in the downtown district, if you could afford it.

Cholla had gotten terribly lucky in that Colette had been gifted "as much as you need, babycakes," for the two-bedroom digs from her father as a graduation gift.

Colette had really just put the ad for a roommate up since she didn't want to ask her dad for any more money and didn't want to get a full-time job. She worked part time at the Wizard's Chest, Denver's premiere costume and magic supply store, and was laser-focused on developing her talents as a writer. She had been published several times in various collections, actually, though they were usually only payable in contributors' copies.

Eventually Doubleday had offered her an advance for her first full length novel, which she had written while still in school. However, she'd scoffed at the initial offer and had sadly hardball-negotiated past their interest level. Now she was searching for another interested publishing house. Had been for months, in fact.

They pulled into the garage, parked the silver Jetta, and walked toward the elevator. On their way, they saw a figure making its way hastily toward the elevator as well. As he drew closer, they saw the pasty-white face of their creepazoid hallway neighbor, Neil. They didn't know his last name and didn't much care to find out.

Since they had moved into the Spire, both had gotten the stock-heebies whenever either crossed his path. Raggedy red hair, so many freckles they all connected, dead eyes, and a Joy Division shirt he wore often enough to notice he wore it too often. He also smelled like Lemon Pledge and possessed a heavy-duty incel vibe, in Cholla and Colette's combined estimation/speculation.

They rolled their eyes at one another as they stopped in front of the door to the elevator. Neil came up just as they did and stood by as Colette hit the button.

He awkwardly stared at the elevator door and without shooting them a look said dryly, "Damn thing always takes forever."

Colette smirked at Cholla and nodded proddingly. Cholla shook her head, then exhaled and resigned herself to defeat, responding, "Yeah, it's, uh, a long way down, I guess. Takes a bit."

She looked to Neil, but he did not meet her stare. That was new. Usually he was always staring. Too usually, and uncomfortably so. He said nothing more after that. All three waited in silence until the lift doors opened and they filed inside.

An equally awkward and soundless thirty-six floor ascent and they all got off on thirty-seven. Neil remained silent as he rushed out of the elevator car and shuffled hurriedly down the hall. He swiftly entered his apartment, then locked his door no less than three times.

As they both walked out of the elevator, which now vaguely reeked of chemical lemons, Cholla let her paranoid imagination take flight, easily visualizing Neil, face pressed up against the door, peering out of his viewing glass at them as they entered their apartment.

Dude was a creeper, squared.

They made it into their abode, then closed and triple locked their door as well.

The apartment was your basic LoDo Denver high-rise homage to post-modern gentrification, right up to the strategically placed false brick showing underneath stylishly torn off-white wallpaper and down to the intentionally weathered, quasi-second hand wooden furniture. It was made up to look like a bourgeois boho artist's loft by way of Wayfair, but without all the used needles or paint brushes.

The two roomies walked in and set down their things, then each began their routine of sprucing up and getting settled in. Colette took a shower while Cholla lit a scented candle and changed into blue pajamas with little white clouds all over them. She microwaved a burrito and scarfed it in a minute flat. She should've eaten more earlier, she realized, and so promptly cooked another Little Juan burrito and ate it with the same fervor.

After kicking on the news on the wall-mounted 4K, she pulled the bottle of the night from the small wine chiller they had near her desk in the living room.

She knew little-to-nothing of wine herself, but according to her roommate with the more discerning palate, the whites from the Marlborough area of New Zealand in the last several decades had been of world renown.

Colette made the selections and didn't give a solitary hoot about how they were consumed, so Cholla chose one of the posh Kiwi whites (Rapaura Springs Bull Paddock Vineyard Sauvignon Blanc, specifically) and popped the top.

Crossing the room, she opened the brushed metallic door of the fridge with the touch screen display embedded in it. The display toggled between HD backgrounds and a live feed of just outside their front door.

She withdrew a charcuterie tray she'd cut up the night before but hadn't made much of a dent in. It would go much better with this white than the diet coke she'd had the evening previous. She yanked the cellophane wrap from the top, and set the tray on the table before the TV.

She got a couple glasses and brought them around to the

living room, then plopped down on the couch. Pouring herself an opening half glass, she watched as the usual roll of semi-sentient pundit dullards that occupied the media ecosphere lit up her TV with their perfectly framed and illuminated faces. Regardless of political leaning, they lamented the jumped-up overreaction brewing about the meteor.

For weeks now, religious groups had been amplifying their rhetoric where the end times were concerned, and it was not making people less jumpy. Quite the opposite. As a result—and perhaps to cynically maintain audience and population numbers right up until the possible catastrophe—the media organizations and governments of the world at large had made a concerned collective effort to tamp down fears and apprehension, thereby theoretically forestalling any riots or zealotry run amok.

It was working, for the most part.

One surprising outlier in this regard was the country of Egypt, whose government had, in recent years, been the target of religious extremists. That was until the meteor, at least. The looniest of the looney-toons over there had swiftly and success-fully usurped the government, using the meteor as a loose basis for their own brand of emergent anarchy in the last several weeks.

It had deteriorated into utter Sodom and Gomorrah-level chaos over there, apparently. At least that's what everyone was hearing. No one had seen live footage or video for weeks as there was a media blackout and every attempt to get intel or on-ground coverage resulted in downed drone planes, or worse.

The columns of smoke and burning cityscapes that they could see—using high altitude planes and keyhole satellites—painted a grim picture. Some other countries were calling it the "canary in the coal mine."

The American media was decidedly more outwardly positive in their coverage. Cholla clicked over to KTOP and saw that they had already begun their 10:00 p.m. lead-in. Mark Protsman, the head anchor, was going through the day's headlines: Religious leaders calling for peace among demonstrators, mass rioting picking up around the globe, unexpected loss of contact with the ISS, and several satellite issues were creating a feeling of unease among basically everyone.

She figured it would be what everyone had expected Y2K to be: essentially the L.A. riots on steroids.

The news abruptly pivoted to local road projects and little league updates as Colette returned from showering and plunked down on the couch. She twisted up her still-wet hair and flipped it over her shoulder, then poured herself a glass of wine. "Checking in with the chicken littles?"

"Yeah. Well, the big three are chirping about the same shizzle as they have been. So was our station at first, but they've shifted over to local now." Cholla sipped her drink and continued, "Jan must've gotten the job with the New York affiliate. Otherwise they wouldn't drop her. I should call and congratulate her when she's off for the evening."

Colette bit into a piece of cheese and said, "Well that's a boost for you, right? Since, as her heir apparent, they obviously think you capable of filling her shoes and matching her level of professionalism and journalistic integrity."

Cholla's nose wrinkled. "That sounded oddly prepared. You scribble that one on a cocktail napkin at some point?"

"Shut up. No, just being half-serious. On the real tip, I'm proud of you. Not sure if I said that yet." Colette took a sip from her wine glass.

"One of your emojis earlier seemed like it conveyed that, but thank you again." Cholla curled her legs under her. "Getting pretty hairy at this juncture. What are we gonna do if we run out of bullets?"

"For our non-existent gun?" Colette asked.

"One and the same. So we're largely fucked if things go tits up. We have some SPAM and candles and that's about it." Cholla laughed, as did Colette. "But hopefully this is all much ado about nada."

Colette sighed and said, "I'm sure we'll be kosher. How long have we got?"

"Till it passes by?" Cholla asked. Colette nodded. "It's gonna be right around 1:00 a.m. on the east coast. I hear Times Square is packed. So I guess right around eleven for us."

"We should turn off the lights right around eleven. See if anybody else does."

"Why?" Cholla asked, rolling her eyes at Colette.

"I dunno, something to do to mark the occasion, at least. Might be kinda spooky and fun." Colette picked up her glass and finished it off, then refilled it.

Cholla didn't reply, returning to watch the tube.

Mark Protsman, of the perfectly applied makeup and blonde waifish coif, spoke from the glowing screen, "And in other news, the DOW sunk to its lowest point in the last fifty years as market concerns still portend a devastating blow to the global economies as a new and paradoxical trend toward what economists are describing as—"

"Hey, you think we should go to Akihabara on Friday? They're having dollar beers," Colette interjected.

"Sounds kinda awful, if I'm being honest. Maybe we hit the

Church for real drinks and check if Oblio is spinning, then see what's what afterwards."

Cholla took another pull of wine and gobbled some sliced meat and crackers from the tray on the table. She looked out the window and saw the glowing outline of the Republic Plaza a few blocks away.

The tallest building in Denver, it had a whopping fifty-six floors. The forty-eighth floor served as the studio and office space for KTOP, and it's where she'd be working for the next several years.

She stood up and walked to the window, glass in hand. Colette grabbed her own glass and joined. They walked out onto the terrace and the cool night air snapped at their skin, giving them goosebumps. They bristled, but hung out for a few minutes and shared a cigarette as Cholla spied the panel windows and glowing offices of the Republic Plaza's forty-eighth floor.

As they walked back inside and sat back down on the couch, they saw that a commercial break was ending and the broadcast had resumed with Jan Johnson, the current on-air meteorologist doing what she did best in a stylish blue dress. She was going over the local and national weather forecasts and had just finished summarizing the seven-day when she started to speak more loosely, going off script.

Using her fingers to guide her blonde hair behind her ears, then straighten her dress sides, she started, "So I would be remiss if I didn't mention that the thing on everyone's minds this evening will obviously be our outer space flyby in about thirty minutes' time. As a student of science first and foremost, I am confident that when I see you all again tomorrow evening, we will all be the wiser about what jumping the gun can do, and have a good laugh at the whole affair. We folks who work in weather can attest as to how unpredictable giving predictions can truly be. And there has been so much that has been sensationalized by—"

In an instant, every source for and user of electricity around them shut off. The TV, the lights, the fridge. Everything. The light from the candle on the counter cast only the faintest glow around the large kitchen/living room space.

It was a moment before either woman could focus their eyes. Cholla felt a deep sinking feeling, like a black hole had opened in her gut. It wasn't a passing feeling. It was a hollow void that was born from her eyes focusing on the window and the city beyond. The lights were well and truly out alright.

Colette whispered, "It's early. Is this the real deal?"

Oddly, Cholla felt it was appropriate to match the volume level and whispered back, "I guess this means the world may be in for some rough riding ahead."

"Are you scared?" Colette asked.

"No, at least not yet. Let's get some candles and set them up on the counter so we can operate normally until we see what's going on."

Cholla stood up and walked over to kitchen island's countertop, with its heavy, pseudo-marble facade. She pulled open a drawer just below the knife block and plucked four medium-sized white candles from it, then closed it. She used the same long-neck Bic lighter to light them up and with all five now going, the room brightened considerably.

She walked over to where she had earlier set down her phone on the small kitchen nook table and saw that it was very dead. Picking it up, the phone was hot. Like left in the sun for an hour hot.

*Shit. Why does that feel so alarming?*

"Phones have gone the way of the Dodo, if mine is to be believed. And it's really hot."

Cholla set the last gen Motorola back down and moved to the supply closet, where they kept the vacuum and the various spray bottles they used for cleaning. She searched for a moment and found another two large candles. She cracked the window to allow for some air to circulate.

Colette shuddered, "Sure that's a good idea?"

Cholla nodded. "Yeah, I read that you've got to keep the windows open when using candles anyway on account of what they do to your lungs. Apparently running a scented candle for an hour is like smoking a cigarette."

"Jesus, really? That's uncool. Not like I can be all too worried with how many nails I'm smoking a day, as of late."

"I was gonna say…" Cholla smiled at Colette, then lit the other two candles and placed them on the table. She walked back to the sliding glass door of the terrace and held her glass in one hand as she looked out across the city.

It was unlike anything she had ever witnessed.

It was a cloudy and essentially moonless evening, and without the lights in the city, the darkness surprised her. Usually, when there was, say, a power outage, you'd still see the glow from the hills of the adjacent towns and suburbs that branched out like tentacles in all directions from the central Denver metroplex. From here, she could often see the lights of Idaho Springs, which were a good thirty miles away from where she stood. But at this moment, in this non-light, she couldn't even tell where the horizon diverged the sky from the mountains.

Cholla hum-sang, *"When the lights go down in the city, and there ain't no sun or no bay*—" She grinned at Colette, who seemed bemused, if a little stressed. It was likely up to Cholla to keep her friend's head straight in the event that this thing was more than a passing day or two hiccup.

Which she was increasingly certain it was.

On that video with Max and the other scholars, they'd said that in a worst case scenario, effects could literally prevent any mass communication or recovery of energy for months. Water, electricity, and all communication would be done and it would cause society to do one of two things: adapt or unravel. The crux of the discussion had them debating which outcome was more likely.

They'd unanimously landed on it unraveling.

The two pulled up a couple of chairs and watched out the doors as they sipped on wine, watching candles start to pop up like fireflies in the darkened windows of nearby buildings. There did not appear to be a source of any electric light.

They watched for about half an hour as some people had taken to the streets and there was a mixture of yelling and cheering coming in through the open window. Not much light still, but eventually distant sources of larger light were springing up. Possibly flood lights hooked up to generators, Cholla speculated.

They were milling about the apartment, and as Colette worked on finding something to eat, a loud, resonant bang came in through the open window and startled them both. Cholla was not far from the door and took a step toward it quick enough to see that some more candle lights had appeared in buildings and on the streets. The bang was a car of some type, many blocks away. She saw the glow on an adjacent building's walls and could only see a tiny piece of the vehicle around the building's corner. It was burning.

Colette rushed over and joined her, Then she spotted the burning car.

*BOOM!*

Another car in a big parking lot, also several blocks away but unobscured from their view, exploded.

Colette whispered, "Holy hell! What's going on down there?" More explosions as several vehicles in the same lot next to the first car detonated into balls of fire. "You know where the binoculars are?"

Taking a cue from the Central Perk crew on the show *Friends*, Cholla had gotten binoculars to creep on people from her high vantage, and on better days, take in all the beauty of the Denver metro landscape. It was easy enough with how high up they were. Now, she ran into the bedroom where she thought she'd left them.

As she flew out of the room, Colette looked over at the small table not far from the sliding glass doors and pulled open the drawer. She rummaged a bit, then withdrew the binoculars. She put them up to her eyes and peered for a moment before coming to rest on a single spot. She heard Cholla banging around in the other room.

"Uh, hey, I found the specs and you better get out here and take a look! It looks like trouble is brewing at the station."

"Republic Plaza? Are you sure?" Cholla rushed out of the bedroom and across the carpet to join her.

Colette lowered the binoculars and handed them over with a sickened look on her usually radiant face.

Cholla took them up and pressed them tightly against her face. She saw that several people were throwing gas cans in front of the building and waving torches around. Hundreds of people were tossing rocks at windows, scurrying and running about like crazed ants after their farm had been shaken.

Another twenty seconds passed and one of the angry villagers tossed your average street-grade Molotov at the front doors of the building and a ring of fire quickly encircled the ground level of Republic Plaza.

As she watched in horror, people fled out windows and down the fire escapes. Many were making it to the ground, but on the north-east side, one exit was seemingly being exploited as a honeypot for a goddamn sniper.

While she gasped, unbelieving of her eyes, she saw that every time someone walked out of a small door coming from the middle of the building out onto a catwalk, they'd be shot and fall right over the railing onto the ground before they could take notice of the increasingly large spot of blood spatter accruing on the brick wall behind them.

"Someone's sniping people," Cholla said flatly. "Holy fuck. It's only been half a goddamn hour!"

"What?" Colette near-shouted.

"And there's those Molotovs you were waiting for. What the actual fuck?" Cholla quipped.

Colette stared at the floor. "I think I'm gonna be sick."

"Yeah, I'm hearing that." Cholla pulled away the binoculars and stood next to Colette, who was starting to shake and sway slightly back and forth. She threw her arm over her friend and roomie, pulling her head into Cholla's shoulder.

"Fucking purge down there. What the hell?" Cholla's blue eyes reflected the twinkle of firelight in the distance.

"Why would they burn the station down?" Colette asked as she stared out the window.

"And who are they in this situation? Is this really how fast it all goes to shit?" Cholla asked.

"Are they gonna do the same thing here?"

Cholla shook her head, then walked toward the kitchen. She had nearly reached the kitchen island when she heard a soft tapping on the front door. She shot Colette a spooked look, which Colette returned in kind, then made for the refrigerator and tapped the screen on the door a few times until she remembered that it was embarrassingly futile. She was gonna have to do it the ol' horse-n-buggy method of actually checking the door's peep-hole.

As she quietly approached, another soft knock came through, and she put her eye against the door.

It was creepo Neil from down the hall. He held a small candle in his hand that barely illuminated his pale face and left the hallway mostly dark. What the hell did he want?

She didn't move to undo the locks but rather shouted through the door, "Hey, Neil, how's your evening going?"

"Dark. Everything is dark. Guess the comet was as bad as they thought." Neil's face was as empty and expressionless as usual.

"It was a meteor, actually. Not that it matters, but I think it's even worse than anyone had foreseen. Something I can help you with?"

Neil was quiet for a moment, then slowly responded, "Just wanted to make sure you were okay. Both of you. Are you okay?"

Cholla looked over her shoulder, but didn't see Colette.

*She must be getting the other candles from the bathroom.*

"Yeah, Neil. Think we're as good as can be expected over here." Cholla felt something like a nervous energy hit her system and her hands suddenly felt sweaty and clammy.

"It's just the two of you in there?" Neil softly asked.

*Weird question. Creepy creeper creepin' all the way.*

"Yeah, Neil, but we're fine and—"

"Armed!" Colette whispered across the room. "Tell him we're armed!" She smiled and finished her glass off again, then began to refill it.

Cholla spoke again, "So, yeah, we're all good."

All the beliefs Cholla had about the stability, durability, and integrity of her front door were suddenly and literally torn asunder as Neil kicked it in.

The hard wood smashed Cholla's face and nose, knocking her backwards onto the floor. Blood leaked from both nostrils and she tried to refocus her eyes. She then watched, semi-dazed, as the dark figure of her hallway neighbor filled the doorway, then leaned down and punched her face.

The darkness and quiet were absolute.

Cholla had no idea how long she was unconscious or that had been at all until she slowly opened her eyes and the haziness around her began to resolve into something recognizable. The kitchen was not far away. She saw the candles she had just lit sitting in a row.

Her head thumped.

Neil sat on the stool at the kitchen island, facing her, slowly twirling a knife in his left hand, the tip of the blade braced against the forefinger on his right. He didn't smile or even look in her direction as he spoke.

"You know, no one will know what happens to most people in the chaos. Without the computers, the cameras, without functioning courts, police, or any one left to help, it will be a blur of death and loss. So many will be shuffled into the deck and never seen again. Easy hunting, for the inclined."

Colette's snoring drew Cholla's attention. Just like her, Colette was tied to one of the dining room chairs, off to Cholla's left.

Cholla quietly addressed Neil, "So what is this now, Neil? Just what in the actual fuck are you doing with us, huh? Why shouldn't I just scream?"

"Because I'll take this knife and shove it through one of Colette's cheeks until it pops out of the other. Then you can watch her drown on her own blood." He raised his eyes to meet hers. "Or you could not. That *is* also an option."

"Okay … fuck, that's twisted. And uh"—she struggled lightly against her restraints—"what's your plan here, man?"

"Best case scenario, I kill then slowly eat you and your girl here."

His tone did not imply he was joking.

"Really?"

"*Really.*"

Cholla decided to go for broke with forced levity. "Right. With fava beans and Chianti?"

Neil didn't flinch, not even a pause as he replied matter-of-factly, "No beans. Salt and pepper."

"You're a cannibal, Neil? That's fairly gross and unseemly and I don't believe you. And if I did, why would that—"

"Shut up, Cholla. Just keep your lips sealed. You wouldn't understand."

"Understand fucking what?" Cholla hissed at him.

Neil stood up. "That if I take of your flesh, then I shall be physically stronger for the battles ahead."

"So no baseline for reality, then? No tether to morality or anything?"

"Morality is relative."

"Psychosis isn't. It's pretty clearly definable, as I understand it." Cholla glared at Neil and his eyebrows pricked up at this. "And currently, it is definable as you. You are one fucked puppy, bub."

Neil sprayed a blur of curses as he jumped up and rushed toward her with the knife held high.

Cholla had two choices, as she figured in that dire moment of realization. It was either death, or fight back hard and now.

She opted for the latter and swung her leg out, connecting with Neil's chest as he lunged her way, taking the air completely out of him. As he went splaying off balance, she cried out and felt something not cool happening with her foot.

She toppled backward, cracking the arms of the chair.

Something down there was fractured and she was feeling it, deeply. Luckily, she sensed the bonds loosened by the impact and started to wriggle her arms free.

Neil dropped to the floor, and in her peripheral vision, she saw Colette stand up with the chair still lassoed around her and run at Neil.

He coughed, rolled to his left, and kept hacking as he tried to catch his breath again.

Colette tripped, falling onto her side with a gasp.

*Must've hurt something as well,* Cholla thought.

Neil was regaining his composure slowly, and as he tried to get up, Colette started kicking out at him with her feet. He brought down the knife and stabbed into the fleshy part of her thigh.

Colette screamed. "Oh goddamn it, you mother fucker! Fuck you! Fuck! Fuck, pull that shit outta me!" She seemed to be straining to push herself away now, though still tied to her chair.

Neil didn't hesitate to yank free the knife, yielding spurting blood from Colette's leg, eliciting another cry from her friend.

He brought it back down again, but this time Colette moved in just a way so that the tip of the blade buried itself in the wood of the chair's leg, instead of hers.

Neil was still hacking, his breathing labored. Cholla was working on her arms and had freed one hand. She was using her free hand to pull at the rope around her left wrist when Neil noticed and pulled the knife out again.

Instead of taking another stab at her roomie, Neil turned his dead-eyed attention to Cholla, and rushed at her.

She instinctively fell to the right to dodge the blow, and much to her immediate shock, Neil passed her by and hit the coffee table, spilling the Marlborough Kiwi White Sauv Blanc onto the floor. And the charcuterie as well.

Cholla pulled her other hand free and just as she was getting the ropes from her legs, she was knocked backward and Neil was on top of her.

He had the knife in his hand, but instead of stabbing again, held it toward her throat and yelled in her face, "This isn't what I want! Not how I want it! You need to stop, bitch! This isn't how this is supposed to go!"

His eyes were wild and angry, and she reflexively grabbed at the blade of the knife. The sharp edge sliced open her palm, but she managed to move it from her throat and Neil lost his balance slightly as he tried to hold her down with his weight.

Her face was near his head, and she could smell that fucking lemon pledge. It made her mad. Really, really mad.

Lemon pledge furious.

Then, as if guided by some unknown reserve of don't give a

fuckery, combined with hatred for this moment and that damn smell, she opened her mouth and curled her head toward his, biting down on anything her teeth could find.

What her teeth found was his ear and she bit down on it as hard as her jaws could handle. She must've gotten more than she realized, because as he howled with pain and toppled backward off of her, holding the side of his head, she realized her mouth was almost full and spit the chunk of bloody ear onto the floor.

Neil twisted and floundered about for what seemed like forever, but must have been all of four seconds.

Still, it was all she needed. She wrenched herself free and stumbled into a standing posture, snatching up the knife in the process. Her left hand was dripping maroon onto the floor, and she clenched her fist to try and mitigate the blood loss.

Colette shouted, "Watch out!"

Cholla moved to one side and pivoted on her feet. Neil was rushing her direction again, but she figured that she'd spent enough time on defense. As he got close, she swung the knife out at him, slashing his cheek, but not stopping him entirely.

He caught her with his shoulder and she fell down again. The knife went flying. Neil fell onto his chest, the air knocked from him as he groaned.

Cholla slowly grabbed for the arm of the couch to steady herself, but he reached up and pulled her long dirty-blonde hair—and by extension, her head—backward, straining her neck.

"You stupid, stupid little whores! This is not what you are supposed to do!" he gritted out.

Cholla kept her hands locked onto the couch's side as he used her hair to further pull himself up.

Colette had righted herself and started to stand up. She slowly kneel-shuffled over toward the two, the chair still tied to her back.

Neil had almost reached the base of Cholla's skull when Colette got close enough to rush him from the side. As she was about to connect, she twisted herself so that the chair would hit him. It did, but her gravity carried her over him and back onto her side on the floor.

Colette cursed, "Fucking fuck!" Her feet had landed not far from him and she gave him two quick shots to the chest with her long legs.

Neil groaned again, but rolled away from the two of them.

Cholla used the couch to raise herself up and limped toward the terrace door. Neil coughed, then slowly stood up and spun around to face Cholla. A thick line of blood drew down his cheek from the slash. His hand rubbed at it angrily, then he coated his digits with the seepage and pushed against his face until it was a smear of his own blood.

He looked demonic.

She knew his pattern now. Just trigger his ass again and use his stupidity against him. "That all you got, Lemon Pledge?"

For the first time, something like real anger filled Neil's normally dead eyes. It wasn't two seconds before he rushed across the room to tackle her.

But just as he had before, he didn't anticipate her reaction time. She lowered herself and put her shoulder out, and Neil toppled over her and through the sliding glass window, landing out on the terrace.

Disoriented, he slowly stood up, rubbing his head and arms. His eyes registered two seconds of the harrowing and dystopian scene in the metropolis below before he was hit from the back and sent flying over the faux-wood railing.

Thirty-seven floors of freefall only lasted about three seconds, until Cholla heard the sickening sound of his body hitting the ground. She stood on the terrace, but didn't cross over to the railing.

Colette was up again and awkwardly hobbling toward her. Her disheveled roommate shuffled through the open hole where the sliding glass door had been a minute earlier. She nudged her back at Cholla and said, "Little help?"

Cholla immediately started to undo the ropes as Colette peered over the railing. Below, illuminated by a nearby burning truck, she saw that Neil had landed on top a large man who was wearing all black, except for an odd white mask. Before his untimely demise, the large dude had been holding a bloodied chainsaw that was still rumbling under their corpses.

Colette scowled and said, "I think you might've killed Cabela's Leatherface down there with, uh, Neil, but I think you likely saved someone too, so it might be a wash. Probably a few someones, now that I'm thinking about it. So it's probably all good. I think it's all good. It's good, we're good, right?"

Colette stared down for another second, then used her hands to undo the rest of the ropes that still tied parts of her to the chair. She yanked free of its grasp, kicking the chair aside, then began to cry.

Cholla wrapped her arms around her roommate, giving her a hug. Her bloody mouth rubbed maroon streaks on Colette's shoulder.

Between sobs, Colette asked, "You think he was gonna eat us?"

"No, he was probably just telling himself he was going to. But who knows? Who fucking cares."

Colette rubbed her now-free wrists, then asked, "I'm just now getting the irony here, but did you honestly just bite his ear off? Was that more Mike Tyson or Hannibal Lecter?" She half-heartedly chuckled.

"More like Dirk Pitt," Cholla said, breathing the crisp, cool air in an attempt to catch her breath.

"Who?"

"Nobody. A badass. It doesn't really matter," Cholla said softly.

Colette raised her head up and looked fearfully into Cholla's eyes, "What just happened? What made him do that?"

Cholla looked past her as their embrace ended and they stood side by side. Her eyes were watching the increasingly distressing sights unfold before her. Crowds filled the streets now, the sounds of smashing windows echoing off the walls of buildings as they looted and rioted. Gunshots all over. More explosions in the distance. And closer, the Republic Plaza was now fully on fire.

Cholla was silent for a moment, then answered, "No idea. But that was likely just the beginning."

They stood and stared for a moment before Colette's hand reached over and took Cholla's as the city continued to unravel beneath a cloudy and moonless sky.

# DEIFIED

Located at 631 Fifth Avenue on the isle of Manhattan—in the city so nice, ya'-damn-sure-know it got named twice—stood St. Patrick's Cathedral. Since its dedication in 1879, it had served as the seat of the Archdiocese of New York and its outer boroughs.

It was the largest Gothic-revivalist cathedral in North America. A supreme testament to the visual splendor of the neo-Gothic movement itself, it drew upon the features and examples of medieval architecture such as decorative patterns, lancet windows, finials, and hood molding. The majority of its composition was made up of Inwood or Tuckahoe marble, a type largely found in southern parts of New York state, which dated from the Late Cambrian to the Early Ordovician ages, or roughly 484 million years ago.

*And people thought that the building was old.*

Shockingly, Scott Weber could recall that much detail from the books and articles he had been reading in the lead-up to his special apostolic apprenticeship at St. Patrick's Cathedral, under the stewardship of Bishop Branford and the archbishop, and which he had recently been the grateful recipient of.

It wasn't an easy internship to acquire, and it essentially guaranteed you a place on the track to becoming a bishop after being granted priesthood.

It certainly made Scott wonder what he had done to rise above the other possible applicants to secure the gig. Several of the others who applied had naturally also attended St. Joseph's Seminary and College with him over in Yonkers, and he personally knew at least three of them to be arguably much more outwardly qualified to receive such an honor. He supposed that it was possible that his humble and unassuming nature, as well as his weary yet tactful way of inter-mingling with others, might have actually helped him in this regard.

However, his mind and heart also knew too well that such self-congratulating thoughts ran the risk of jockeying the ego and inflating the head. So Scott quickly and humbly assumed it was, as everything would ever be, but the lord's will alone that he had been given this gift, and thanked Him quietly for His grace.

The bronze doors at the cathedral's front were beset on each side by towers with spires rising toward the heavens. The northern tower contained nineteen bells, while the sprawling interior had dual pipe organs.

Beyond the ornate doors, a long nave flanked by several chapels, two transepts, a chancel and apse, as well as a crypt below the altar. On the east side of the property was the archbishop's residence, which faced Madison Avenue.

The cathedral was truly a New York staple. The crown jewel of the Archdiocese and a landmark for generations.

The gratitude he felt for this opportunity was something he had already expressed to the cardinal as well as the archbishop when they had met briefly a week before at the archbishop's residence.

His parents were also unabashedly proud. Being devout Catholics themselves, they had been encouraging his faith since he was a child and saw this next step as the bearing of fruit from seeds sown long ago.

It was with this joy in heart and hand that he walked from the street, up the steps, and to the large and heavy bronze front doors. It was almost 11:00 p.m., and the cool breeze felt good on his face. It was enough to ruffle his brown hair, so he quickly straightened it with both hands.

He was wearing a black tracksuit as he had just come from a solid two hours at the nearby gym after he had gotten off the subway.

Above the doorway before him was a bronze relief of an open-armed Jesus surrounded by his disciples. And beset in the intricately carved doors themselves were the relief sculptures of six saints and martyrs, from St. Patrick himself to the Mohawk maiden, Kateri Tekakwitha. Both doors were firmly secured and closed.

He walked to the right of the main entryway to another set of doors. The left door in this set was just slightly ajar, and he knew it was on account of his after-hours arrival. There was a small sign atop a short, movable brass post warning off others and blocking entry. He moved it aside and stepped through the doorway into the interior, replacing the post behind him.

As he walked in, he heard music he immediately recognized echoing off the high vaulted ceilings. Piping in "Hymn of the Cherubim" by Tchaikovsky through the modern speaker system may have been a bit heavy handed, but it certainly set the tone.

Filling the halls with the faint, reverberating notes of classic music's past, it felt all the more holy and grand in its scope. The reverence one felt as they walked through it was resonant and permeated every nook and cranny of the ornately designed interiors.

The long corridor of the church's nave, or main area, ran west to east and was separated into four sections of pews divided by three walking aisles. Scott moved into the nave's center aisle and marched east toward the direction of the altar in the sanctuary, located about fifty yards away.

There was no one else occupying the pews or inside any of the side chapels that he saw as he walked along. He was struck by how bright it was every time he had been here.

The restoration project launched a decade ago had come to fruition about seven years prior, with the Pope visiting shortly thereafter its completion. Now, the once yellowed facades were gleaming white with a freshly-renovated pearly sheen. Thirty-two marble support columns, roughly five feet in diameter each, rose up and met with the adjoining buttresses and arches of the high vaulted ceiling. In the last few years, all of these columns had been fitted with vertically mounted, high-definition TVs for announcements and to display hymnal lyrics during services.

A sign of the times.

Scott walked quietly along and glanced at his watch. It was 10:39 p.m. He was to meet with the cardinal around eleven, but hadn't been fully informed as to why. Bishop Branford had told him to expect to meet with a few others and do one last bit of introductive administration stuff, so he had zero idea what exactly was going to happen.

He briefly thought of a scene he had watched when he was researching organized crime for his finals paper titled, "Moral

Decay in the Twenty-first Century," the previous year. The movie he had screened was called *Goodfellas*, and there was a part where a loud and distastefully obscene little man was lured to his death in the basement of a building under the auspices of being elevated in the hierarchy of his organization.

It certainly didn't work out for the short Italian, but this wasn't that.

Obviously.

The thought was really quite silly and he wondered why he had even had it. The truth was, he barely watched movies, and generally only if they were on one of the Christian networks. He was assuredly more of a reader. He'd tried to finish all the classics: *Moby Dick*, *Lord of the Flies*, *Catcher in the Rye* (he never understood what the big deal was with that one), *Jane Eyre*, *Red Badge*, etcetera—some of which he certainly enjoyed more than others.

One thing he did have a soft spot for was fantasy. In his youth he had absorbed any and all fantasy novels he could get his hands on. He'd gotten the bug from the *Lord of the Rings* trilogy which his father had gotten him when he was just seven, espousing it as an allegorical retelling of Christ's struggle. And he had spent countless days imagining he was slaying multi-fanged, big-eyed monsters in faraway kingdoms.

When he was eight, he had proclaimed to his amused parents that he would one day be the greatest dragon rider in all the land. After that, his parents stopped buying him so many Anne McCaffrey books.

Scott strolled up to the elevated chancel and high altar and walked past it. He could see the archbishop's pulpit and the apse. Harder to see were the small, semi-concealed copper doors on the backside of the altar. Opening to the small space under the altar known as the crypt, it was where several deceased archbishops and former high-ranking church officials were interred.

Scott had only ever seen it once, a week ago when he was granted a private tour when it looked as though he may be in serious contention for the position. That was the day before he got the confirmation call to meet with the heads of the church.

He walked around the altar and behind it lay the smaller Lady Chapel. It was the furthest east of the cathedral's side chapels and was adjacent to the apse with the altar.

Standing before the chapel inside, facing away from his approaching footsteps, was Bishop Branford. He had a small purplish mitre upon his brown-haired head, as well as a house cassock of black with similar purple piping and red buttons. He wasn't kneeling, but his head was lowered and his hands were together as he mumbled softly, likely in prayer.

Hearing Scott's approach, he turned on his heels. Scott could now see the purple sash hanging from his waist and the big wire-rim glasses hanging from his nose.

The bishop walked to meet Scott with his hand held out and a big, disingenuous smile stretched uncomfortably across his face, which was something new. Scott noticed because generally the bishop was a paradigm of chastity, virtue, and unyielding charisma. Not false and certainly never awkward.

Something was off…

"Hey there, bright boy! My apologies—bright *man*. It's hard sometimes to shake off the inclination to adopt a paternal affectation when speaking of or to younger members of the holy order."

"Yes, well, a good evening, your excellency." Scott nodded politely but didn't know what else to say. He was caught somewhat off guard by the detectable difference in the way the bishop was acting. He seemed … nervous.

"Was your trip enjoyable? Did you find your way in easy enough?" A gold chain crossed his chest on which hung a small golden crucifix. Bishop Branford's right hand was rubbing it, again and again.

"Quite an enjoyable subway ride, yes. It only vaguely smelled of urine, so that was good. Or perhaps about as much as one may ask for. How are you doing this evening, your grace?" Scott asked.

"We're… I'm—rather *you're*—going to, uh… Well, you've seen the crypt before, yes?" He nodded past Scott back toward the back of the altar in the previous area.

"Yes, but…" He raised his hand up. "Excuse me, your excellency. My apologies, but may I ask one question first?" Scott's voice was soft and did not betray the true depth of his curiosity.

Bishop Branford said nothing but folded his hands and nodded for him to continue.

Scott did: "What is this we are doing here this evening? I thought we had discussed next week as when I would begin all of the—"

"Listen," the Bishop cut him off, "we need to make haste to the crypt."

Scott was surprised. "Why are we going to the crypt, sir?"

Bishop Branford walked past Scott, but did not answer.

Scott looked up at the crucifix upon the altar inside the Lady Chapel and made the cross on his head and chest before turning to follow.

The crypt was secured by two imposing copper doors fitted with large bolts. The metal had oxidized green over the decades and had left the door looking like an entryway in the city of Oz.

As it was only a few yards away, they quickly reached it. The bishop then used his right hand to search through some hidden pocket amid the big black folds of his cassock. As he withdrew it, he held a small golden key which he then promptly inserted into a discreetly placed lock inside a small keyhole, built into the wall.

An audible click, then the rolling of tumblers as a mechanism started up and released some bolt behind the marble wall. The right door softly cracked open.

Branford opened the door the rest of the way, but stood back so that Scott could enter first.

"You know, there used to be a big stone slab in front of this crypt's entrance that required six men to move," the bishop said.

Naturally, Scott had read about this in a tome about the first one hundred years of the church's operation, as well as other readings he'd assigned himself. One thing they had never been specific about in any of the articles was why the past keepers of the crypt had felt it necessary to secure it so. No time like the present to end the suspense on that count.

"What do you believe was the reason that they felt they needed to put such a heavy stone in front of the door?" Scott asked as he passed into the brightly lit, white-marble-walled passage that immediately opened to a low ceilinged, badly illuminated square room with rows of crypts in the opposing wall.

"They were doing their best to keep the place hidden," Branford quickly replied.

Scott paused and turned slightly to face the bishop. He decided to play along and see where this odd discussion was headed. "And why would that be?"

"Despite their wisdom, they did not possess our modern

day's current level of technology to accommodate the security measures needed to safeguard the Church's greatest secret. And so, they used a stone. Taking a cue from Joseph of Arimathea, one imagines."

The bishop walked in behind Scott and drew the doors closed. He tapped three times in rapid succession on one of the square marble slabs on the wall and a panel popped open. Not unlike a drawer, it was about five inches by ten inches long and had a small jet-black keyboard-like input array, but the characters were all Greek letters.

The bishop pointed past Scott at the wall in which most of the cathedral's former archbishops lay in their eternal slumber behind dense blocks of stone.

Scott turned to look and Bishop Branford tapped a few keys on the keyboard, then a grinding sound of stone rubbing stone echoed through the tiny chamber. The lights dimmed.

On the wall before him, along with the occupied tombs, were several spots that appeared to be ready and available to receive future church heads. To take up their eternal residence.

The lowest right panel receded an inch or two into the wall, then slid to the right. The hole was small, a foot or two in height by the same in width. He saw what appeared to be a faint, ethereal orange glow flickering beyond the opening.

"I do so hope you forgive my inquisitive nature, your eminence, but this seems unbelievable, and if I'm being honest, a bit frightening. This isn't like one of those college fraternities that make young men eat laundry detergent, is it?"

The man in the black cassock had affected the disconnected and frozen grin of a ventriloquist's dummy. It made Scott nervous, so he forced a smile of his own.

"No, it isn't that," Branford flatly stated.

"Should I be worried?" Scott asked.

"Well, of course you should!" Branford weakly snickered, then fake-broke into emotionless laughing. "I'm just not kidding."

Scott's eyes cocked suspiciously. "You're kidding?"

"No. Or am I? Maybe, but who's really to say? And what's it matter anyway, eh?"

The smile he bore in that moment might have been that of Lucifer's, as Scott saw it. This whole situation was becoming dangerous somehow, though he couldn't really figure why or how he knew this. He just knew his spidey sense was tingling every time the bishop spoke.

"Are you joking, your grace? Because I'll again be honest in saying it isn't wildly funny, sir."

"Let's go down the staircase and find out. How about it?"

His smile was about as comforting as razors in apples, but what could Scott do?

"What staircase?"

"The one you'll see when you crawl into that hole."

"Into the hole?" Scott asked, dumbfounded.

Bishop Branford nodded. "Into the hole." His smile narrowed to a scowl.

"Your grace, if you please, I must insist that you explain yourself and what is currently happening before I crawl into a hole near the floor under clandestine and starkly obtuse pretenses. Please, Bishop. This is starting to cause me concern and your demeanor isn't helping."

Bishop Branford's cold and detached grin softened to something more human, and Scott saw clear pain behind the holy man's eyes. A deepening sorrow, unnameable and unfathomable, but quickly disposed of and replaced with a burgeoning fury and resolve.

"I'm sorry about this, Scott. It ultimately wasn't my call, but this is important enough to get right and expedite. So much so that we simply must shuffle this along." The bishop withdrew a small pistol, an old Walther by the look of it, from the black layers of his cassock and pointed the business end at the younger man. "We need to get moving, son." He then flicked the barrel twice toward the orange lit opening.

Scott's mind suddenly became as clear as the holy water that bubbled within the font upstairs in the cathedral. This wasn't good and he needed to form a plan. Time was sludgy and the bishop's words were almost predictable.

*Is this what adrenaline feels like? Who knows? Doesn't matter. What matters is survival now.*

*Grab the gun? No good. That's gonna be the easiest thing to defeat where plays are concerned, by virtue of predictability alone.*

Fleeing was now fully moot, what with the door closed behind them and the bullets able to move quite a lot faster than he was able. It was time to follow directions and reassess once he had more options.

Scott sighed and threw a look of resignation up onto his face, then made for the hole. He kneeled then walked on all fours through the marble-plated tomb's walls.

The tunnel beyond the mouth of the passage immediately opened up and he was able to stand again. He considered kicking away the gun from the bishop as he also crawled in, but the sound of voices from further down the corridor drew his attention.

They were in a narrow hallway that extended about fifty feet, then met the top of a spiral stone staircase, widening down from the top landing. There were fresh candles in wall holders every ten feet or so, and Scott even thought he heard laughter echoing up from below. The walls and ceiling were dark gray cobblestone, mortar and little else.

He started down the hall toward the stairs with Bishop Branford following, pointing the gun at Scott's back.

"Keep your hands to your sides, where I can see 'em, my boy."

"I'm not your boy, Padre," Scott snapped back.

"I suppose not, but I always considered you a good man. A little dim, sure, but certainly friendly enough."

"Dim?" Scott's voice cracked as he spoke. His thoughts raced.

*Snatch a candle and jab it in the pudgy man's face? Nah, still the whole gun thing to deal with,* he realized. *Yep, keep waiting for an opening. Patience now. Steady.*

"Well, not *Forrest Gump* dim, of course, but I noticed on your transcripts that your GPA was only 3.9. So, ya know, yeah, you're not exactly going to cure cancer anytime soon, either."

"That's sort of rude and unlike you, your excellency," Scott said softly. He had almost reached the top of the stairs and the orange glow was much brighter now and appeared to be flickering against the brick walls.

"Keep walking, son. We're almost to the land of milk and honey."

That line actually made Scott very frightened, and he paused once he reached the stairs. The bishop stopped as well and might've been about to say something when, from some unseen place down below, called out a voice:

"Is that you Bishop?"

It was the cardinal's voice. Scott would know it anywhere.

Branford's reply was immediate. "Yes, it is! Had to go with plan B!"

A round of laughter came from the bottom of the stairs and the cardinal called out again, "Well don't scare the poor boy. This is a night of much celebration, isn't it? Send the young Mr. Weber on down!"

Scott's mind was a flurry of curiosities. *What in the world could this possibly be about?* he wondered.

His rumination ended as Bishop Branford spoke, "You heard the big dog. Time to enter the unknown."

"Why are you speaking like that?" Scott asked.

"Cognitive dissonance. Separating the ego from the id for sanity's sake. Move."

Scott started to descend the staircase, and as he did, the walls changed from intersected bricks to a more earthen appearance. The chamber he stepped down into was carved from a solid rock by some ancient hands. It appeared to be a huge circular tomb with a massive hole in the center that must have been fifty feet in diameter. The hole looked colorless, it was so devoid of light as it toppled into the unseen abyssal depths.

The rocky stairs ended on one side of the chasm and there were large, flattened sections on the cavern walls interspersed with hanging torches that provided the flickering light. Upon these square, level areas were frescoes depicting many scenes of Judeo-Christian iconography: Angels, demons, cherubs, parting clouds, the crucifixion, Sodom and Gomorrah, and light casting down from the heavens onto burning villages.

But, there were other things Scott noticed that didn't quite mesh with those images. In one picture, he could see what looked like several DC-10 type airplanes in the sky over a volcano, with what looked like small ghosts pouring from the mouth of the eruption.

In another, he saw a man holding up golden tablets he had dug up from the dirt.

Scott saw an upside down cross behind a large-breasted goat-woman with twisted black horns. He saw greenish blobs against scenes of the cosmos, with hundreds of eyes and multifarious tentacles extending outward like a flower opening itself to the first rays of dawn's light. And he saw iridescent sugar skulls and voodoo dolls alongside Shiva, the Hindu god of destruction.

*But why? What, in the good name of the Lord, is all this?*

As he stepped off the final step onto the ground, he saw that on either side of him, in areas further back from the edge of the hole, were at least fifteen people in black hooded robes with shimmering gold trim along the seams, collars, and cuffs.

He couldn't immediately see any of their faces, save for one. To his right stood the tall and broad shouldered cardinal with his hood drawn back to reveal his big smiling face and bald head topped with a red and black mitre.

"Hello Scott. How are you feeling?" The cardinal grasped his shoulder in one large, hairy, claw-like hand—with enough pressure to flash pain.

Scott spoke quietly while glaring at the cardinal. "Terrified. But pretty curious as well."

The Cardinal bellowed a bone-rattling laugh that echoed loudly around them. His eyes were unkind and erratic. "Good boy. There's nothing to worry about. You're gonna help us with a sacred rite that will help to forestall the unfortunate demise of untold scores of others. We need a man of your character and composition, that's why we've called you here."

"At gunpoint?" Scott nodded toward the bishop who had come to the bottom of the steps, but kept the snub-nosed Walther trained on Scott's back.

The cardinal waved his hand at Bishop Branford. "Come now, Theo! Put that silly thing away! It really shouldn't have come to this, Scott. I apologize."

Scott's mind raced as he surveyed the area. His eyes noted the sources of light on the wall.

*Torches and robes. Bingo.*

*There's one avenue of attack that might work. And who knows where this giant, gaping chasm drops down to?* he figured. Without being able to see the bottom, he knew it was far enough to permanently deal with anyone who tried to restrain him.

*Forgive my willingness to kill to stay alive, my Lord, but I think you'll likely understand where these feckless heretics are concerned.*

He made the sign of the cross on his forehead and chest and the bishop and cardinal shot each other a look of suspicion.

Scott's eyes completed a circuit of the area and saw that along the walkway surrounding the hole were two wooden flagpoles adorned with black flags that had the symbols of half the world's religions randomly cast about the fabric, like planetoids against the pitch darkness of space. Each was set into pole-holders in the stone floor so they hung out over the mouth of the abyss. Both ended in a sharp blade, making it more of a lance.

*That's it,* he realized. *Easiest to reach and the least risky to employ. Whenever the opening appears…*

Across the area from him, running the length of the wall's circular interior was a narrow, three-foot wide catwalk (also called an allure, as Scott suddenly recalled). And something else too. A spot for a person, like a cavity in the stone wall.

Bishop Branford walked up to his left and held the gun to his side so Scott could still see it. "Off you head to the other side. And by that I mean use the walkway to go around to the cheeky little niche on the wall there."

"Why would I do that, Padre?" Scott's tone shifted to one of obstinance.

Bishop Branford grinned. "Well, because that's where you go, naturally." He moved his hands in a shooing motion with the gun's barrel, not quite aiming it at Scott.

Plenty of trepidation and worry coursed through every fiber of Scott Thomas Weber's being. His desire to flee as fast as his legs would carry him was all-consuming, and yet he remained where he stood. The gun might've been put away, but he wouldn't be able to get past the mob of figures now effectively blocking his escape the way he came.

*How many people can you throw into an abyss before you tire physically?* he wondered.

"In the small space, just over there?" Scott pointed across the circular, brick-lined chasm. Carved into the slick, porous stone was a concave indentation that was enough for a man to stand inside of. There were two sets of dense chains and iron cuffs attached to the wall with rusty red metal fixtures, panels, and bolts.

He felt a sinking feeling, but readied himself to snatch up one of the lances and swing for the first person he could reach—if this was going where it sure seemed like it was.

"That's the spot, Scott." The bishop sounded impatient now.

"Again, my apologies, sirs and madams as well as whoever and whomever, but this seems to bear all the hallmarks of paganism."

A collective groan rolled from one side of the group to the other.

"So does the Bible!" someone scoffed, and giggles rattled through the assembled lot of shrouded loons. Scott was now certain that this was going to go south, one way or another.

The men and women pulled back their green, gold-rimmed hoods to reveal their mostly scowling faces. His eyes traced around the room and he thought he half-recognized some of them, but then his gaze went to a man in his sixties, whose perfectly coiffed blonde hair made him look like a grown-up boy scout. This man spoke first, and with a slight lisp.

"Can't let you get in the way of the money machine, my man. Not when there is a spiritual war ahead. Gotta squeeze all the lemons whilst they are still able to be squozen." He smiled, and while several around him rolled their eyes, some nodded in agreement.

Scott had lost his patience. "Okay, someone explain to me what the fuck this is, now!"

Without waiting for a reply, he used his elbow to smack the bishop in the eye, which caused him to drop the gun. Scott snatched it up and slipped it into his pocket as he ran up to the lance on the left and ripped it free from the placement on the rock floor.

He turned and began to back slowly along the outer wall on the allure while keeping the lance pointed at anyone who came close.

For the most part they all stayed where they were, but the cardinal and the bishop both stepped forward. The cardinal shot a look to a few of the others and two of the black robed figures, one woman and one man, started toward Scott.

The woman was African American, and had her hair woven into intricate braids that were tied up with a black band. She had icy mirrors for eyes and slowly removed a jewel-encrusted dagger with a crucifix for a hilt from under her robe and crouched as she stalked around the opposite side of the catwalk to cut off his means of exit.

The man was before him and followed him slowly as he backed up, staying just out of reach of the lance's blade.

Scott yelled, "You better stay back, you two! I will hurt you if you attempt to hurt me!" He jabbed the lance at the man before him and kept inching backwards.

The blow missed the man, who smiled a fully-bearded smile. He had bronzed skin and dark circles beneath his unfeeling eyes.

The cardinal took a small step toward the pit and calmly spoke in the same soothing tone he affected whilst upon his pulpit before the congregation on Sundays. "No one wants to hurt you, Scott."

Jabbing the flagged lance at the nearest follower, Scott yelled, "From your mouth to God's ears! What is this bullshit, Cardinal? I need some answers here and now or you are all going to regret it! Who are all these people?"

"Well, you know several of us, Scott, but the rest are the representatives and/or heads of various religions. A council, if you will."

"Why?" Scott shouted.

"No need to yell, my son," the cardinal cooed.

"Damn it! I'm not your son, crackpot! And you are no one's father. You are but a father of lies! Are you all insane?"

"We don't have a lot of time here, Scott, so to save as much of it as I'm able, here's the sum of it: We may seem different, but we all serve the same master. No God you would know of, it's true, though some primitive cultures have written and spoken of it. No one takes them seriously, so that's a dodged bullet. Beyond that, we've successfully and collectively preempted the broader knowledge of our deified benefactor for millennia. Hidden from the eyes of the world, the secret of the beast lies with us."

Keeping his weapon ahead, Scott scoffed and asked, "You're saying the religions of the world, all of them—seriously?—are actually part of a massive faith-based pyramid scheme? Yeah, right! I certainly don't envy you for having to sell that line of horse pucky, right there."

"It's true, and by golly, it's profitable!" a man with angry eyes and a black head of hair said.

Scott knew all too well who he was, and wondered what his oddball Aunt Rose would think if she saw him now. It was Kenneth Copeland, the kooky (to dramatically understate it) televangelist she used to watch on Sunday mornings—*religiously.*

The cardinal continued, "The leaders of all North American churches and/or religious organizations can shear the wool from the lambs to their heart's content. However, they all must, at minimum, pay monetary recompense for their profiteering idolatry as their part of the ancient compact. As such, we have the heads of all mainline denominations: the Moron—ahem, excuse me—*Mormon* Church, The Jay-hos, Baptists, Jews, even the Evangelicals over here, accounted for." He was pointing at the man with a curly tuft of black hair and a devilish, if somewhat unsettling grin.

"Hallelujah!" Kenneth Copeland shouted, winking at Scott. It sent a chill down his spine.

The cardinal finished, "And, uh, the Protestants too."

A short, mustachioed brick of a man next to the TV preacher snapped, "I don't think us Protestants should be listed after almost all the others every single time."

"Well imagine our mother-humpin' surprise, Bob! We'll store that one away with the other complaints filed by the constituency of malcontents!" hollered the short blonde boy scout-looking guy.

At once, Scott finally realized who he was.

Of course, it was David Miscavige, head of the Church of Scientology! Husband and possible murderer of Shelly Miscavige, confidant to and likely blackmailer of Hollywood lunatic Tom Cruise, and quite possibly the least empathetic and most sociopathic man in the room.

*No small feat in this company,* Scott thought to himself.

Miscavige's beady eyes rolled and whipped about as though he was high on something, but it was likely just thetan-mania.

"Compact with what? What beast is deified?" Scott returned to the initial topic of discussion, waving the lance at the man, then rushed toward the woman coming from the other direction. She smiled and bared her teeth at him as she withdrew, then said something he couldn't understand under her breath.

The assembled group of people, all twenty or so, bowed their heads, even the two trying to trap him in a pincer move on the catwalk.

The cardinal twisted his head, as if being possessed, and spoke in a hollow voice, "The beast of the half-formed moon, Scott, my boy. The timeless and formless darkness from the depths. It's hungry, Scott. So hungry."

"What are you saying? And what does this have to do with me?" Scott yelled. His mind raced. The current mental plan read as follows: Impale one zealot with the lance's blade, pull the gun and take out as many as you can till you run out of bullets, then toss as many into the hole as you are physically able. May not be foolproof, but what plan is?

The two members flanking him had slowly driven him toward the niche in the wall. He could see now that the chains and cuffs were stained with dried blood, which had initially been hard to see against the rust from further away.

"If we don't feed the beast, he unleashes terrors you would not imagine, nor would you wish to. Unspeakable horrors that could rend the earth in twain. And, he can control the ocean tides and flood continents."

Scott almost laughed in spite of himself. "That's not... *Jesus*. That's not possible, you fools!"

"Well that's what he tells us and we do not question him, for he is eternal," the cardinal scoffed.

"Eternally jerking your chain, it sounds like. And what about the father, the son, and the holy spirit, Padre?"

"Merely a convenient cover story."

"Ah, right. Okay." He shot a look at David Miscavige. "You're Tom Cruise's friend, right?"

David smiled broadly and took a more lackadaisical tone suddenly, "Oh, yeah! Me and Tom, we hang out all the time! Why, I was on the set with him the other day and it was just the best, ya know? The best. He's the best. He's my *bestie*."

One of the other robed figures made a retching sound behind David. Without turning toward them, he raised his middle finger and flipped off the crowd behind him.

"So you don't believe in those alien things at all, then? They don't inhabit you and all that?" Scott asked, truly curious.

"Nah, no way. What do we sound like, crazy people?" David asked, with a craven look in his eyes.

"Yes, that. Very much that. That, and twice on Sunday," Scott answered swiftly.

Kenneth Copeland raised his arms above his flat head and shouted, "Amen!"

The cardinal rolled his eyes and spoke up, "Enough of this! We need you to take your position."

"No, Padre. This is where you and I get off this train, so to speak. I mean, my God, what has happened here? What have you all become?"

Boy scout man with the coif chimed in, sounding ruffled, "Well, I'm gonna tell you this—David Miscavige doesn't like what David Miscavige is hearing. That kind of debased, suppressive ranting makes David Miscavige nervous."

The archbishop shot out a finger on his right hand and pointed at the scientologist. "Silence, interloper! I will not allow gratuitous and dubious overuses of third person in the presence of the forsaken one, for he draws nigh!"

Copeland shouted, "Yessir. Amen!"

"Can it, Copeland," the cardinal scolded.

Kenneth nodded and murmured, "Consider Copeland canned, your eminence."

Scott held the lance in his hands and watched as the two robed figures started to slowly creep along the catwalk on either side of him.

"What's forsaken?" he shouted as he made a lunge at the man to his right, catching the man's hand, slicing it open. The man recoiled and hissed at him. "You mean the beast thing?"

"Stalagmaw!" the Cardinal called out as a rumble from somewhere deep in the depths of the large hole echoed up to them. The others in robes repeated the word.

"Sta-lag-maw!" they said in unsettlingly perfect harmony, much as an unholy choir might.

"What the hell is that?" Scott shouted as he swung the lance swiftly from left to right. The man and woman in dark green robes kept taking false starts at him, but he was not letting either draw nearer. However, even he began to worry about the growing sound coming from the pit before him.

Air began to move through the chamber and the whoosh of wind caused the torches to flutter and struggle to remain lit. The room dimmed as a result.

Just as he wondered if the whole thing was an elaborate mechanism of some type, the head of a giant insectoid creature rose up from the hole and peered at them.

Everyone in a black robe hit the ground and knelt before the monstrosity.

Scott was unable to move or speak as the segmented thing rose up until it filled much of the room. It bore the appearance of an enormous brown centipede-like body and head, replete with pincers, each the size of an earth-mover's arm, and antennae that must have easily been a foot in diameter or more. It had several eyes on either side of the head section of the carapace. The thing's body must have been thirty or forty feet wide. Its arms were also massive.

The insect face looked upon those kneeling, then turned to face Scott. It clicked its massive pincers and beheld the source of its name. As its mouth flicked open, he could see big, sharp, rough teeth—rows and rows of them, much like a shark would possess. But these were more like long, slender daggers made of what appeared to be marble. Slimy tendrils of viscous sludge accumulated on the blades of the teeth, then formed large drops which dripped from the alabaster-hued tips.

"W-what?" was all Scott could manage. He dropped the lance

and shook like a leaf as the thing's head shot to either side, spying the robed figures who were on the walkway with him. It's eyes closed (*It has eyelids?*) and the two antennas twitched. The orb-shaped ends of each antennae began to glow.

The cardinal, who had been kneeling and facing the stone floor, looked up and stood. He slowly inched toward the hole, saying, "Stalagmaw, oh benevolent whisper on the lips of dying men. Oh wicked eater of the—"

A hiss from the creature's mouth silenced the cardinal mid-sentence. His body shuddered as he cowered from the beast, which spun around to face the holy man.

Scott watched on in shock as the braided-haired woman and bearded man slowly stood up and turned toward the creature. Their eye sockets were now black voids of obsidian. Mouths hung open and arms limply at their sides. Guttural sounds emanated from their throats and coalesced into whispered words that spoke thunderously in unison.

> *"Salt of the ground, hear me. Why have you brought*
> *forth an unclean specimen for me to consume?"*

The cardinal risked a glance upward and asked feebly, "My Lord, our most egregious of apologies! Of what uncleanness do you speak?"

The creature hissed and the robed figures spoke for it:

> *"This man is unclean. He has taken of the carnal.*
> *He has known the touch of another."*

Huge gusts of air passed by Scott and he realized the thing was sniffing at the air. It winced and blinked its sets of eyes rapidly.

*"He stinks. He will not do."*

Scott regained something like coherent human thought long enough to take this somewhat offensively.

"Yeah, and what do these heretics smell like then?" Scott wore Paco Rabanne, and he knew he didn't stink, despite what this Empire State bug was saying.

*"They smell like loyal subservients. They also reek of incompetence, though they usually don't screw up this badly."*

Kenneth Copeland stood up and pulled his hood free and narrowed his eyes as much as his heavily botoxed face would allow.

"We didn't screw up! This little shit must've lied when we asked him, any number of times, if he was a virgin! I read his dossier. I read it! I never read anything, but I read that! It said no humping! He reported that he was a virgin."

"You never asked me anything, you devious little shyster!" Scott glared at Copeland as he reached into his pocket and slipped his fingers around the Walther's wooden grip.

"I meant the royal 'we,' obviously, you dolt. They asked you, so we asked you, therefore I basically asked you. And you should shut your mouth, lest the beast devour your soul and then set up the tides to flood the shores of the coasts with the rotten carcasses of the—"

One of the creature's arms reached up out of the hole and swiped at Kenneth in a flash of movement. A second later, the wacky televangelist's head was gone and rolling across the floor as blood spurted out of the ragged stump. The twitching body fell to the ground.

*"I can't listen to that guy any longer. His delightfully wretched faith has been replaced by wanton lust for petty materialistic gains. Have you seen that gaudy jet he flies around?"*

David Miscavige was slowly backing toward the stairwell and had almost gotten to the bottom step when the creature called out:

*"Not so fast, Davey! You stay right here.*
*We are not done with you."*

The cardinal started to weep mournfully. Others in robes whispered to each other without raising their heads to look. The cardinal asked, "Are you saying that our sacrifice is not virginal? If so, then he did indeed betray us on this count."

Scott smiled, in spite of himself. "You didn't ask me that exactly. It was my senior year and I had a crisis of faith. And since I'm as likely as not to die in the hole, I don't mind saying that I was as horny as a ten-peckered owl, so it was what it was! Unlike with you lot, God still loves me!"

"See!" The cardinal pointed and glared directly at Scott in an accusatory manner. "He admits it, my liege! What would you have us do?"

*"I would have virgins upon which to dine! Not this*
*annoyingly honest boy, here. He may possess much virtue,*
*but stinks of the carnal. He is unclean and mouthy."*

The cardinal cried out, "How do we please you, oh sanctified sovereign—oh, deified doom?" He raised his fists in frustration and shook them as the creature gazed down upon them. The cardinal feebly whimpered, "How may we satiate your hunger?"

The creature bristled and clicked its tens (or hundreds, Scott couldn't see to tell) of arms against the walls of the hole it had emerged from. It leaned its head down, air whooshed by, and it seemed to be sniffing again. It clicked its pincers together and the antenna on its head wiggled.

The two robed figures on either side coughed and gurgled and the voice came again from their open mouths.

*"You smell clean. In fact, almost all of you have never known the carnal. Some stink too, but you would do as my meal, I suppose. Prepare yourselves to be devoured!"*

The walls shook and with his eyes utterly transfixed on the unfolding chaos before them, Scott watched Stalagmaw lower its head down to the cardinal, who shouted something unintelligible as he was sucked up into the seething maw of the huge dirt-brown arthropod and crushed between the porcelain-white stalactite teeth. His body twisted and splashed blood all over the creature's mouth, mixing with the dripping vines of saliva.

Scott heard crunching and tried not to focus too much on the exacts of the slaughter that then took place.

After it ate the cardinal, it set about snatching up the other robed figures, taking two at once several times and swallowing them after chewing them for only a few seconds.

Oddly, they did not try to resist, as if they knew this was inevitable. Still, one or two made for the stairs and were readily snatched by the thing's pincers and fed into its clicking mouth. Muffled screams, crunching, cracking, snapping bones, and dripping bloody slime rolled out of the creature's mouth and down its body.

Amid the chaos, for the first time, Scott took note of an oddly shaped bump on the insectoid's chest area.

The bishop had remained kneeling since the beast had appeared, but then made a quick dash for the stairs. He was stopped by a long appendage erupting through his chest and making a huge hole. He gasped, and the creature withdrew its arm, sending the freshly impaled bishop crumpling to the stone floor with a THUD.

Scott's mind had tuned to a razor-wire wavelength of flight or fight. He knew neither would do until he got the perfect opening. One that might never come. Of what use he was now to this ancient life form was anyone's guess.

Only Scott, Mr. Miscavige, and the two robed mouth agapers remained.

The creature straightened up and turned back toward Scott. He felt his stomach sink, knowing this was probably the end. Oddly though, he heard the mouth of the two robed figures gurgle more and then clear their voices out. What came forth from their mouths sounded like a normal-ish human voice, though two at once, harmonizing:

*"Is that better? I can speak more clearly if I don't exert too much of my own will upon them."*

Scott blinked, stunned. "Sure."

*"Good. That's good."* The voices were sort of genial and folksy.

Everyone stood there, silent for a moment, and the Stalagmaw's pincers clicked.

"Okay, so are you going to kill us?" Scott tensed as he asked, awaiting an attack that never came.

*"No. You stink and I'm full. I won't be hungry for a good while. Plus, I prefer to leave a witness or two to serve as a warning to others."*

The robed figures hummed the words. It made the voices sound like they were coming through a tube.

"And what about the operating thetan, over there?" Scott pointed at David Miscavige who was shaking with a creepy, crooked smile on his lips, but was otherwise unharmed.

*"Bishops, cardinals, imams, rabbis and the like are a dime a dozen. But sick bastards like our cult leader over there are increasingly rare these days. Now the ones with potential all become mass murderers—going on shooting sprees and such. Waste of potential, if you ask me. We need them to draw attention from our slumber and men like this do that quite effectively. You can't just go and pick up a David Koresh at the local sporting goods store, know what I mean? Believe me, I've had followers try, and it's embarrassing. What do you even request to get good help in these harrowing end times? 'I'll take a pound of Jim Jones and some sliced Gouda'? Nobody says that. Nobody says that."* The massive creature shook its head and sighed.

Scott's eyes were wide, his mouth now agape as the two speaking figures.

"Yeah, it's true that, uh, nobody says that. That is … accurate." He saw the flap of loose plating that he noticed before twitching. He pointed at it. "What is that thing upon your chest, uh, Stalagmaw, is it?"

The creature's eyes all blinked in unison at him. The robed figures spoke, *"Yeah, Stalagmaw, with an "S." And that's the source of our power. The Jewel of Babylonia."*

"What is the Jewel of Babylonia?"

The creature hissed and chortled from its mouth opening. The sound was high-pitched and blood-curling, but Scott didn't flinch. The beast reached down with one of its massive claw-like appendages and slipped it under the twitching spot, then ripped at it and turned the flap upward, revealing a brilliant, shimmering red jewel the size of a small car embedded in its chest.

*"Well, just after the time of the last global extinction, deep within the magma trenches of the subterra did there sit, upon a throne of—"*

Scott's mind came alive again with steely resolve. *Dear Lord, give me the strength to do something crazy now, or who knows how this goes, so let's go, here we go, Amen!*

He pulled the gun out and aimed down the sights as he steadied the muzzle with both hands. He fired the gun as fast as he could.

The target was big and at least three rounds struck the gemstone before the creature hissed, howled, and then swiped out at Scott's head.

He had anticipated the attack and had already ducked down. The blow glanced off the wall behind him. Pebbles, dust, and bits of rock kicked up and hit Scott on the head. He shook them off as the ancient Stalagmaw whipped about the walls and howled. It crashed into the frescos, demolishing them.

The two robed figures were knocked over in the commotion and lay on their sides, possibly—dead.

Probably dead.

The creature shook and Scott could see that black, oily goo trickled in drips from the cracks in the Jewel of Babylonia, opened up by the gunfire.

Scott aimed again and fired at the cracked gem, further opening up a wide hole in the center.

The oil streamed heavily now and a sickening gagging sound echoed off the cavern's walls. The creature leaned over and orally ejected a truck bed's worth of blood-soaked, dismembered, half-digested human pieces onto the edge of the chasm in a steaming pink pile. Then it stiffened and curled up as it fell straight down into the darkness. It made no sound as it plummeted toward the unseen bottom.

Ten or more seconds later, a whoosh of air followed immediately by a reverberating THUD.

Finally, the room fell silent.

David Miscavige stood up cautiously, looking around, and brushed off his brownish-blonde hair. Dust and detritus flew from it and he shook his robe, then pulled it up over his head, walked to the rim of the chasm, and tossed it into the hole. Underneath, he had a perfectly tailored blue Armani suit and red tie that looked no worse for the wear.

He eyed Scott. Scott, in turn, eyeballed the head of the church of Scientology. Then David's eyes went to the gun still resting in Scott's grip.

"How did you do that? You basically just killed a god, young man." David spoke slowly, clearly shocked.

Scott shook his head and corrected him, "No god. Just a big bug. Huge one, but a bug all the same. And I'm not into bugs. So I shot the bug."

"You actually killed it, didn't you? I didn't think it could be killed. Holy moly—that's crazy. I didn't think it could be killed. Wait till I tell Tom." He glanced nervously at Scott. "Am I gonna be able to tell Tom? Are you… Are we, you know, are we cool, dude?"

Scott nodded and tossed the gun into the void. He began to walk around the catwalk, over the dead woman with the braids, then stopped a few feet from David, close to the stairs.

"Yeah, we're cool, David. You aren't. But we are. One question, though."

Relief washed over the Scientologist's face. He shot his cuf-flinks, straightened the cuffs, and smiled as he said, "Anything, man. Anything. I'm in your debt, so fire away."

Scott put his hands on the pants of his black tracksuit and sighed. "You believe in that Xenu shit at all?"

"Fuck no. Hubbard was a loopy twat. SeaOrg is a front for the cartels. I just want money." David winked.

"Fair enough. Where's Shelly, David?"

"Safe and secure at the compound. Thanks for asking." David peeked over the edge and whistled for a few seconds before making a crash sound with his lips. He straightened up and clapped his hands.

"Well, I appreciate the assistance. You're quite possibly a sup-pressive person, but I can still say I'm glad you were the, uh, you know, lamb who wasn't sacrificed and all that. Feel free to stop by the Church sometime." He turned to the stairwell, raised his fist and loudly called out, "Next stop, infinity!"

Looking utterly pleased with his own nonsense, he walked toward the staircase.

Scott followed him and they began their ascent. As he climbed, he thought about what had just occurred and, surprisingly, was filled with nothing. All the day's madness and stimulation had somehow zeroed itself out and he was just tired now. He wanted to sleep.

Too many questions to consider in the aftermath. What of the church? What would the press make of this mess? The Pope—how much did he know about this sacrilege? What would Scott do now? Should he call someone? If so, who? Would the ancient creature's death have any lasting impact? And given his spiraling faith, did he even care anyway?

Barely.

And there it was: Eons of deification undone in an instant by piss-poor planning and blind faith in the subservience and stupidity of man by some dead bug.

*That's the life of a false idol for you,* Scott mused to himself, then smiled.

But, a single thought caused the brief smile to drop from his face, replaced by a pained look of deep concern.

*Oh Jesus, how the hell do I explain this to my parents?*

# VENERATED

t was a dark and stormy night.

Seriously, it was.

Fat droplets of rain and rushing wind struck the exposed brick-laden outer walls of the centuries-old castle that lay at the foothills of the Romanian Carpathian Mountains. Nestled along the eastern side of the Transylvanian Plateau in a small and unassuming valley, lush with wet, green overgrowth and situated against the rugged cliffs of the east, the remote mountain fastness had been largely carved from time-worn rock to keep it concealed from the world's view.

Tall tree canopies, thick underbrush, and one of the most cultivated landscapes in all of Eastern Europe meant that even modern-day inventions such as aerial photography and thermal imaging were not capable of locating the hallowed site. Its geologically sturdy and geographically discreet design had allowed it to remain both improbably intact and wholly undetected for over 900 years.

To that end, it lacked the typical features one would associate with such a building. It had no rising towers, no cathedral spires, and no curtain walls or ramparts. Absent were the stylistic trappings of the Classical, Gothic, Byzantine, or Romanesque decor that predominated the architectural landscape by the year 1050, when the castle was first carved from the stone of the earth.

None of the standard flourishes that would make the structure more livable or suited to repel attacks were present, in fact, because neither of those were the function. Remaining isolated from the world's view was the only attribute that mattered to those who would occasionally occupy it, and in that regard it had excelled spectacularly.

The valley that beset the keep on all sides was a good many miles from the nearest road or trail, and even then, one would have to brave dense forest that was nearly impassable to arrive at the valley's mouth. Then, that same industrious person would, hypothetically at least, have to be cognizant of, weary to avoid, and capable of crossing a ten foot-wide chasm that ran diagonally from one end of the area to the other.

Local fauna including brown bears and wolves, to say nothing of the snaggle-toothed wild boars and the odd Eurasian lynx, completed the perilous gauntlet that made the terrain nearby so treacherous. Even more so when the mists of the low-lying clouds swallowed the dew-dappled green canyon and further enshrouded the area in invisibility.

The history of the castle from antiquity to modernity—from conception and creation in 1050 Anno Domini, to the current status as the most sacred location for the leaders of the European vampire covens—was something that Stefan Voslo had memorized half a century before. He had applied for, gone through the appeasement trials of, and waited five decades with statue-like patience for the venerated position of council scribe to open up.

With the elevation of the previous holder of said position to the equally enviable title of council edict officiator (essentially the presiding rule enforcer), his promotion was all but assured. This emergency meeting of the family leaders would be his first council assembly dictation since he was informed of his appointment three months prior.

He had ordered a set of custom ivory-inlaid Montegrappa quill pens and was delighted when he was emailed weeks ago that his order was finished and ready for prompt collection in Bassano del Grappa, a city in the northern Veneto region of Italy. It was always a pleasure to visit Europe's oft-spurned peninsula.

How he did so enjoy Italian cuisine. Slow to drain and bursting with delicious nectar upon which to suckle. Yummy to the last drop. A veritable cornucopia of veiny flavors and subtle notes.

He could always taste whether the victim had had a lemon or onion within the last twenty-four hours, and every so often he could nearly tell the vintage of the wine that they had last consumed. He'd stayed for five extra days just to really absorb and savor the taste-milieu of the boot.

His wandering mind snapped back into the here and now. Out of habit alone, his pale hand ran down the long blonde ponytail running off the back of his head. He wore a tailored suit of black with gray pinstripes and red piping that had also been ready for this night.

Well, not precisely this night, but essentially so, for his position was not set to start for another two months and even he was as yet unaware of the purpose for which tonight's meeting had been called.

When you got the call though, you answered it.

And so it was that he stood before the unseen palace of stone in the failing half-light of the waning moon. He walked along the thicket, across an unseen bridge of carved stone, long-ago layered with an ever-densening carpet of soft moss, to the cave opening that led to the hidden castle's interior.

Before he reached the inner antechamber, he crossed under the piercing points and bronzed-hued metal latticework of an ancient portcullis. He could already hear voices deep in the fortress's belly. Out in the open, he heard for miles. Inside, less so, but still sufficient enough to hear every beating heart within a skyscraper from the bottom floor.

Though he heard no such pulsing rhythms tonight. No one in attendance had what you would describe as a well-functioning heart, literal or otherwise.

Walking inside, he saw dusty and musty unadorned stone walls with no pictures and barren rooms with no furniture. He crossed a small marble-floored vestibule into a larger chamber that served as the keep's main foyer, lined with modest matrone-oms and smooth pillars holding upper walkways aloft.

It was spherical and emptied into a maze-like array of narrow passages and corridors. He chose and hastened toward one, making a path toward the voices, yet he already knew from previous visits where to head.

He strode down halls, every so often passing wall torches, though none were lit. Down a spiral staircase and through another long corridor dotted with wall niches for candles, also unlit, until he arrived at a door which was red wood lined with gold fixtures and bracing. It had one large bronze ring hanging from the center.

He pushed the door open easily and crossed into the source of the sound.

Entering the area, he saw the lined balcony level elevated

above the circular floor. It was designed to accommodate exactly one hundred, but Stefan knew it had never been host to more than twenty-five.

The room was much the same round shape as the foyer, but had no other exits, just rough, torch lined walls. All of these were alight with a faint orange glow.

Before him, a staircase that emptied down into the round central area of the room, from where he stood inside the doorway.

To his left and right, two daises, each with five lords and five ladies, all representatives of the ten global vampire clans.

Standing tall at a lectern near the dais' end, with an imposing frame even for those gathered, was Dark Lord Vanivos Tiberius, first High Lord of the African Continent. He served as the high lord to the council and was the oldest and most powerful vampire of those assembled. Second in rank only to the Old One, he was the head voice of the undead commission.

Tonight, his was the voice that took the lead.

"Welcome scribe-elect." He stood in a black robe with red piping similar to Stephan's, and motioned for the new addition to take his place on another raised podium not far from the dais where the lords and ladies sat.

The new scribe made his way across the room and ascended the steps at the podium's back, taking a seat and setting down his small velvet carrying case. He popped the latch, removed a crystal inkwell and his dual ivory quill set, then readied some parchment already set upon the desktop before him.

"You have received all of your mandated background on the council's current action items and we unanimously approve of your induction into our ranks as council scribe, edict historian, and dictator of record. Welcome, Mr. Voslo."

Stefan felt something akin to a swell of pride in his cold breast as the congregated vampire lords and ladies stood up from their stone seats along the dais and clapped in a harmonic boom-clack that reverberated off the cold walls and high dome ceiling.

He bowed slowly and graciously as he felt he should, and then smiled as he nodded in gratitude to Tiberius.

Then he clapped his hands twice and the chamber fell silent as he spoke. "Accounting of attendees shall be the first order. On this count what say you, Lord Tiberius?"

"We are missing one, obviously, but we may rest assured that he shall join us momentarily. He mentioned that he was going to grab a bite en route, so, yes. Everyone else is present, I see?"

Nods from the assembled group.

"Okay then." Tiberius nodded to Stefan.

The Scribe dipped his quill into the inkwell atop the flat surface of the raised podium and began to make soft scratching sounds on the parchment before him.

As the mahogany-skinned Tiberius sat down at the dais, there before him lay a heavy book with metal clasps securing it closed, grayed from centuries of use.

"As the second order, it should be revealed to the members of this council the purpose for our unscheduled gathering this evening. Vérbulcsú himself did request that we meet to discuss a tragedy that has befallen our collective."

Surprised glances shot between the robed figures.

One lady, who exuded the air of and matched the ensemble of a Japanese suit-class businesswoman stood up. Stefan noted that Lady Sasaki had assumed the floor.

"Of what tragedy does the lord speak?"

She sat back down and crossed her arms. Having employed

daily telepathic training exercises for decades, Stefan could certainly read her enough to know she already knew the answer to her question.

Tiberius spoke again, "It is with heavy heart that I bring to you truly disappointing news this evening, for two nights ago, the entire American coven was essentially wiped out by hunters in one swift attack. The slaughter lasted less than ten minutes. As a result, it seems that North America is again without leadership. In fact, there are no adjuncts or consults left to assume the role, either."

A gravelly voice, vaguely Russian sounding, called out, "How could this have happened?"

Stefan jotted down the time and that Lord Mikkhal Adrik of the Euro-Soviet clan was speaking. He was big, husky, bearded, tiny eyed, and huge (as well as hairy) handed.

Tiberius replied, "I have preliminary reports that seem to indicate that again our former friend was responsible."

Hisses filled the air.

"He was never a friend!" shouted the Euro-Soviet lord. "He was ever but a cancerous undergrowth that should have never been elevated as he was! I, for one, foretold this very moment, did I not?" Mikkhal scoffed and slapped the table with his large palm.

Stefan jotted down that Tiberius nodded and conceded in that moment that, "Yes, Lord Adrik, yes, of course you did. And rest assured, we will assume that we need not worry about you forgetting to remind us about that fact anytime in the near future."

"On this point you may rest quite assured, High Lord," Mikkhal agreed, flashing a wry smirk.

A small, short-haired middle eastern man with a long, curly mustache stood and Stefan marked down that Bilal Abbas, Second High Lord of the African Continent had the floor.

The short man spoke quietly, "Forgive my directness, High Lord, but what becomes of Lady Marius?"

Tiberius shook his head and answered, "She is gone, felled by Gregor's hand directly—with a purple heart stake, no less."

A collective, guttural hiss rose from the throats and mouths of those assembled in disapproval of this news. Stefan dipped his quill and hastily made note of the hisses.

Lord Abbas's face fell expressionless as he sat back down.

"Despicable, contemptuous, vile wretch! I would have his eyes to shine my teeth!" the scratchy vocal chords of Danica Tenebrasa, Queen of the South American Clan rang out.

She stood up and the black blanket of her silky hair dropped to her sides, brushing against the thick strands of turquoise beads that ringed her neck.

Her eyes were inky-black with hatred as she growl-spoke, "I would implore the members assembled to consider a charge of high treason for our former colleague and henceforth commit to ending his life by forming a death squad before he can continue with his reckless and puerile vengeance. This is getting out of hand!"

The Russian vampire laughed. "It was out of hand when he wasn't put down to begin with! This really was entirely avoidable. He should have been tried and executed. Now we reap the seeds of that mistake, as did our late Lady Marius."

Tiberius imperceptibly winced at the none-too-subtle implication in Mikkhal's words. Stefan took note, but did not note it down in the record.

The High Lord then quickly moved to assuage concerns by saying, "We have seen the consequences already, it's true. I would remind all those gathered that it was this council that forgave his initial trespass and voted to exile him, making us all responsible for the destruction he has wrought since. We may yet send an assassin to handle this, however creating a larger contingent to do the same risks the appearance that we cannot handle this situation ourselves."

"We can't." Lady Sasaki straightened the sides of her gray business suit as she stood. "If we could have then we would have. That's what the lady was sent to do herself, and now this."

Queen Tenebrasa snarled, "So Gregor kills Ezekiel and we, in turn, send our own Lady Maurius—our greatest will manipulator, I might add—to hasten the heretic's demise. And as a result, now she too is dust in the dirt? It's a tragicomedy of errors that has long since ceased to be funny! What stops him from marching down to pay my coven a visit with his fucking doom trucks?"

Stefan was keeping up, but paused momentarily as he wrote down "doom trucks," not knowing what that was.

He didn't have to wait long to find out.

Mikkhal rubbed his beard and grinned widely as he asked in a brusk Soviet tongue, "Doom trucks? What is a doom truck?"

Whispers among the other members at this term followed.

Tiberius replied, "The queen speaks of the means by which the coven was dispatched." He cocked an eyebrow and glared suspiciously at Tenebrasa. "Though it remains curious as to how the lady would already possess such information."

Danica flashed a cold, crooked smile in Tiberius's direction and tilted her head just so as she said, "I know you'd like to know, and yet you shant! Suffice it to say, I possess the means to keep myself as informed as any gathered here. For one apparently cannot be too careful. Dangerous days, these, what with vampires killing vampires and all—"

Tiberius raised his voice slightly as he cut off Danica's words, "There is but one defiler of the edicts and he is the only member of this order in five hundred years to challenge the authority of the Old One! Do not speak as though there exists any broader contagion upon this council beyond the hypocrisy and misfeasance of a singular would-be martyr."

Voices from both sides of the room called out in dotted agreement, "Here, here!"

Stefan wrote down upon the record that, in this moment, the room did agree with the high lord.

The tanned, black-eyed queen glowered for a moment before softening her features and saying, "Forgive me, my lord, but I express only my deepest concern for the safety of every member of this council, to say nothing of my brethren on the southern continent. If this demon must be dealt a death blow, I would humbly ask that it be sooner rather than later. Please understand, I say this not as a purveyor of fear, but rather as the only member of this council who shares a land bridge with this dangerous fucker!"

The Russian interjected, "Excuse me, but before we move on, I would like to first hear more of these doom trucks. Did they have ultraviolet headlamps? What's the story with those?"

Stefan wrote that Lord Tiberius then said the following: "They—the hunters—arrived in shipping vehicles full of light weapons as well as large vacuum trucks. A platoon of the rats surrounded the Aspen-Starwood compound and after they dispatched our kindred, they sucked up the remnants into the aforementioned doom trucks—HVAC trucks, actually—then packed them off to, well, anyone's guess.

"Gregor led the group and has amassed a large number of cohorts. At least fifty strong and mostly made up of either former kin or humans who have had a relative, or several, taken from them by a darkborn and seek vengeance. We only know this because we successfully infiltrated his ranks. Our operative was with the group for several weeks leading up to the assault, but a week before the raid we stopped receiving any communication from him and so must assume they discovered his true intent and have neutralized him as well."

A very dark skinned woman in a black robe with purple piping and short, curly black hair stood and spoke in a soft, soothing tone. "What light weapons, High Lord?"

Stefan logged the statement from South Asian coven leader Mila Jussou. Her eyes were golden rings of piercing inquisitiveness.

Tiberius bowed his head toward the lady, then replied, "They use beam-projecting handheld UV light cannons. Essentially laser guns. But the beam is thick enough to vaporize a darkborn in under a second. Some fifty to one hundred in total. All legal consults, all manipulators and adjuncts—anyone who could succeed to at least keep the new darkborn in line are gone. We'll need to send an interim lord. Then, as a matter of procedure, they wiped the security footage and—"

Lady Sasaki interrupted, "My apologies, Lord, but what type of laser exactly?"

"What does that matter?" asked Mikkhal loudly.

"Just curious. Unless, of course, the high lord does not know exactly what type was employed." Lady Sasaki cocked an eyebrow and smiled.

Tiberius, always the advocate of due diligence and cognizant of the ever-present need to assert his own authority within the council, replied, "Specifically, it's a type of chemical laser, but in solid rather than gaseous form. Excited bromide in an argon matrix. As soon as the field is applied, it is coupled to a state that is radiatively coupled to the ground state yielding a five megawatt beam at one hundred nanosecond intervals. Does that sufficiently answer your question, my lady?"

Lady Sasaki remained smiling as she sat. "It does indeed."

Stefan dipped his quill tip in the crystal inkwell and noted the language used in her dubious challenge to Tiberius's standing without describing it as such in the official records.

"We're being killed with laser guns now? Like villains in a sci-fi film, laser guns?" inquired the perturbed queen.

"Not laser guns per se," Tiberius explained. "But yes, in a way. The problem is not the means, but rather the thorn in our collective—"

South Asian clan queen Mila interjected, "Why would they have all gathered in such great numbers? What in the hallowed halls of Hades were they thinking?

"They may be our kin, but they remained tempestuous Americans through and through, with the exception of Marian. She was usually more cautious than this, and it remains mysterious as to why she would allow such a meeting to occur without anticipating the risks. The charter has clear directives in this regard."

Tiberius reached out and slid the thick tome on the table to the space before him and swiftly opened it to a page marked with a red ribbon. The yellowed pages audibly cracked as they split wide. He moved the blood-colored strip of fabric aside and ran a wiry tendril of a finger along it, then found purchase halfway down the page.

Tiberius's eyebrows piqued up as he cleared his throat and began to read, "Yes, on page 203, right here, below the daylight feeding provisions. Article Four, section B, items one through four. It reads as follows: 'Should any coven, covens, larger congregation of council leaders, or darkborn individuals numbering fifty or more, seek to meet under the auspices of sharing information, dictating policy, prosecution of crimes against fellow undead, or meeting for celebratory purposes, they should endeavor to never have more than fifty percent of correlated coven members involved in said—"

"Yes, yes, we understand the edicts in this regard," Mikkhal interjected. "And like with all American endeavors, it was only a matter of time before it was a victim of its own lofty hubris."

"Said the pot of the kettle," murmured Lady Sasaki.

"And what does that mean, good lady?" Mikkhal asked swiftly.

Sasaki's eyes narrowed. "It means that it takes a fool's hubris to spot a fool's hubris, and in that regard, you've got enough for—"

*"Silence."*

A sound like that of splintering metal spoke one word and all obeyed the command as a massive breeze swept through the chamber and blew back the hoods on all the robed figures gathered upon the two daises.

Stefan dipped his quill and wrote down that at precisely seven minutes into the meeting, the Old One, last fang standing of the original seven darkborn lords, Count Vérbulcsú, arrived.

As the gusts swirling around the circular room died down, they heard the echoes of sucking noises above their heads. Snapping and slurping sounds amid a swirl of dark red and blue fabric.

The group patiently waited for their master to finish his meal. About twenty seconds later, a woman's whimper rattled through her dying teeth and with a hard thump, the modestly-clothed body of the young blonde woman—whom the Old One had been draining high above the floor for the last few moments—dropped straight down upon it. Sucked ash-dry, the body, despite falling thirty feet, did not create any spatter on the ground.

As the ten lords and ladies looked on, Count Vérbulcsú floated slowly down from the ceiling. He wore crimson and navy blue robes that wrapped about him in a bumpy swell of fabric. Pale, wrinkled skin, but chiseled features and a warm smile held fast beneath needle-sharp eyes. A long gray beard that hung halfway down to his waist and equally long gray hair tied up in a single long ponytail hung over his shoulder and down his front next to the beard. He glided down and his thick, nearly cloven feet found purchase on the stone floor.

Stefan and the others stood and bowed in solemn reverence for their dark father.

As they did, the Old One's eyes ran over them as he kept the smile fixed up on his lips. His voice was razors on metal, but clear and calm as he said, "You may sit."

They all did as he bade them without a word.

The vampire that ruled them continued, "Since we seven Chieftains of the Maygars arrived in this valley at the turn of the previous millennium, our commitment to the secrecy of our society has been at the forefront of our decisions worldwide. It has been long and it has been grand. Save for a few foolish fallen, like that impetuous impaler, our way has remained unknown."

The Old One spoke swiftly, and Stefan scribbled furiously to keep up.

"And yet the paradigm shifts with every sunfall. Humans have created a world teetering on the brink of sociological, ecological, and societal collapse. This planet has forcibly mutated into a tinderbox of nuclear saber-rattling, laughable class division, rampant corruption, and enslavement of most for the financial benefit of few. All in the vainglorious pursuit of an immortality they shall ne'er possess. Which is all well and good, so long as we are the primary benefactors of all that forced misery for profit. As it stands, though, we no longer are and may yet see our way of existence threatened by the eternal stupidity of the blood bags."

Tiberius nodded and bowed. "Here here, dark father."

The others nodded and bowed.

The corpse on the floor did nothing, obviously.

It's a corpse.

Vérbulcsú lowered his smile and an indescribable tension fell upon those gathered in the castle's belly.

He spoke again, voice wholly absent of the quasi-pleasant tone he'd begun with. "To address the issue at hand, Gregor has had his fun, and now it ends. I'll handle him myself so that he might see with his own eyes the disappointment in mine before he dies. Though ultimately I have called you all for a correlated cause this evening. As my faithful children, I know you'll all see the wisdom in my decision."

A pale, older looking vampire with long, silvery-black hair raised his hand and spoke up. "Father, may I speak?"

Stefan wrote down that it was Lord Dorian Hanniver of the London coven that had asked the question. He also noted Vérbulcsú's reply of, "Of course, my son."

Lord Hanniver adjusted the collar of the button-up shirt he wore under his black and purple robe and said, "We did not mean for this to escalate as it has and I apologize for my unwillingness to see the err in allowing Gregor's trespass to go—"

The Old One's hand came up and Lord Hanniver went silent and still. The metallic hiss came again, "No need to assume too much responsibility, my children. For was it not on account of this council's knowledge of my fondness for my first child that you based your judgment?"

No one spoke.

Vérbulcsú continued, "Perhaps I should have seen this coming centuries ago. Gregor has been with us longer than any of you, and has proven his merit through the many facile human ages. It was only when we took from him that which he loved too dearly that this tragic tendril of vengeance took root. That fault lies with me alone."

Stefan noted this, without entirely understanding what the Old One meant. It was not the place of a council scribe to ask questions during a conclave, so he would look over the parchments from previous meetings to understand what the impetus for this statement was at some later time.

Queen Tenebrasa, speaking much more softly than before, slowly stood and asked, "Would it please my lord if I quash the heretic? I would savor the chance to honor you, dark father." She bowed her head and her hair made the black robe she wore all the more absent of color.

Others among the two dais' benches watched for the Old One's reply.

"No, daughter." He tsked and she raised her head to meet his laser-focused gaze. "He is mine, in all ways. And I haven't been to the Americas since the early 1900s. I hear New Orleans is as full of culture and life and succulent treats as it ever has been." The ancient vampire rubbed his hands together. The sound was that of rough sandpaper.

Lord Mikkhal stood and nodded. "Very succulent, father. I was there last year, and the tourists are so dense and faceless that it's a fine buffet table they've turned the city into. Too many kitschy voodoo shops, but still, you won't be disappointed. And yet, my lord, not that I would ever doubt your capacity where handling heretics is concerned, but I would ask that you consider having some of us assist in your travels to avoid any cultural hiccups you may encounter."

The council was still and quiet. Count Vérbulcsú smiled again and took a step toward Mikkhal. "What sort of hiccups do you foresee, my son?"

Before the large Soviet vampire could reply, Lord Abbas stood and said, "He's right, my lord. Even flying on private planes is not as easy as it once was to the Americas, specifically."

The Old One turned to face Lord Abbas and asked in his raspy tone, "And why is that?"

"9/11, my lord," sighed High Lord Tiberius. "It happened in New York about six months ago. An attack by a group of terrorists blew up several buildings, killed thousands, and as a result, air travel to the US has become…" He paused, then said, "Bothersome."

The group of assembled vampires all nodded and murmured in assent.

Lord Abbas spoke, "They check the cargo holds of every plane coming in and out of the Americas for bombs, though ostensibly for drugs as well. And if your skin is not alabaster, they often want to do personal searches. Our will manipulators can handle it for the most part, but we have taken extreme precautions to travel in safety as a result of the event."

"Religious zealots are ruining my travel plans?" the count asked, as all took the cue and laughed in unison at their master's humor, such as it was. He finished, "Same shit, different day, one could say?"

More laughter.

Tiberius smiled and concluded, "In essence, you're not wrong, Father. We would only offer to aid you in safe transport. Americans are not any more reasonable than when you last visited."

Vérbulcsú continued to watch Lord Abbas, whose face remained sullen despite the lightened mood in the room. He asked of the shorter man-pire, "How are you holding up, Bilal? We all know you suffer as greatly as anyone present at the loss of our dear Lady Marius."

Lord Abbas rubbed his mustache, stood, and looked at the Old One. "Better than I've been, worse than I've been, and so it goes. Your grace in asking is all the comfort I am able to appreciate for now, Father, so thank you." He bowed his head and sat back down at the dais.

Queen Tenebrasa stood again and asked, "Father, of what other news did you seek to summon us this evening? For I would relish the opportunity to serve you in some other way, since you do not wish me to rip Gregor's unbeating heart from his ribcage and swallow it whole with some mint fucking jelly." Her eyes remained black as pitch.

"Yes, my seed. Might I inspire a new age of emboldened views with this decree, so council scribe—Vérbulcsú paused and pointed a finger at Stefan, sending a spike of frost through the scribe's own unbeating heart—make sure to get this down clearly."

He stepped back to the circular center of the room, and with one long-nailed foot, casually kicked the body of the young woman aside, sending it into the stone footer of the stairs, the impact eliciting another audible spinal crack from the dead body. Then he faced them all and raised his hands up.

All the members of the council, along with Stefan, waited

eagerly for the next words their master said unto them. And yet, none could believe it once he did.

"Henceforth, the covenant of perpetual darkness is nullified and the seal of silence is to be likewise undone."

Surprised looks passed between the darkborn, but no words arose from the group. The master's words hung heavily in the air.

Stefan filled the quill tip from the crystal inkwell and wrote down what the Old One had said, disbelieving it still. In a quill stroke, the new scribe was being tasked to essentially discard one thousand years of policy pertaining to the broader world's knowledge of not only their way of life, but their very existence. It was the bedrock upon which much of their foundational views and policies involving humans were built.

Queen Tenebrasa was the first to stand and break the silence of the chamber. "Such knowledge, such power, such wisdom, my lord! I hope one day I might see for myself as far as you do, Father, for your tactical mettle is beyond reproach!"

She clapped and the others started to join in, cautiously at first. Then, upon seeing the Old One hold his place, still framing a cold smile, they all stood and applauded openly.

Tiberius stood as well, but his face was filled with concern. Stefan left that detail out of the record.

The high lord carefully chose his words. "There may be some under our command who would wonder about the specifics of such an order. And so as to not dilute or distort the message, I would only ask for further clarification, my lord."

The clapping slowed and stopped. Everyone fell silent once again.

The elder vampire lowered his hands and sighed. "Well, I can't be more all-encompassing than that, my son. But I shall expand upon it since you'll all need to know my reasoning and certainly deserve to understand fully my will.

"When I say that we may walk in the light—save for the literal meaning, naturally—I mean it in every way. We needn't hide our faces, nor our existence, from the world any longer. Mark my words here and now that this will benefit us greatly in the coming decades. Our own climate scientists, engineers, economists, and global risk assessors agree that no more than another fifty years can be expected at the current rate of degradation before humans bring long standing chaos upon themselves, if not the ecostasis. Their numbers will dwindle.

"We aren't meant merely to ride the tide of time, but rather to change its very current and tailor its direction to our advantage. It is our divine destiny to rule them, and by extension guide the hand of the future. Until now this has been better done in the shadows, *but no longer!* We will be known and will be feared. I know what it is to have this power, for my time before the shadow was cast saw me subjugating them like sheep for over two hundred years, and frankly, it was awesome."

Several of those assembled chuckled at this.

"Admittedly the diet of the average world citizen was so lackluster that the blood didn't taste as good back then, but I digress. It wasn't until the church gained its legion of adherents and developed the means to hunt our kind that we formed the law we have all held true until this very hour.

"As it stands today, the church hasn't seriously believed in our kind for over a hundred years. They possess no institutional memory upon which to draw and will not be able forestall our shift in posture. Darkborn agents have already assumed various government positions. We shall maintain some level of anonymity for the first decade or so, but by the second decade of the new millennium, the world will likely know of our existence. And we will embrace the newfound notoriety by taking control of world affairs."

Lord Tiberius and Lord Hanniver shot each other the briefest of looks as they and the other vampires stood again and applauded this new edict from their creator.

Stefan caught sight of the exchange between the two lords, but as with so many things he had noticed this conclave, abstained from making it part of the historical record.

Lady Jussou wasn't applauding with the rest, and did not hesitate to ask the obvious question no one else dared:

"Why now, Father? What changed?"

The others stopped clapping and watched, waiting for the Old One to either verbally dress the South Asian lady down, or worse, but he was exhibiting something they had not seen in him often, if ever: true excitement. Almost giddiness, at least for him. His frosty smile endured.

Vérbulcsú eyed Mila for a tense moment, then explained, "Even if this trouble with Gregor ends as swiftly as I intend it to, the time has come. In truth, we may be a decade or two behind, but that is so much water under the bridge, as one might say."

Lady Jussou watched and waited for more, unsatisfied. The Old One did not disappoint in this regard as he admitted, "And if I'm being completely forthcoming, I'm ready to rule them again. They spend so much of their short time frivolously busying themselves with self-created crises and manufactured fear that they've really lost all perspective. Why should we be relegated to the shadows when what they could use—and indeed what they need—is some real fear. Fear that, my kindred, we can provide in spades."

The council members nodded and mumbled affirmatives in assent.

"However," the Old One said, "make no mistake that our moves will be coordinated, subtle, and will provide only improvement to our unlives, all of it approved by this council. The council shall naturally retain supreme decision-making authority."

A collective relief spread amongst all those in the room at this last statement. For fear had begun to grow, and knowledge that there would be continued collective involvement in the decision-making process moving forward was welcome news to all. But the shock of the night's initial decree still hung heavily in the air.

Stefan, for his part, was burning through parchment pages with all this gabbing and had nearly emptied a quarter of the inkwell—much more than he expected to. Still, he feverishly notated every last word into the record, for this was a momentous occasion and he knew that he was part of living history in the making.

He also realized that two lords and one lady had still not spoken during the entirety of the meeting: Lord Bejuis, Lord Ghosh, and Lady Emëxu. Not that it mattered, but he noticed it just the same.

The big Soviet vampire clapped his hands once loudly and feigned a smile as he said, "It is the dusk of a new night, my lord! And I thank you for your timeless wisdom and guidance. I would only ask to humbly serve you in this new chapter of your Empire." Mikkhal bowed and sat back down.

Vérbulcsú slowly walked forward as he spoke, "*Our* Empire, Lord Adrik. Our Empire. Serve you shall, at my side. All of you. You have made me proud over this last thousand years and I thank you all for your loyalty." The ancient vampire walked up the steps that parted the two daises. "I'll return in two days' time and we can handle getting me over the water to end Gregor's malignant reign of heroics. Good evening, my children."

Before the final word hit the ears of those gathered, a torrent of air swooshed through the chamber and the elder vampire disappeared. Those that remained shot each other nervous looks and Stefan knew this to be the end of the conclave.

Lord Tiberius stood and closed the old book before him. "With that, I would draw this conclave to a close and ask that we meet separately afterward to go over specifics of this…" he hesitated, then finished, "…exciting new era we've been thrust into. Are there any other matters before the council this evening?"

No one said anything. Someone coughed.

"Right. So it is closed. Take the time, Scribe, and we thank you for your work." Tiberius clapped once and everyone stood.

Stefan sketched out the last bit and hit the tip against the parchment one final time before lying the quill down on its side. *What a meeting!* he thought to himself.

The many lords and ladies stood and began to muster for departure, a murmur taking over the room.

"So that was, um, surprising." Tiberius admitted as he remained at the podium upon the dais.

"You can say that again," quipped Queen Tenebrasa as she slipped a black shawl around her turquoise-laden neck.

Tiberius obliged, "That was surprising."

"Cute," the queen hissed.

Lord Hanniver spoke, "Oh yeah, that was not something I would've expected. He's really very pleased about all this. Just so very pleased. I've never seen him that way."

Tiberius nodded. "No one here has. To say that that cheery

vampire we just saw was the same dark father who helped initiate the Crusades and gave us all life eternal is just … yeah. I don't know, that was, as the youth might say, weird."

"Uncharacteristic, truly," mused the business suit-clad Lady Sasaki. "Now it's up to us to figure out how to do this without giving up the ghost."

Stefan gathered up his quills and capped his inkwell as silence deafened the room. It was a good ten seconds before someone volunteered a suggestion.

"Killing off all the major world leaders would be a good start, would it not?" asked the short, curly mustachioed Lord Abbas.

Lady Jussou rapidly replied, "Couldn't hurt. As an opening gambit, anyway." She stood and walked toward the exit.

Those that remained in the chamber smiled wickedly and began to nod to each other, breaking into fits of laughter. Even the queen smiled as her eyes flashed from black to white with gold irises.

The vampires started to file out of the chamber and broke off into smaller, gossipy conversations as they exited the red door—with the exception of Lord Tiberius, who watched as Stefan loaded his velvet carrying case and started toward the exit of the room.

Everyone but the two had left when Stefan spoke.

"My lord." He hesitated, then resumed, "Father, I cannot help but wonder…"

Tiberius looked upon his firstborn son of darkness and smiled at him. "What is it, my son?"

Stefan scrunched his nose and asked, "Are all conclaves as eventful as this one?"

Tiberius started to descend the podium and laughed loudly, the sound echoing off the stone walls of the castle's belly.

"Oh heavens, no! No! This is crazy shit. I don't even…" He shook his head. He walked up to where Stefan stood and clasped the younger vampire's shoulder as they walked in tandem up the steps. "I don't quite know where to begin; so much work lies ahead. But I'm certain that our dark father has a larger plan and he'll provide more detail in the coming days. Worry not."

"I'm not worried, just curious," Stefan lied.

"About what?" Tiberius inquired as they reached the red door.

"There's absolutely no way that Gregor could… Well, that he could actually kill the master. Could he?"

Tiberius pulled open the door as he assured his darkborn child, "Of course not, Stefan. Of course not."

He knew that this was possibly a lie and regretted that he could not admit freely that he was deeply concerned for the fate of his master. Their master. He'd known Gregor for enough centuries to know that underestimating him was a sucker's bet—pun intended—and that the threat he posed to their way of life could not be discounted out of hand.

Stefan walked ahead as Tiberius held the door open, then disappeared into the adjacent corridor as the heavy red slab slammed shut behind them. Inside the chamber, the candles remained twinkling.

The body on the floor still did nothing.

For how could it?

It's a corpse.

# RUIN

Chris Bejarano had never seen much outside of Colorado. For all of his thirty-two years, he had lived in the Roaring Fork Valley. He'd been outside of the state once or twice on various vacations, but the siren song of the snow-capped peaks called to him at all times and he could never imagine moving too far away from them.

To boot, he was an avid snowboarder, hiker, biker, rafter, spelunker, and climber (though just a novice at the last two). He figured he'd be those things right up until the moment the ground swallowed him up in perpetuity, and he was fine with that. More than fine.

He loved where he lived and would spend much of his free time either taking or planning trips to various off-the-trail locales hidden among the lodgepole pines that dotted the rugged Colorado landscape.

Several of his friends and he had formed a collective of nature-loving thrillseekers that regularly went on such sojourns as a group. Not many of them shared his love of caves, though.

Still, never lacking curiosity about the world beyond the

square borders of his home state, he spent much of the rest of his time indulging his interest in the history of fallen civilizations, especially those that time had not been careful to preserve. The ones with the mystery embedded into the history. The lost South American tribes of the west, the mysterious sea people of the east, the ancient inhabitants of Easter Island, the Etruscans and the Babylonians, all of them. He couldn't get enough. If you existed as part of a pre-Christian civilization thousands of years ago, it's likely that Chris thought you were just terribly fascinating.

His bookshelves at home were filled largely with written histories, James Patterson paperbacks, and trail maps of Colorado.

For work, after graduation from Roaring Fork High School then a brief stint as a hair stylist at his dad's barber shop in town, he'd found a job he really enjoyed when he was hired by the local forest service station to help maintain the areas around the valley in which he'd spent his formative years.

Stationed at the Sopris Ranger Outpost, located right next to Sopris Park, which in turn stood not-at-all coincidentally beneath the imposing peak of nearby Mt. Sopris, he had taken the job just as soon as they had offered it to him.

It was his dad's friend Bill who had managed to finagle the job for him and the application process was largely a formality. In the valley, sometimes it came down to who you knew.

A lot of times.

He found the opening to the cave system the first month he was on duty. Assigned the none-too-enviable task of clearing overgrown trails up Prince Creek road, just south of town on Highway 133, he had been working his way down from the top, slowly clearing one trail after another for about two weeks.

One day, he was working on a trailhead just down the slope

and between the trees, about a hundred yards away from Dinkle Lake. It was more of a tiny man-made pond than a lake. The fish hatchery at the bottom of the hill kept the waters stocked year-round with trout for the angling enthusiasts.

When nature had called to him, he jumped off the trail and stood behind a tree to shield his private moment (and parts) from any looky-loos who might pass by on the main road.

As he was shaking out the last few drops, he noticed that under some brush, just about twenty feet away, there was an unusual rock formation. As he looked closer, he saw that one rock seemed to be jammed into the center of another.

Upon investigation he saw that the smaller stone could be pulled from the other like a plug being removed from a drain. Oddly, there were small notches in the rough sides of the rock and he was able to slide it out without much resistance. When he did, he heard a reverberating sound from below him and the other stone slid down, revealing a narrow passage about two feet by two feet and clearly not naturally formed.

He pulled a headlamp from his pocket, strapped it on, and looked into the dark mouth of the cavernous hole.

The opening had almost definitely been made by some hand other than Mother Nature's. Yet as he stepped carefully into it, the interior was a near-pristine passage jutted with stalactites and stalagmites. The floor was smooth and seemed as though it had been formed by hand.

He was very excited, and decided to return with more supplies and friends. However, five of his buddies had taken a trip to Ibiza and other Euro-locales for three weeks and his other friend was fishing for a month on the Colorado River with his father.

Chris's girlfriend (in so much as they were possibly becoming more than just another summer fling) was—and she was fairly vehement on this count—Hardly interested in squeezing myself into some damp grotto to see if I can induce myself into a flight or fight panic mode, á la *The Descent*. No, thank you."

So he resolved to do some preliminary checking himself. He knew better than to go down too far into an unknown cave system alone. However, he was as curious a man as any other, and when he innocently did another check two days later, he found something he had never expected: A clear indication that the place was, in fact, manmade.

Not fifty yards into the first passage, against the far wall that ended the tunnel and seemingly covering a smaller passage, lay a shaped piece of dense stone, roughly four feet tall, two feet wide and one foot thick.

All over the tablet were inscriptions that Chris, in his initial haste, had barely been able to register, other than some cryptic writing of unknown origin. He was too excited by the possibilities this undiscovered system might contain.

Giddy as a proverbial schoolboy with a shiny apple for the teacher in hand, he told his lady and best bud about it the next day. Both cautioned him to get others involved before he did anything else. His girl was worried for his safety, which was nice and made him like her even more.

His good friend Ryan Jervis, while excited at the prospect of Chris getting to name his own cave system, said that if what he was saying was true, it likely had some scientific and/or historic value that he may do well to check out before he went barging, half-cocked, into King Tut's Tomb.

After several weeks of contemplation, he decided that he didn't hate the idea of the Bejarano cave system being, you know, a thing, and resolved to take another trek just a little further into the tunnel with the tablet.

He waited until the moon was full and had let his friends (disapproving) and girl (half-disapproving) know that tonight was the night that he planned to find out just what kind of mysteries lay dormant in the fertile subterra beneath Dinkle Lake.

In his defense, he never lived to regret it.

Finishing up with a particularly bramble-ridden trail near the Thomas Lakes turnoff, he shooed some weed-smoking teenagers off from where they had congregated near the trailhead, eliciting moans from the group. Afterwards, he bagged up the trail debris and loaded it up into his vehicle.

He was only a quarter mile down the road from Dinkle, and as the failing light of the day disappeared behind the high ridges to the west, he knew that he should do this while he still had the energy and focus to keep himself safe.

His watch read 8:15 p.m. when he pulled his Motorola phone from his pocket and hit the number for his lady friend, currently holding down the fort back in town.

At the ranger station, about five miles away, a beautiful and curvaceous young redheaded woman in her twenties sat behind a 1970s-era metal desk with chipped harvest-yellow paint coming off in strips, filing down her red-painted nails as she eyed the clock on the wall.

The station was small and beyond racks of pamphlets for trailheads and river networks, as well as several "ONLY YOU CAN PREVENT FOREST FIRE" signs with Smokey wagging his finger your way, the place was fairly bare.

And that wasn't by accident. No new money or resources

were going into the decades-old station. Despite it being in work-able condition, it wasn't long for this world. Several years prior, some officious little business-suit clad pricks, distinctly of the monetarily-gluttonous mindset to gentrify every historic and unique piece of classic Carbondale charm right off the map, had recommended and sadly gotten approval for plans to demo the three small buildings that made up the Sopris Ranger Station.

They planned to replace it with some gaudy monstrosity that looked like every other bit of nouveau-trendy, cold, grayscale, dystopian crap that had slowly polluted the iconic skyline of Avery Katz's hometown since the early aughts.

Now, in 2023, it seemed that these old and dusty yet beauti-ful landmark buildings (which were directly adjacent to the park where the town held it's annual fair) were sadly going the way of the Dodo. A half century of history set to be torn to literal pieces by meddlesome and profiteering property developers, determined to make a good commission, despite their pandering excuses for do-ing so. The bastards never let up. Death by a thousand transplants.

Where once, growing up, there used to be a field of cows grazing across from her small house between the high and ele-mentary schools on Highway 133, there was now a well-to-do, upper class neighborhood replete with an over-watered golf course and cheaply constructed tennis courts.

It made her queasy to watch the town's charm go tits up, as it seemed to be going. Still, the whole affair was truly above her pay grade, as far as she was concerned. Thus, she had zero intention of chaining herself to the trees out front (which the history-razing bastards were also determined to plow from existence), as some of her more eccentric friends from Colorado Mountain College were planning next month.

She had about two hours until she could lock up the station and head to her apartment she shared with a college friend of hers, Beth. Just like the eponymous KISS song—her personal favorite of their catalog, despite its oft-dubious standing amongst diehards in the KISS fanbase. Which hardly mattered in the moment; it obviously didn't make time go any faster.

And that's what she could use right now. A little chrono-nudge to expedite the *tick tick tick* of those clock hands.

With black lace-up, knee-high boots kicked up on the desk, she rubbed her nail file back and forth, listening to the electronic beats of the local radio station, KDNK (K-Dinkle to the locals). Jam after jam pumping out of her little Sanyo radio on a nearby shelf.

A group of industrious locals volunteered to fill in as DJs for the grassroots radio outfit, and the guy they had on right now, DJ Oblio, had a penchant for EDM that gave Friday nights in Bonedale the same background soundtrack as a rave in 1999.

Despite the thumping 4/4 beats distracting her, she nearly flipped onto the floor when the corded telephone on the desk suddenly rang loudly.

Startled from her quasi-reverie, she righted herself, swung forward in her swivel chair, and snatched up the heavy receiver from the base, putting it to her ear. "Sopris Ranger Station, how may I help you?"

"Hey, cutie. I'm thinking you know how you can help me, though it might prove tricky at this distance."

Avery smiled and leaned back in the squeaky black, faux-leather padded chair. "You almost done with your *Hardy Boys* adventure?"

"Oh yeah. Just about to head down to the second ring of Dante's Inferno."

"Which one is that? The one with the ice and Satan and all that?"

"Nah, that's number nine, I think. The second is for the lustful and sexually wanton to be blown eternally around by violent winds or some such shit, if I'm correct. Provided you cotton to that particular brand of mumbalarkey."

"I cotton to no such mumbalarkey, sir," Avery assured him.

"Good, I'd be worried. How's the terminal ranger station holding up?"

"Still chipping paint and pleading for a stay of execution. Doubt the governor's gonna call, though." She flicked at her nails, eliciting tiny clicks. "Other than that, it's your usually cold Carbondale evening. Nothing but the smell of Peppino's beckoning me to go grab a slice before they close. You gonna be much longer?"

"Less than an hour. Does that mean I should come back by the station before you head out?"

Avery replied, "Of course, you should. You know you should."

"Why's that?" he asked.

"You know why," she mused.

"Humor me."

"No."

"Is it my manly abs?"

"Maybe it's simply your taste for good sauvignon that draws me to you time and again." Avery did enjoy playing coy.

She could imagine Chris's grin. "Wouldn't be the fact that I can make you hum like a banshee in heat when I—"

"Yeah, okay, okay, ya big fucking galoot. Radio silence while I'm on the clock. Just keep the Lone Ranger on standby until you get back or you're liable to burst a teste tendon between Dinkle and here." She stopped filing her nails and picked up a cup of coffee from the nearby shelf, taking a sip.

"I'll hurry my ass and see if I can't snag up some of that mighty fine wine on the way."

"Sounds good. I could use some. And if you hurry back on down here before I have to head home, I'll make your cute little head spin."

Genuinely curious, Chris asked, "How's that?"

"Wouldn't you like to know? Otherwise, back at my casa, we have to be quiet for the roommate. She's gotta get up early and is being a real … ya know. Whatever."

"I'd much rather perform with you at full volume, so I'll be hurrying my happy self back, post haste. Checking the cave, then I'll see if I can move that stone I told you about before I come back. My trail shit is done for the day and I'm ready to come and, uh, well, you know … cum."

"Enough dirty talk, I'm getting dizzy. Shut it and I'll see you in a bit, babe. Seriously though, don't be a dipshit and get yourself stuck like that guy in that James Franco movie. I don't know if I'd like you as much with missing limbs. Just being honest, here." Avery's voice was concerned, but playful.

Chris finished, "Can do. I appreciate it, cutie. See you in a bit."

They hung up. Avery leaned back in her seat, unconsciously pulled her curly red locks behind her freckled ears, and smiled.

*Getting some tonight, for sure,* she thought.

Good. She knew she deserved it.


Five miles away and under the moonlit glow casting down from above, Chris opened the rear door of his state-issued White River Forest Service Ford Bronco.

He pulled out the small bag he had brought for his trek into the cave, with a few "what ifs" accounted for. He had some rations, a radio, a couple lights, and a very sharp US Army Ranger knife with a compass in the hilt that his father had gifted him on his eighteenth birthday.

And lastly but arguably most important was a large black crowbar. Essentially the same kind that the burglars in *Home Alone* had used. That thought amused him.

Checking everything twice, he made sure he had some batteries in the front pouch of the bag, then walked over to the opening under the thick brush and stepped into the cave. He placed the headlamp strap around his scalp and flicked on the light.

His eyes adjusted rapidly to the surprisingly bright bulb's beam. He saw the same cavern jutted with pointed rock protruding from the ceiling and floor. The same narrow path between the stalagmites that was too smooth to be naturally formed. Not that the tablet at the end of the room left any doubt that once upon some bygone time in the storied antiquity of the American continent, someone very purposely had set it there. Why remained a mystery.

One he was determined to begin unraveling.

The flat tablet-shaped stone that lay diagonally at a pitched twenty-degree angle against the oddly tilted wall was too smooth along its edges and almost looked as though it had been machine-cut to uniformity.

It was nearly beveled along the edges, and the etchings that filled the front face of it were like nothing he'd ever seen.

Oddly, the only thing his mind could reach out and grab to equivocate it to was, silly though it surely might sound to some, the handwriting of the Coneheads from the 1993 film of the same name. Largely remembered (like nearly all SNL films) as something best left in the dustbin of history, Chris had always had a soft spot for the outright goofiness of those movies as a kid. Now, looking at the otherworldly script on the stone, it was the closest analog he could muster.

Still, the characters were almost all unique, and just glancing at it, he saw no repeat uses of any single glyph. He wished he'd thought to bring some tracing paper so he could make a rubbing of it to take with him. Instead, he settled for taking a few snaps with his smartphone.

While he still had a bar or two, he shot the images to his vacationing friends across the pond. Since they were only eight hours or so ahead of him, they might catch a glimpse of it before they passed out sometime before sunrise and went into a full blown conniption with jealousy.

He pulled the precariously protruding crowbar from the black bag he'd brought and set it against the wall. Setting down the bag, he picked up the crowbar and stood to the side of it while he tried to get an angle on it that he could use to start prying it from the wall. It felt stuck fast, though, and he couldn't get it to budge.

Luckily, this was one of the "what ifs" that he had accounted for and from the same black bag, he soon withdrew a small, yellow, rubber-handled chisel. He lined it up against the wall and used the curved end of the crowbar to smack the black plastic end cap of the chisel.

After five whacks, the slightest of cracks appeared, forming along the spot where he had lined up the edge of the chisel's tip.

As it split from further hits, he realized that the tablet was affixed to the wall with some sort of rudimentary cement-like adhesive or something of the like. But it was giving, chip by chip. He figured he'd have to work at it for a good half hour to get it loose at that rate, but was surprised when, after just another minute or two, the limestone-looking mortar substance around the tablet's perimeter began to break down.

He had only cracked it for a few moments, but, as though a vacuum had begun to take hold of the air outside, he felt and heard the slightest of drafts whistling between the perforations made by his chisel.

He stepped to the side, and much to his astonishment, the tablet fell forward and dropped onto the cave floor with a resounding boom that rattled Chris's nerves something fierce.

He was surprised—no, *stunned*—by the dull greenish glow that poured out of the now open passage that led further in. A little worried that the stone would've cracked from the fall, he saw that it seemed intact from the back.

Standing upon it, he peered into the opening. He could see that a mossy substance covered the inner walls of the tunnel that led away from him. It must have been about fifty more feet, this new tunnel. The opening, a perfect square, a few feet by a few feet, ended when it opened into a much brighter chamber beyond.

A smell similar to rotten fruit hit his nose and he wondered if this was a burial crypt of some neolithic civilization. It wasn't the craziest thing to deduce, he knew, and the sour odor emanating from within almost made him stop his advance. But his nose quickly acclimated to the pungent aroma and, after a few moments, he crouched and shuffled into the hole.

He recalled that the catacombs in Paris were said to be wide, musty, stale, and with notes of malaise. However, *sour* or *rotten* weren't words he had ever heard in reference to them. Possibly something organic was the source of the befouled odor.

As he crouch-walked down the narrow passage, he saw that he was leaving footprints in the half-inch thick, greenish glowing algae under foot. It squished and slooped and slurped, and he had to use his hands to steady himself for fear of taking a nasty tumble and having to limp back out the Bronco. Which would suck. A lot. He'd never live it down, in all likelihood.

He came to where the brighter light spilled in through the far hole and he stepped through the square portal into a larger room. Much, much larger.

This interior chamber was so large it resembled the space needed for a small city. It was easily a couple of miles to the far, green-slicked wall. He could see it because the whole area was unbelievably well-lit. The size of the ceiling did not seem structurally feasible.

Every surface within the giant cavern was illuminated by a faintly greenish-blue glow coming from what looked like iridescent algae coating every surface from floor to ceiling.

In the area between the rocky walls was a city. A small one, but a city, nonetheless. Ancient, and remarkably well-preserved. Absent any residents that he could see from his vantage high above it, here it was. Like the lost city of Zinj or El Dorado. Yet slimier and more foreboding.

The blueish-green glow was not bright, per se, yet still accented every feature and angle of the various buildings he saw filling the chamber.

During a raucous and rowdy class trip to Mesa Verde back in middle school, he had visited a sizable collection of cliff dwellings. Ancestral Pueblo people began moving into these dwellings, which they built into natural cliff alcoves, in the late 1100s. The villages hewn from said rock had been largely preserved by time. These glowing buildings before Chris bore a similar neolithic settler look that the cliff dwellings at Mesa Verde had, but simultaneously quite different.

Otherworldly, in a way.

Their design was unfamiliar and non-Euclidian, with aberrant angles and odd weight bearings that made various walkways and oddly pitched landings seem unnatural. Hard on the eyes and seemingly structurally unsound. He could not understand how any bipedal creature would have found it to be a suitable place to live at any time, past or present.

And why in a cavern beneath the lake?

As he calculated the odds of an unknown civilization occupying a damp cavern in the subterra—below a body of water that didn't exist when these buildings were carved from the rough rocks in the chamber—he thought of something that Ryan had said to him two days prior:

"Man meddles endlessly and makes the bed, then doesn't want to lie down when the shit hits the fan and they risk getting egg on their face."

In response, Chris had said something like, "Well that's a helpfully jumbled and cryptic amalgam of bumper sticker slogans and all, but what's the bottom line, Haus?"

His friend had quickly snapped back, "We keep fucking around with things that time has tried to forget and we're likely to find something we wish we hadn't, ya know?"

Then his animated hombre had launched into a blathering aside about how the prehistoric bacteria which were being released from the arctic ice shelves—the result of global climate change—was likely to start a pandemic that made COVID-19 look like the mumps.

*Ryan, always the dramatic type.*

Though Chris took the point all the same.

His friend simply hadn't seen what he had seen though. Ryan

might think the whole thing a fanciful endeavor of limited pay-off, but Chris realized he was about to do what only famed archeologists and frontiersmen had been privy to in the past. The discovery of something that, for all intents and purposes, no one knew of, let alone had ever seen.

And so he walked to the edge of the large balcony-like outcropping he stood atop of, and gazed out at the vast and asymmetrical field of old buildings and other indescribable formations.

Hanging from the top of the slick and iridescent ceiling were uneven and roughly formed links, making up massive chains that held aloft metallic dishes. The concave, circular disks—fifty feet in diameter and also colored with the same iridescent algae—held purple, bulbous, blue-veined orbs with glowing green leaves that looked like some sort of alien fauna. A displaced and invasive interstellar species that no one had prevented from Earth entry.

They pulsed with a repeating pattern, glowing brighter for a moment, then going nearly dark.

Interspersed between the disks were unholy, ovoid-shaped grotesqueries and vagaries of geometric form. Columns and jutted rock-like curls of stone. Reddish veins of rope-thick sinew connecting architectural abominations like muscles hewn to flesh.

It struck sour in his mind to gaze upon them. Chris's eyes, now wide with equal parts excitement, wonder and encroaching terror, also felt a bit itchy, as though something in the air was irritating them. He rubbed his eyes.

His head felt a smidge-bit woozy, as it sometimes did when he was on the border of dehydration. Though he knew he had kept himself watered during the hot day, so he figured he needed an aspirin.

His eyes hurt too, and the feeling was not like anything he'd ever felt. It wasn't a familiar stinging; it was heavier and sort of disorienting, like a migraine.

His lips tasted like metal while he ran a tongue over his teeth, and that wasn't good. Not good at all.

Yet something even worse became starkly obvious to Chris at that moment. Because that's when he saw the blackness.

At first, from his extremely high vantage overlooking the unnatural—and one might even say ugly—city of dilapidated ruins, he could see a blob of something that the light could not penetrate.

Amid the cracked, crumbling, and disproportionately designed columns and under the eaves of a slanted portico that lay a mile distant, the shape began to grow like an amoeba absorbing adjacent organisms and swelling in size as a result.

The air tasted freshly sour, which meant that it was getting stronger. Also not a great sign.

The blob spread and formed into a rolling arc, like a wave that began to cascade out in all directions. It spread out unevenly, and as it did, the forms of the buildings flattened out and almost appeared to vanish in the wake of the blackness.

A line, like a rippling twilight-tide of dark waters rolling onto a beachhead, composed of unseeable pitch blackness, consumed everything it reached. The void-wall of onyx emptiness pushed across the necropolis, up the walls, and extinguished the light coming from the bluish-green algae all around.

The massive chamber began to rapidly dim and it only seemed to hasten the imposing darkness's consumption of all that the chamber held.

His head began to really hurt.

Something was off.

Something was wrong.

His breathing became increasingly labored and panic filled his chest just as the air began to leave it. He felt the latter of his fight or flight response taking his will in its steely grip and he turned to run from the chamber.

The black rot that had begun to crumble the buildings was moving in his direction at an alarming rate. He rushed to the exit but stumbled and grasped onto the walls for purchase. As he tried to steady himself and pull himself up using the wall, he was suddenly aware that all the light had gone out except for his headlamp.

Turning, he saw the rolling black and managed to hit the number for the ranger station on his phone.

It rang only twice before the torrent of darkness befell him and all was gone.

At the ranger station, Avery was turning lights off in various rooms when she heard the old handheld phone ring again. Despite rushing to it, when she picked up the other end, there was only a flat dial tone, which then went to silence.

She slowly set the handset back into the cradle and stared curiously at the door, though she didn't know why.

Something. Something.

As Avery stepped out the front door of the Sopris Ranger Station into the cool night air, she raised the binoculars to look toward the direction of Prince Creek and Dinkle Lake to the south-east. The clear moon shone, pouring blueish light onto the ground, making clear the ridges in the far distance.

As she rolled the adjustment wheel on the lenses to focus on the horizon, her eyes located the ridge right near the lake.

She was immediately startled to see that a wide black envelope was swallowing the hillside. The lush green forest was rapidly giving way to a wall of death that sucked the color and life from the vegetation as a blight swept all too quickly down the hills.

Her horrified eyeballs watched helplessly as the trees toppled, bushes curled, and howls of various animals cried out in a sickening symphony carried on the wind from her place in the heart of the small town.

As the black curtain seemed to speed up, enshrouding the entirety of the southern hills, lights of small homes went down, moonlight disappeared from the ground, and what life she saw was extinguished in a stunning flash of withering decay.

The black did not stop at the bottom of the hills, but began to run the length of the fields that lay on the outskirts of town. Through the binoculars, she beheld as it roared down 133 toward her town. At the rate the all-encompassing blackness was moving, she would be swallowed in less than a minute.

The last thing Avery Katz saw was an impenetrable fog of onyx mist, like a dense swarm of black flies blotting out her vision and taking her oxygen, her life, her cells. And indeed the very memory of her, as if they'd never existed.

The plague to end all plagues blossomed out in all directions, fueled and hastened by the life upon which it fed, and started its circumnavigation of the globe. As it spread, killing everything in its path and sucking the life from the Earth itself, it only sped up.

It hit mountains and sped up. It hit grasslands and sped up. It hit oceans and rivers and snowfields and cities and towns and children and pets and mothers and trees, and all it did was speed up.

The whole thing took but two hours to biologically decimate the world, extinguishing all life on the planet. Even the cockroaches finally got theirs.

Nothing was left.

*Nothing.*

Not even this story.

# ASCENT

"**E**ric says you need to hustle your butt up to control. Something's up."

The tall-figured man in the break room doorway wore a white button-up shirt, a blood red bowtie, and a bristly mustache that was straight out of a seventies police procedural. When he spoke, the dense red tuft over his mouth hopped up and down.

Across the room, Jeff nodded and stretched a thin smirk across his face without looking away from the coffee machine. "That's nice. A little bit of aviation levity just to change things up?"

"Well, I surely aim to please, Cap'n. But seriously, he did say ASAP," the tall man said, 'stache a-bouncing.

"Did he now?"

"He did now, and how. And iffin' he's comfortable sending me down to get you without delay, then—"

"Yeah, okay. He knows I'm on in fifteen and not late, yeah?"

"Just trust me, Jeff. You're gonna wanna come up now."

"Okay! Roger, Roger."

"You have your vector, Victor." Daniel Burrows and his

bushy facial hair walked out of the entryway, letting the door close softly behind him.

Jeffrey Caramacci picked up the small paper cup that had just rattled out of the sunbeam-striped, eighties-era java vending machine, which had sat unchanged by time in the corner of the sky jockey break room since the late 1800s. In actuality, probably the early nineties, but who was asking? The still-operational relic fit cozily with the rest of the retro-chic decor which filled the space of the control tower lounge. Disco drapes, hardback swivel chairs, and a modest table long enough to accommodate the five to seven person crew.

Turning his blue eyes to the large sepia-toned picture on the wall of the Wright Brothers' first airplane flight attempt, he blew softly on the coffee in the cup, but did not sip at it. He knew better, as here was a rattlesnake that had bit him on more than one occasion. Best to give it a wide berth for a spell.

He spent another moment enjoying the warmth of the cup in his palms, then turned to head upstairs to the top deck.

Crossing into an ascending spiral stairwell wrapping along the inner walls and secured with an iron railing, he began the short but laborious jaunt up to the operational control room, or OTC.

One minute, two landings, and sixty steps later, he hit the top landing. Just before he entered the door, he straightened his short blonde hair with one hand and used the other to tap his passcode into the electronic keypad outside the heavy metal door. A soft click and it swung open of its own accord, sucking in a light swoosh of air as he stepped through.

Inside the cylindrical-shaped control tower, a vast array of colored diodes and control mechanisms surrounded by rings of glass panels offered a 360° view of Denver International Airport, its runways, and its many terminals.

At least, it normally would have, but for the flowing sheets of driving snow obscuring the tower's view that evening, prohibiting the controllers from seeing much more than the lights outside.

The snow had been predicted, but had come harder than anticipated. While they had been taking in some flights earlier, most were now being rerouted due to the inclement weather to nearby Eagle/Vail Airport just an hour or so west, down the I-70 corridor.

Fat square buttons that glowed green and red were legion and the whir of fan-cooled electronics was constant. The room layout was essentially several terminal stations—work desks flanked by banks of screens which comfortably accommodated the team that Jeff had come to know as his reliable running crew over the last several years: Sam, Eric, Cherrie, his gal Mon, Daniel, and Juliet. The latter was apparently the only one running late and currently unaccounted for.

Walking in, the short, pudgy body of Eric Sturess appeared from seemingly nowhere, blocking his passage. In his thirties and built like a brick shithouse, the young man was quite thick round the middle. Not really fat, just thick. One hell of a flight data jockey, he'd supposedly once tried out for the Broncos but was possibly too short to make the cut.

But, he didn't like to talk about it, so…

"We've got a shit storm brewing, Jefe." Eric's black hair was combed back to mask a thinner patch on the top, and he regularly ran his hand along his scalp while speaking, as he was now.

Smiling, Jeff blew on his baby-blue paper coffee cup and peered through tiny wisps of steam at Eric as he took a sip. His tongue lightly recoiled.

*Damn it. Still needs another minute. Goddamn snake strikes again.*

"Happy to see your penchant for glowering and hyperbole remain intact and operational, Eric. Good evening to you as well. Meds working?"

"I'm not kidding."

"I never think you are, nor am I. But give me a second to set down my things before you lay down your whole Chicken Little spiel. That work for you?"

Stepping aside, Eric snorted and crossed his arms. "Funny you should say it like that. And we don't have a minute." The thick gentleman trotted toward a bank of screens before a sparse metal desk and took a seat.

"Why funny?" Jeff asked, though Eric did not respond, but rather plunked his silver headset on and started to dial a number on a glowing numeric keypad with his right hand.

Passing by Eric's desk, Jeff threw glances to the rest of the crew, equally enamored with their respective screens and read-outs, and walked over to two terminals seated by one another.

Wearing a headset and leaning into one bank of screens was a lovely brunette in a black tank top and blue jeans. Her hair was tied up and she wore large, stylish glasses.

"Hey, babe. You been here long?" Monica Sanders leaned back in her chair and unconsciously rolled her finger over the small but appropriately pricey engagement ring she'd been wearing for about a month now.

Jeffrey leaned down to kiss her, noticing her fidgeting with the ring, then settled into the nearby terminal where he set down his bag on the floor and plunked down his coffee on the desktop.

"No. Just walked in and got coffee and *boom*." His eyes glanced out the big paneled windows at the falling flakes. "You thought about where you want to go yet?"

"For the honeymoon? Uh, meh. I don't know. Sky's the limit, right?"

Jeff snorted. "And there's my daily quota on aeronautical puns reached in no time at all! Thanks, babe."

"'Kay. So, did we rise on the wrong side of the flight deck, mi amore?"

Jeffrey sighed and smiled at her. "Yeah, no, sorry, I just…I dunno. Yeah, maybe. I think I need more sleep, is all. But who's trying to hear that old rap?" Reaching over and taking her hand in his, he kissed it softly. "Sorry, I'll be fine. I'm good. Valerian root. I need to try some Valerian root."

"You haven't?"

"I haven't. But I should, and I shall. Could be the ticket. Surely though, we digress. What's the problem up there?" he asked as he turned to face four sixty-inch screens mounted before him with a smaller terminal monitor beneath them atop the desk.

His eyes scanned the timetables and radar scopes. Up to date software and modern instrumentation providing real-time data to he and his team ensured that flights to and from Denver International ran as smoothly as possible. Still, despite such modern advances, his team remained as integral to the safety of passengers and flight operations as the pilots themselves.

The air controllers, Monica and Sam, pushed the tin on their approach and through when they touched down, while his two ground controllers, Cherrie and Daniel, handled taxiing on the runways as well as any other movement-heavy areas of the airport. Lastly, his two flight data geeks, Eric and Juliet, as their title implied, were the eyes, ears, and comms of the tower.

His humble role was that of operations manager—essentially the whip cracker of the motley lot, though he rarely, if ever, had to flex any of his dubious authority. Really he was the tower's long-time jack of all trades, and therefore a master of none. Perfectly suited for middle management.

His position certainly did little to dissuade Eric from testing the limits of their occupational disparity with languid regularity. A right smartass is what he tended to be, truth be told.

"Hopefully nothing," Monica relayed. "But we got a ding from Pitkin County Airport. They claim to have dropped a plane a few minutes ago just outside of their range and haven't been able to raise them on the radio."

Jeff nodded, pulled on his headset, and adjusted the microphone next to his lips. "Anybody else confirm it?"

Eric stood and called to him from across the room, "Nobody else is seeing it right now, either."

Jeff wondered who was confirming this, so he simply asked Eric, "Who's giving us that?"

"Cheyenne."

Pleased, Jeff asked, "You've got Cheyenne on the line already?"

"Seemed prudent."

"Quite. Good work, Eric. And it's off their scopes as well? Same flight?" Jeff asked, already knowing the answer.

"Same flight. Delta 275. Aspen to Chicago, direct." Eric sat down at his terminal once more.

Looking at his screens, Jeff saw that they only had a handful of flights crossing in and out of their scopes. Guiding his mouse to open and click through applications on the big screens, he switched his focus from ground radar to the more powerful LRRS (long range radar system) and, using a satcom relay that communicated between hubs, pulled up the area around Aspen/ Pitkin airport. His top two screens filled with the short range radar seen by those at the other airport. And just as he was being informed, no 275 transponder appeared active on the screen.

He swiveled ninety degrees toward Monica. "Well, shit, this doesn't sound very good now, does it?" he delivered flatly.

His fiancée shook her head. "Not too good, no." Monica shot him a pained half-smile that, after six years together, he knew all too well. It was enough to trigger the slight, albeit familiar sting of reality hitting him square in the sternum. She wasn't betting on this having a happy ending. And now, by extension, he wasn't either.

Everyone in the tower knew of Aspen/Pitkin Airport's reputation as one of the trickiest runways in the continental United States. A dicey little strip wedged between two hazardous mountain walls, plagued by crosswinds and unpredictable weather fluctuations, it had experienced more than its fair share of aviation tragedies over the years.

In early 2001, an Avjet Gulfstream III had crashed next to the runway killing all eighteen on board and the resulting litigation had led to performative procedural changes at the airport, however hardly for the better. It did nothing to improve the conditions of the runway nor the difficulty that inclement weather provided to any approaching aircraft. The tragedy was but the worst of the many that spanned the decades.

Noting that Juliet was officially late, Jeff asked, "Where for art thou Juliet?"

Monica smiled and replied, "Mayhaps she found her man dead and offed herself, forthwith."

"Okay. About this plane—what's the scoop? Who's the closest other than Pitkin?" Jeff asked, rolling around his mouse on the pad to dispense with the screensaver of Singapore's neon skyline he'd had going on his primary terminal monitor, below the other, larger screens.

"Junction's still closest, technically. Sam is getting them on now." Monica pointed to the young man with the horn-rimmed specs, stylish black vest, and onyx fauxhawk rapidly typing at one of the nearby terminals.

Jeff nodded. "How's the weather in Aspen tonight? Worse than we got?"

Monica adjusted her glasses and leaned back as she answered. "Surprisingly not as bad as what we're experiencing. Who knows for how long, but they're still taking touchdowns."

Jeff winced at the thoughts rapidly coming together in his mind and asked, "Have we gotten anything from the TCAS? Any crash data?"

"No." Monica shook her head briefly, clearing her throat, then finished, "We're still getting flight data from TCAS and ACARS. It, or rather *they*, I guess, think she's still in the air. Just zero coming in on the airwaves and no transponder relay. The pilots didn't send out a distress signal on the emergency frequency either."

"Do we know if we—"

"They have another," Samuel Tibbits called from across the room. He was their lead air controller, and with all the traffic on the runways essentially at a standstill, he had been contacting other airfields for flight confirmations and releases.

"Really? Pitkin?" Jeff asked, disbelieving.

"Yeah. They said they've lost two on scope. Nothing from the secondary surveillance radar either. I also have Junction on, and they're saying they've lost the same flight as well. This one is, uh, Delta 715."

"Somebody better get Robert Stack on the horn, cause we've got us an *Unsolved Mystery* a-brewing!" Cherrie Temple teased from the semi-secluded spot her terminal occupied, nearest the western windows. Goth-chic with shiny raven hair and matching attire, her disposition was eternally bubbly and vivacious, despite outward appearances.

"That's a little premature," Jeffrey passively scolded her for the morbid quip. "We can't count on their scope being on the fritz. Though two in one night would be quite something, wouldn't it?"

Monica asked, "Which? The two scopes or the two flights?"

"Take your pick." Jeff looked out the windows at the snow-saturated conditions. He picked up and sipped his coffee without worrying if it would nip him this time.

Alas, it did not.

He cast a look at Monica who, grinning ear to ear, was clearly quite taken with the mode he'd suddenly snapped into.

"You're my eyes on ACARS, babe. Lemme know right away if something comes up. In the meantime, can you get the NTSB on the line, just in case?" Jeff asked.

Monica winked his way and, without a word, started to dial the number on her phone keypad.

"Okay," Jeff spoke, standing up and walking over to where Sam was seated. While clean shaven, well-dressed, and reasonably handsome, Sam's desk always looked as though an energy drink bomb had gone off on it. Tall, slender cans of every variety were sprawled in all directions.

Jeff was able to linger nearby, outside of the aluminum blast zone, as he asked the seated man, "What kind of equipment are we talking about for the two that have gone AWOL?"

"Looks like a Cessna Citation and, wouldn't you believe it, a Gulfstream."

"And?" Jeff pressed.

"Hold on." Sam sat back down and touched a button on his terminal. "Junction Tower, this is Denver Tower, please confirm the last transmission."

Jeff tapped his foot nervously as his eyes traced around the room to his five-person crew, (was Juliet even coming at this point?), waiting for Sam to speak. Finally, he tapped the mute on his phone control and stood up again.

"Junction just lost two themselves."

Stunned silence in the tower for five pregnant seconds.

Sam went on, "So, yeah, that's gonna be four total between the two airports…"

Several hushed gasps and curious looks popped up around the control room. All eyes darted searchingly to one another for some answer, yet this fresh info only lent tself to more questions.

"Sam, come on…" Jeff muttered, disbelieving.

"What do you want from me, Jeff?" The operations manager sighed, raising his arms up at his sides in a dopey shrug.

"What do I want? Um, okay, well what I really want—or rather need, right about now—is confirmation that what we have here is some massive radar mishap losing tin left 'n right and not one of the largest aviation tragedies in human history unfolding before our goddamn eyes, *Sam!*"

Standing up, Daniel shook his red head as he covered his headset mic with his hand.

"It wouldn't be just ours. It can't be. Salt Lake says they're losing dots the same as Aspen. They're dropping out of the sky, sir."

Jeff frowned. "Don't call me sir."

"Yes, sir." Daniel went ahead and took the extra little step of saluting the senior man in the tower, just to bristle his bacon. Jeff, unamused, returned Daniel a hostile look in kind.

"We know that they're dropping?" Jeff asked the room.

Dan said nothing.

Monica jumped in, "Nothing yet from the flight data. Not one alarm, actually. I haven't checked the new ones yet."

"Okay, so what's happening here?" Jeff asked, turning Eric's way.

The stocky man's eyes went wide and he shrugged. "You're asking me?" Eric stood up again as everyone's eyes shifted to him at his station.

"I'm asking you, Eric. You were pretty hot to trot about this whole thing and you've got Cheyenne on. What are they saying?"

"Nothing right now. I'm on hold."

"Seriously?"

"Completely."

"Why—"

"I don't know, man! They just put me on hold for a second. Probably, *hopefully*, piecing something together so that this starts to make sense sooner than later."

"Odds of that in your opinion?"

Eric snorted. The closest he ever dared to approach actual human humor. "A snowball's chance in hell, Cappy."

Jeff let out a sardonic laugh. "Shit."

Daniel raised a curious eyebrow to Eric and asked the obvious. "What makes you say that?"

Eric's normally unflappable demeanor was one of his defining character traits. It's what made him a top tier flight data man and, despite his generally gruff demeanor, earned respect from the others in the tower. Yet now, for the first time Jeff could recall, he was noticeably wavering, his voice loosely cracking as he replied, "This is… Well, this could be something pretty serious."

"We all get that," Dan shot back.

"No, I mean *big*, big."

"Explain *big*, big," Jeffrey pressed.

Eric turned to face Jeff directly. "Well, what we could or maybe even *should* ask ourselves right now is one question."

"Okay. And what's that?"

"Is this an attack or something else?"

Jeffrey rushed across the room to his terminal and sat down, pulling on the headset. He dialed a few digits and waited a moment. After nothing came from it, he stood back up. "Dan, we need to get a read on the military response. You should see about getting the Pentagon for us once your line is freed up."

"Sure, but with the chain of command such as it is, and since Eric already has Cheyenne on, Nellis is who I should be getting on the line first, right?"

Jeff nodded, "Of course. Good. Do it."

Dan gave a quick thumbs up, then sat back down at his terminal.

"Sam?" Jeff called out, spinning on his heel to face the dapper, overly caffeinated young man amid the Red Bull wastes. "Pass your call with Junction off to Cherrie. Cherrie, please get us confirmation if you can."

"On it," Cherrie said, signaling digits to Sam with her hand so he'd know which line to transfer the call to.

"Sam, you make damn sure to log times and keep feeding me anything you can, yeah?"

"Naturally." Sam nodded as he took his seat again.

Turning back to his fiancée, Jeff inquired, "Monica, what about the NTSB?"

"They're aware of what's happening and are being updated every sixty seconds. But until we have something to report..." Monica made a funny half-scowl and went back to re-checking the ACARS readouts.

Dan piped up again, "Yo! I have Nellis, who gave me an update on the response. They're scrambling jets out of Cheyenne Mountain and Schriever AFB in C. Springs. Maybe ten minutes max before they're doing visual confirmations near Aspen. But we just lost another two in the space over Grand Junction."

From across the room, Eric confirmed, "He's right about the jets. They've left the ground at both. A few minutes and we'll have some confirmation."

Cherrie held up her thumb and clicked a tiny red button on her headset. "The tower in Junction is saying they have zero visual confirmation or reports of any crashes so far."

Jeff sat back down at his terminal, and without looking Cherrie's way, asked loudly, "How's that possible?"

Unseen by Jeff, Cherrie's black lips curled up into a broad smile. "What do you mean?"

"Isn't Grand Junction just a few miles from end to end?" Jeff clarified.

"Yeah," she confirmed.

"Then how aren't they or we seeing them yet? Some of those flights should be within visual range. Have we confirmed with Nellis about the radar losses that Utah is experiencing?"

Jeff's eyes ran over the screens before him. He used his mouse to toggle between the ground control radar and the data readouts from the TCAS systems. Nothing on TCAS was signaling anything amiss, and yet transponder dots began to drop off his scopes as well, both through the short range ASR as well as the LRRS.

Across the room, Daniel called out, "Nellis has confirmed the loss of several flights on their end as well."

Standing, Sam removed his headset and rubbed his forehead with his fingertips. "Fuck, this … this is really happening, isn't it?"

Jeff shook his head. "Not until and unless we have wreckage. Not to sound indelicate, but I need somebody in this room to give me at least one downed flight to start with. One fucking crash site. Or at the very least let's ask what Cheyenne wants us to do at this point. Because if the system is randomly disappearing flights inaccurately like this, we may soon start to lose the real thing."

Aside from the whir of electronics inside and the breeze outside, there was quiet among those in the control tower.

Cherrie broke the silence. "Could it be a solar flare that's taking out the electronics?"

"We are not doing that!" Jeff called to her from across the room. "Alright? Let's keep the wild speculation to a hard zero and work on resolving the issues we can. Everyone clear?"

A hushed chorus of agreement filled the room.

Eric stood again and covered his headset with his hand as he spoke, "Cheynne just gave me a, uh, unique update. We—they—have a visual from one of the jets. Or *had* a brief visual."

"Had? Why had and not have?" Jeff demanded, more harshly than he would've liked. He made a note to chill the F out a smidge.

Eric shook his head and shrugged.

Danny seemed not to notice the lingering question as he said,

"We've lost contact with the jets from Cheyenne and Schriver also. No radio. Transponders off. Nellis's confirming."

"Okay." Jeffrey removed his headset and rushed over to where Daniel and Eric were.

Monica heard a telltale beep coming in through her headset and looked at her short range radar, spotting a dot moving in from the northeast. "Jeff, my love. Not to pile on, but we got a flight coming in from the northeast. Delta 236. And they're hailing us on a distress frequency."

Jeff didn't hesitate. "Send it through and put us on intercoms."

Monica clicked her mouse a few times and tapped at her phone keypad. A whizz of static came pitching through several small speakers that lined the ceiling of the circular room.

"Why a distress frequency?" Cherrie asked, to which no one replied.

Touching her headset, Monica spoke into the mouthpiece softly, "I'm putting you on the intercom. Please repeat, Delta 236."

"What the hell is going on?" Sam asked aloud of no one in particular, yielding no reply.

After a second, another hiss, then a voice cut through the audio mist of the ceiling speakers:

"Denver Control, this is Delta 236. Repeat, this is Delta 236 to Denver Tower. We have been—" Silence and light static for a moment, then, "We are stopped in midair. I repeat, we are stopped in midair. I have no control. Repeat, I have no control of the aircraft."

More static. Then the pilot's voice returned. "I don't know if this is… This can't be what it—"

Three agonizing seconds of quiet, then:

"Denver Tower, we have begun a rapid ascent from twenty

thousand feet. Now at twenty one thousand and climbing. In the air above us is what appears to be a large… It's a large black craft of— Now at twenty two thousand feet. Still climbing. The— Is that a ship? Is that…"

Static again hissed in the circular room for an instant and then no more sounds came from Delta 236.

Jeffrey walked to Monica's terminal as she handed off her headset to him. He held the mic to his mouth and immediately started to hail them.

"Delta 236, this is Denver Tower. Please acknowledge."

Nothing but muted static.

"Delta 236, this is Denver Tower. Acknowledge."

Inside: silence. Outside: snow.

Jeff handed the headset back to Monica as he walked right up to within a few inches of the big tower window. Looking out, he started to walk along the perimeter of the room while eyeing the snowy sky for any sign of Delta 236.

"What the hell did he just say?" Cherrie asked, voice trembling.

Still surveying the skies beyond the glass, Jeff spoke softly, "He must've, I dunno. Something is obviously very wrong up there but I don't… I don't know." Jeff rubbed his eyes and stopped, still looking outside. "It doesn't make sense. None of this is making sense. I mean, if anyone else has any ideas, jump right in, but why would he say that he was in rapid ascent if he was going down?"

Monica chimed in. "What makes you think he was crashing? He said the exact opposite!"

Jeff spoke without looking back. "Either the info on his gear or his own sense of gravity made him say that, in all likelihood. He couldn't have been ascending, obviously. I'm guessing he was headed down, but couldn't tell because of…" He paused. "I don't know. I can't square any of this. Cards on the table, I'm just tossing stuff out."

From his place before his own set of glowing screens, Dan finished quietly speaking to Nellis and shouted loudly to Jeff, surprising himself. "They're not crashing, cap'n!"

"Okay? Clarify, Danny, and fast."

"He's right," Eric called from his terminal.

"Right about what?" Jeff asked.

"They're not going down. They're going up." Danny's face remained solid while saying this, though his eyes reflected his fear.

Another wave of stunned silence filled the room as anxious looks danced back and forth between those in the tower. Snow flooded the outside air in choking white billows.

"What do you mean, 'up'?" Monica asked, before Jeff or anyone else could.

"I mean the opposite of down," Daniel deadpanned, red bushy mustache flat, face terribly unamused.

Monica warned, "Daniel, I swear to God that of all nights, this one is absolutely *not the one* to—"

"I'm serious, Mon! These ones I'm tracking are at increasing altitudes with no sign of slowing. If you were still watching ACARS, you'd see it confirms the flight data we are seeing in each tower. Same shit there. I got Nellis saying they've begun tracking at least six with rapidly increasing altitudes, but they can't hail them either. I don't know what's happening, but all of that is true."

"How the hell is that possible?" Jeff asked, mostly to himself.

Around him, nobody spoke, several shrugged, and Monica frowned. She looked at her screens and highlighted the ACARS data.

Dan sat back down and started speaking quietly into his headset once more.

"I want to start having fewer questions and more answers. Let's turn this around!" Jeff asserted, calmly this time. "Has Washington been informed?"

Eric swiftly reported to him, "Yeah, they're…" He paused, listening to his headset for a moment before finishing, "Okay, yeah, they have Washington tied in. The chairman of the Joint Chiefs is being briefed right now. Some staffers are being moved to Cheyenne."

"Christ. I mean, *good*. That's good. Then we can start taking orders and stop improvising. Any more from Nellis?"

"They're saying that planes all over the globe are going up. It's not just ours. And they…" Dan trailed off.

Jeff stopped looking at his screens, stood and looked over at Dan. "And they what?"

"What they're saying is crazy."

"We're in a loopy goddamn field of crazy right now, so what's another acre? Tell us what they're saying, Dan."

"They're claiming that they are tracking at least twenty massive objects entering Earth's atmosphere and NASA has taken the lead now. It's taking longer than it should because several comm satellites have disappeared as well."

"Holy shit," Eric grumbled.

"There's something you don't hear every day!" Sam finally chirped up.

Dan nodded. "They're currently working with the White House for a response. President's gonna go live to address the public shortly."

Cherrie jumped on it. "Hah! So, UFOs? They have UFOs up

there? Just sucking up our fucking airplanes? This is real, right? We're really being attacked from outer space?"

Everyone in the room wanted nothing more than to disagree with this conclusion, but as they all did their own mental math on the matter, no one could.

Cherrie concluded, "That's sort of fucking horrible and awesome all at once, isn't it?"

Jeff shot Monica a sweet look, somewhat out of place with their current predicament, and calmly asked, "Hon, can you please put up a couple newsfeeds on your monitors and have it ready to go to the intercom?"

Monica returned a fearful look to him, but dutifully clicked closed a few windows, then opened up the browser tabs to display the live newsfeeds.

Before she could fully finish resizing the app windows, her sixty-inch screens displaying said news channel feeds, suddenly cut to a short test pattern drawing everyone's gaze directly to them. Then, the emblem of the Office of the President.

Two more seconds and it switched over to the president himself, seated with his hands folded atop the Resolute desk, fingers interlaced. They were visibly shaking.

"My fellow Americans—" was as far as he got before the screens went jet black.

But not just the two displaying TV channels. Every screen in the room went dark and was filled with green spirals that danced about the darkened screens, much as fireflies danced through the warm summer air. What would be an otherwise mystifying or enchanting sight on the displays seemed utterly alien and unwelcome in this moment.

Inside the largely darkened tower, the backup lighting system kicked on, shrouding the control room in a soft, pulsing orange glow. Absent the ambient whir of electronics, the outside wind now audibly roared past.

Nobody spoke for nearly an entire minute. Not one of the people staffing the tower that evening had gotten where they were by lacking in intelligence, and the implications of what had just happened were slowly sinking in for all assembled.

Jeff knew it was his task to keep team morale high, even in the most unpredictable and precarious of scenarios. Qualified or not, that was his charge. As such, he offered up the minimum assurance he could bring himself to muster, given the circumstances.

"So, you were saying, Dan, about unidentified objects?"

"Uh, yeah. They, uh…" Dan paused, scratching his thick mustache before finishing, "They basically said that Cherrie was right. Somebody should've called Robert Stack."

Cherrie whimpered from somewhere in the mostly dark room, "I fucking hate being right so often."

"So do we," Eric agreed.

Without saying anything else, everyone slowly congregated near the front of the room, before the large, slanted windows facing the western horizon. The snow had slowed somewhat, offering a hazy, yet improved view of the airport.

Red and orange emergency lights, flickering against the snowflakes, lit up much of the runways, while the rest of Denver International remained shrouded in darkness. All of the landing strips had been cleared. Still, many of the concourses were host to scattered planes via extended passenger boarding bridges, and essentially ready for takeoff once the storm subsided.

If it ever subsided.

Monica was somewhere nearby, rifling through her desk audibly, when Jeff heard and asked, "You okay, babe?"

Banging about, she answered, "I think I have a Maglite somewhere in here."

Eric, Dan, Sam, Cherrie, and Jeff stood next to the window, and while Monica continued to search, they saw something start to happen in the darkness.

The first indication was the unmistakable sound of screeching metal as the boarding bridges began to buckle and break.

All eyes focused on the main terminal with its many offshoots.

Defying any and all ideas the assembled lot had developed about such niceties as gravity and the tensile strength of airport-grade steel fabrications, ten or twelve airplanes slowly began to rise inexplicably from their metal moorings. Spinning and twisting in an almost zero-gravity fashion as sparks and pops of light blazed through the snow cover, they caught tails and noses and wings on the jetways.

The group collectively gasped as the planes floated skyward in virtual synchronicity, trailing metal wreckage and falling debris.

The effect on the larger terminal was disastrous. Catching and tearing away at several places, the metal sky bridges—crumpled, torn, and in jagged tatters—shredded from the terminal with varying degrees of destruction. Some remained clung to the sides of the planes, while others fell completely to pieces on the way up, raining down fiery metal debris. More still were sparking enough to create small fires at several spots along the concourses.

Monica clunked a final drawer closed and joined them, nearly stumbling over something in the dark as she watched in mystified awe at the sight of the ascending aircraft.

"Oh sweet Jesus in a manger. What the actual fuck?"

Jeff tried to sound calm, "Babe, it's gonna be fine."

One spinning plane began to flame, and before they knew it, it exploded in midair, sending a boom and a wave of orange light their way through the snow. Everyone reflexively recoiled for a moment.

Watching as the other fires spread and the planes started to disappear into the white veil of the night air, Monica shook her head vigorously. "No. Nope. This is not okay at all."

"She's right," Eric confirmed for anyone who was curious.

This made half the room involuntarily giggle and seemed to inject some much needed levity to balance against the tension of the moment.

Once the planes and pieces of the terminal disappeared into the sky, everyone looked over to the burning terminal fires that were slowly spreading.

"Someone should really put that out," Cherrie observed.

Sam spoke for the first time since the lights went down in Denver. "I'm sure somebody is handling it. You could always go help 'em."

Cherrie snorted in the dark. "Or not. Like the waitresses say, *not my table.*"

Along a far mountain ridge highlighted against the sky by moonlight, a spear-shaped object suddenly lifted up and left the Earth, racing skyward.

Out of his peripheral vision, Jeff noticed just quick enough to point at the distant sight, calling to the others, "Look! There!"

The seven controllers followed the direction of his finger and watched as the distant projectile continued up, briefly illuminating the snow-dappled mountains below with the bright light of its exhaust's flames. It quickly disappeared into the clouds.

Eric was the first to speak, his voice low and less confident than usual. "You don't suppose that—"

Before he could finish, another missile-shaped spear shot out from further north, along the same rocky range, and they beheld its rapid ascent with equal parts awe and fear.

Once it too vanished from their collective view, Eric asked, "What was that?"

"Shit," Jeff flatly replied.

"Didn't look like shit to me. Looked like rockets," Sam called out through the orange dim.

"No, I meant this is as serious as it gets, now," Jeff clarified.

"Why?" someone asked.

Jeff sighed. "Because I'd be willing to bet all the money in my pockets against all the money in your pockets that what we just witnessed was several of our warheads heading straight up to engage Cherrie's UFOs in the opening gambit of an intergalactic dispute over territory or resources."

"Seriously?" Sam asked.

"I mean… Well, you know, I have no idea what's happening, really. It's important to remember that. But odds are fair that if we really lost the planes and satellites—if they're being drawn up to those ships in the stratosphere—then it's as likely as not that we might've just launched a nuclear attack on them. An act of reciprocity for their preemptive strike against our air capabilities."

"Just like that?" Cherrie quietly murmured.

"Makes sense in a theater of war scenario. They've already taken out our ability to attack and likely disrupted global communications."

"We would just launch a nuclear attack that quickly?" Dan mused.

"Wouldn't you?" Jeff quickly dealt back.

"Where does that leave us?" Monica asked softly.

Unseen by all, Jeff shrugged. "Like an ant farm that's about to be shaken."

"Seriously?"

"I don't know. You've seen the same movies I have. Anybody's guess really. But I doubt it's all good news up there. I do doubt that."

"Think so?" Dan asked.

"If they were able to suck up our aerial defenses and disrupt or even entirely disable communication, I doubt those missiles, nuclear tipped or not, will ever hit their intended targets."

"He's right," Eric agreed.

Jeff smiled and said, "Thanks, man."

"No problemo."

Monica drew toward her fiancé, wrapping him with her arms and holding him tighter. "I'm scared."

"Me too," Sam echoed.

"Me three," Cherrie agreed.

"Yeah, this sucks," Eric said to no one's disagreement.

"I know guys. I know. Obviously that's the only reasonable response. So, yeah, me too. It doesn't look too good," Jeff agreed.

The six-man crew unconsciously drew closer to one another as they stared out from the saucer-shaped tower deck into the dark, frosty abyss, masking an uncertain fate in a world now well and truly under hostile extraterrestrial invasion.

Juliet never showed up.

Who knows why.

# CICADAS

On Electric Avenue in Mountain City, Georgia (population: 247), your average citizens generally felt completely safe. Each yard had a tree swing, each porch had a rocker, and nary a front door among the thirty or so houses that made up the town proper ever had the lock thrown. And just like that song from '82 by Eddy Grant—which shared its name with that eponymous stretch of asphalt—the area imparted unto its residents the feeling of there being no immediate dangers in the world around them.

Nestled within the kudzu-choked trees and dense overgrowth that enshrouded the wet, hilly land making up the tiny town were a handful of streets of varying inclination and zig-zagginess. The highway south led to nearby Clayton. The way north led to the state line.

And that is where this particular tale begins. In the drizzle-dappled hills of Mountain City.

It's the story of a young boy and his loving, if somewhat surly, grandfather who felt the need to impart a little raw wisdom one dark summer night. And the place where we intersect with these two is on that relatively cool evening with whipping winds and a high buzz of chirping cicadas hitting such a fever pitch outside that the thick window panes were lightly rattling.

Inside an old post office from the late 1800s that had eventually been repurposed as a residential home by the 1950s (once the Second War had finally ended) is where we lay our scene.

It's also inside the musty walls of this classic cottage on Electric Avenue—with its gorgeous, all-too-southern wraparound deck—that the man and the child were milling about after having eaten a fine dinner of fried chicken, mashed potatoes, and butter rolls at the Clayton Cafe. The boy was visiting his maternal grandfather that evening while his mom stayed at his aunt's nearby cottage, just two doors down.

And while the mother and her sister drank blood orange mimosas and watched the newest episode of whatever brain trash on the boob tube at the other cottage, at this one, the boy was wrapped in a warm, snuggly, fuzzy blanket and nursing a small Atlanta Braves coffee mug full of hot cocoa which was steaming from the top.

As the grandfather walked about setting out candle holders, the boy watching the television in the living room sat with his legs crossed on a small woven rug. One of those down-homey, warm kind that looked like an endless spiral of braided rope smashed down into an oblong oval shape.

"Whatcha doin', Grandpa?" the boy asked as he watched the old man pace about the room.

Shuffling around and placing the last brass candlestick holder on the shelf above the fireplace, the older man smiled warmly at his grandson. "Just keeping the candles lit up. When the cicadas get this loud, you can't be too careful."

The boy blew on his cup, though sensed it still too hot to venture a go. Instead, he asked, "Why's that?"

"It's a full moon," his grandfather replied simply.

"Does that make the bugs louder?"

"Yes, and more dangerous by a mile."

"Dangerous?"

"Yep. Very. Now while I can't speak to what it's like in other states—say, out in Colorado where you guys live—I can surely attest that up here in the humid climes of northern Georgia, our cicadas get to be a bit nasty once they get this riled up. And riled up is what they are. Spooky riled. D'you hear 'em?"

The boy turned his head as if to lend an ear to the ever present outside hum, which was largely unnecessary. He could hear them as loud as an engine running just a few feet away. The chirp-hiss coming from the opaque blue of the night cried out in chorus for sweet release while a million sets of eyes peered into the darkness.

"Yes, I can hear them."

The grandfather hacked, swallowed some spit, then deepened his voice. "It's a rare and dangerous night to be walking around, even more so to be caught in the dark."

"Why can't you walk around?" the boy asked, genuinely curious.

The older man walked over to a nearby cabinet between the bedroom hallway and the kitchen, pulled some long white candles from the top shelf, and closed the door.

"Truth be told, the damn things tend to gnaw people right on up."

"They *do?*" the boy asked, long frightened at the prospect of killer insects, without being able to fully articulate such at his tender age of seven.

"They do. They do. Damn shame, too. One kid I knew growing up—name was Michael; he was a nice kid. Sister was a candy striper. But he got chewed up by the filthy little creepy crawlers on a night just like tonight. After that, his family moved away. Guess they didn't cotton to losing another kid to them. The bugs, I mean. The cicadas."

"Are you joking around, Grandpa?" The young boy with the snug blanket wrapped around his shoulders took up the cup of hot cocoa in his hands and blew on it again.

"Heck no! No, sir. I wasn't kidding around back in '43 when I used the machine gun pipper on my Hellcat to line up that Japanese zero in my sights and blow that kooky kamikaze to bits all over the Pacific, and I'm not kidding now."

"You blew somebody to bits?"

"Several. All over the Pacific. You're welcome for that, by the way."

"Really? Well, thank you … I think. Do cicadas even have mouths?"

"Yeah, boy. But not all do. Actually almost none do. Basically none. Just the ones you hear on a night like tonight. And most folks never see it coming. They don't know that these are the human chewin' kind until the cicadas are already swarming 'em. Burrowing into the skin, they peel back flesh in a thousand little strips, like you're being dragged over a big ol' cheese grater. The blood comes from all directions, just pours outta ya. Truly."

"Holy moly, Grandpa! That sounds so scary! They don't really do that, do they?" The boy was so nervous he forgot about how hot the cocoa was. As he sipped it, the liquid chocolate made his tongue recoil and go slightly numb.

"Why, you damn well better believe that they do! Oh yeah, you betcha boy. And once they got your skin in tatters, they use the strands of sinew connecting your muscles with the bone to floss their rows of razor sharp teeth with."

Maybe it was the fantastic nature of what he was hearing, but somehow, even to this young man, this particular part of the story told by his maternal grandfather simply wasn't passing muster.

"How many?" the boy asked, now testing the elder for holes in his tall tale.

"What?" the grandfather (George Kittredge was his name-o) asked.

"Teeth. How many teeth do they have?"

"Thousands."

"Woooow," the boy said as his eyes went wide at the mental image his brain painted for him.

"But the worst thing—by golly, the worst thing they do—is make short work of your internal organs!"

"What's that?"

"What's what?" the old man asked.

"An eternal organ?"

"Oh. It's internal, not eternal. And I just mean yer guts. The soft things inside you."

"Ew! Like your brain?"

"Sure, but mostly it means your heart, liver, lungs, your spleen, your pancreas, and your spongy little gallbladder. All that gooey filling, even the soft bits like your eyes and tongue. Little monsters target those parts so that the medics can't donate any of the organs when they find the corpses—or what is left of them."

"Gross! That's super yucky!" The young man giggled as his grandpappy plugged candles into the seven or so candle holders he'd placed about the room and lit them with a small white Bic lighter in his hand.

"Yeah, yeah, you're right. It is. And now that I'm thinking about it, might not be the sort of thing your mom is gonna want to hear about you hearin' about. Sure you wouldn't rather me show you how to do another magic trick? I can teach you how to disappear a penny under a cup covered in paper."

"No way! This is way more interesting. They don't tell us this kinda stuff in school."

"I'd think not. Probably don't want a lawsuit on their hands."

"How do they make that sound?"

"By running their ribs together super fast, causing them to click."

"Why do they make that sound?"

"Cause they're DTF."

"What's DTF?"

"Nothing. Next question."

"What else do they do?"

Pausing to think while he lit another candle wick with the flick of the Bic, then chuckling softly to himself, the older man said, "If you believe what the old forest folk used to say about 'em, they can steal your dreams and sometimes your money if you aren't careful."

"What are the forest folk?"

The older man shook his head in response. "I'm just half-kidding about that last bit, really. Probably a legend—almost assuredly a silly legend. Celtic nonsense from the old country of your forefathers. Hardly matters anyway; I doubt if anyone has ever had their dreams or money taken away by any cicadas. It's very unlikely and very silly." He sighed, then cleared his throat again and finished, "But they do eat your face. They'll eat it clean off. That they *do* do."

"Gosh, but aren't they just bugs, Grandpa?"

"Sure. But so were my pubic lice and they made life hell. So are those huge spiders that they got in the Sahara that leap onto camels' throats and drain them like Dracula!"

"They have spiders that suck the blood from camels? Holy moly, Grandpa, how big are they?"

"Bigger 'n you, I tell ya that much. They'd probably eat you up in a single gobble."

"Grandpa!"

"It's true! Look it up next time you're near a set of those Encyclopedia Britannicas! I'm dyin' if I'm lyin'!"

Genuine concern now flashed over the young boy's face. "They don't live near here, do they?" he asked, his high voice cracking.

"Nah, the Sahara is a good distance from here. Besides, I'd protect ya, just like I'm protecting you with these here candles."

"Are there enough lights to keep the cicadas from eating our skin and eyes and internal organs, Grandpa?"

"Oh, sure! I wouldn't worry about it. I'm not worried. Nah, we should be good. Unless they chew up the electrical lines between here and the plant outside of town. Then we'd just have the candles to keep them bloodthirsty chompers at bay. Lucky for you, I'm all too prepared. We got lots of light."

"Are you just trying to scare me, Grandpa?"

"Course not, boy! I got little to gain from givin' you the creepin' willies or the heebie jeebies. Nah, just trying to keep a few monsters tucked back."

"Mommy says there are no such things as monsters."

The grandfather smiled warmly at this and finished his candle lighting rounds. Walking over to the nearby recliner and taking a seat, the older gentleman placed his forearms on his legs and leaned in toward the sitting boy as he said, "Your mom's a good woman and her heart is in the right place. That said, on this count, she's more full of shit than a leveled off saloon outhouse."

The young man shivered as a cold chill ran up his spine at his grandfather's words. "Really?"

"Look, there are most certainly monsters everywhere. All corners of the globe and everywhere in between. They just don't look like Godzilla or the Wolf-Man or anything quite so obvious. They tend to look like your neighbor or a politician or even a tiny single celled amoeba that gives you some fatal illness. Sometimes it's a crazy man flying an airplane toward you over the Pacific and sometimes it's a swarm of bugs. They come in all shapes and sizes."

Shaking with the warm mug in his trembling digits, the boy confided in his grandfather, "I'm really scared now, Grandpa."

"I would be too, if I were you, but you really don't need to be. I promise. We're fine. I got your six covered, good buddy. Plus we have lotsa backup flashlights in the closets and the electricity hasn't gone out in years."

"Will the glass keep them back?"

He could hear the slight shake and rattle of the windows. It sounded to his fearful ear even louder than when it had first started.

"Sure. They won't try it if they see the lights. Now c'mon, let's get us something else to focus on. We could watch a movie? I use VHS tapes to record whatever is on the premium channels, though I never watch them. Got one recorded from the other night we could put on."

"What kind of movie is it?"

"A space movie, I guess. That's what I think it said in the TV Guide. It's called *Total Recall* and has that guy from *Kindergarten Cop* and *Predator* in it."

"Arnold Schwarzenegger?"

"Yeah, that fella. You wanna give it a go?"

"Yeah! That would rock! But can we watch it in the bedroom with the door closed in case the bugs come into the house?"

"That's not gonna happen. Trust me. They're just making lots of noise because they ain't got nothin' better to do. We're good. Let's grab that tape from under the TV stand there. It's marked with the name. Bring it into the bedroom."

And that is exactly what the boy did. He grabbed the VHS cassette from under the seventies-era TV stand and followed his grandfather into the bedroom. And they watched *Total Recall*, a sci-fi adaptation of a Phillip K Dick novel with a hard "R" rating. Not what you'd normally prescribe a first grader, but still.

The following morning, both boy and grandpa woke up in the very same bed they'd fallen asleep in, while watching ol' Arnold try to outrun the gun-wielding denizens of the red planet.

Rising and getting ready for the day, they had a light breakfast. An hour later, while the grandfather filled out the day's crossword and his grandson sat watching morning Nickelodeon cartoons, the boy asked his grandpappy, "Can we get some ice cream?"

"Uh, yeah, why not?"

"With sprinkles?"

"Oh, yeah. Just like you prefer it. That doesn't sound too bad at all."

And to him, it didn't. He'd never lost his sweet tooth.

Getting into the car, they pulled out onto Electric Avenue and got about two blocks down the road back toward town when the grandfather began to slow down his classic gold ragtop Oldsmobile convertible.

Noticing the same odd-looking thing on the road that had caught his papi's attention, the kid rolled down his window and was immediately struck by an awful smell that made his eyes water.

"Grandpa, Grandpa! What's that? It smells so gross! What is that?"

"Looks like something that met its maker in a hurry. That smell is the desiccation of the flesh, withering and wasting in the unrelenting Georgia heat!"

"Is that an animal that somebody hit?"

"I don't—" the older man began. But as he pulled closer, he saw half of a black baseball hat with the NY Yankees logo on it. He also spied what looked like a belt buckle and colored cloth mixed in with the largely reddish mound of chomped on body.

Noting the telltale markers of being worked over by a swarm of hungry creatures, the old man laughed and pointed. "I think that's that dope-peddling dipshit who works at the Saucer Stop. Steven something…"

"That's a person?"

"*Was* a person, son. Was. Now he's fly bait."

"That's disgusting!"

"See! I told you that they basically tore you up from the inside out!"

"Oh my God! That's so horrible, Grandpa! I don't think I should be seeing something like this!"

"This is real life, my good boy. Real life—all day and all night in three dimensional technicolor. And while generally everything is as easy as peach pie freshly plucked from a Georgia oven, you do gotta be wary of a few things. Three specifically."

"What's that, Grandpa?"

"One, don't ever wear suspenders with plaid shirts. Just don't. Two, never buy roadside blueberries—*ever*, no matter how good the deal seems. And three, when it's a full moon in northern Georgia and the cicadas start to shake the windows with their hissin', you'd better light up the room as much as you can because they will chew off your dang face, then fill up on whatever they run into after they get through that."

"Did they eat his face?"

"Oh, yeah. Big time face eating."

"And his eyeballs?"

"Popped like cherries in his ocular cavities."

"And his tongue?"

"Well, he ain't gonna be whistlin' Dixie anytime soon, that's for sure."

"I'm gonna be sick."

Peering past his grandson out of the passenger window at the bloody heap of chewed up person lying on the ground, he saw the flies buzzing around the body and cocked his head to one side. "That's a completely understandable reaction to seeing this kinda aftermath of a body that's been eaten alive by plagues of the biblical variety."

"That's horrible, Grandpa."

Laughing, the old man howled with amusement, "You bet it was! And goddamn painful as all get out. Slimy little sucker suffered all hell right up to the very end. You can bet your sweet Aunt Susie's ass on that one!"

Using the old hand crank to raise the glass back up, the young boy, now irrevocably changed, gave his grandfather a look of despair mixed with horror. He mumbled his next words:

"I don't think I'll ever be the same after this, Grandpa."

"Yeah, yeah. Probably somethin' to that. Think I was about your age when I saw my first dead body, and I still wish I'd never seen it neither. But maybe it made me more okay with blowing people to bits over the Pacific, so who knows? Still, I bet yer wishin' you'd taken me up on the magic trick instead now, huh, bub? Hah!"

The boy nodded.

"But come now, boy—enough dead body bullshit. Let's go get us some ice cream with sprinkles!"

# STORY INSPIRATIONS

KUDZU - I used to spend summers with my family at their cottages in northern Georgia, specifically Mountain City. It rains all the time there and when the grey clouds coalesced overhead, it felt as though the green which surrounded on all sides was pushing in on you. I never forgot that.

FLANNEL - This one was inspired by traveling with a friend of mine to a place his family owned way up in the wilderness outside of Denver. There was this one fire watchtower nearby and I wondered what the occupant would do if some random creature attacked him. Now I know.

VAUNTED - Almost anyone who lives in the Roaring Fork Valley will eventually end up visiting Starwood Estates at some point—either for work or due to being invited to a soiree like that depicted in the story. And everyone knows that there are vampires up there. It's just a fact.

P38 - I caught the new Indiana Jones film and it was truly one of the worst things I've ever seen. I felt that anyone, myself included, could likely write a time travel story involving Nazis and an old artifact that would be much better than what those jokers had done with half a billion dollars. A very low bar, to be sure—though I believe I cleared it with room to spare.

CHOOSE - I read every *Choose Your Own Adventure* book I could get my hands on growing up, and was absolutely obsessed with them. I still read them with my daughter and sons to this day. And they are always very wholesome and most of the endings are upbeat. I decided on a story that wasn't quite so wholesome and that doesn't have that usual happy ending. Channeling a little Clive Barker, admittedly.

UGATS - The base idea with this one was to have two sets of mid-level guys confront one another. Once I chose the setting of Las Vegas, it seemed obvious that it had to be made men and extraterrestrials given the towns close proximity to Area 51. Vinnie and Vito also appear in another story, set ten years later called *Rats*.

LOBO - This one is based on a real school trip that my friends and I took in the seventh grade, and Gene Schilling *was* in fact the bus driver. He was also terribly tolerant with our adolescent shenanigans, unlike our science teacher who was decidedly *not* as amused, and incidentally played the bad cop of the two. Minus the werewolf stuff, a lot of this is on the mark. However, Cody is, in reality, quite brave and a good man. And yes, Gene is why we all wear tie-dye to this day.

METEOR - One of my favorite horror movies of the 1980s is a film called *Night of the Comet.* I suppose this is almost a love letter to that film as well as a chance for me to demonstrate what I suspect would happen if anyone ever tried to mess with the real life Cholla and Colette. They also appear briefly in a story called *Harvest.*

DEIFIED - This one required a bit of research and is meant to be more absurdist than anything. I find Scientology and nearly everything related to it to be absolutely hilarious, minus the family separation bit, of course.

VENERATED - I had never intended for any of the stories to be interconnected. However, as soon as I finished *Vaunted,* I knew what the next part of the story was. So this came quite quickly, and ended up being a personal favorite of mine. The next part of this story is likely to be a full length novel.

RUIN - Chris Bejarano and Ryan Jervis are two of the mellowest, coolest, most down-to-earth dudes that I had the pleasure of growing up with. So naturally I had to kill them and the rest of the world off with a biblical plague unleashed from a closed off ecosystem under Mount Sopris, right? This is largely drawn from one summer I spent working at that very ranger station(which the town sadly tore down recently). It was the same summer that a firebug park ranger lady accidentally started a massive forest fire that burned down a sizable swath of the Colorado landscape. Perhaps that played a bit of a role in the inspiration as well.

ASCENT - I do not particularly enjoy flying, and haven't for many years. This was my stab at writing a good Twilight Zone episode, as they often had plots which revolved around airplanes. I believe it to be a prequel to a much larger story.

CICADAS - My grandfather, George Kittredge, was a hoot. He taught me magic tricks in his cottage on Electric Avenue in Mountain City, used to show me movies like *Total Recall* that were arguably inappropriate for my age at the time, and did indeed tell me all these unsettling and wild stories about escaped convicts and killer bugs in the wilds of the surrounding Georgia landscape. He, like my other grandfather, was a WW2 Navy man and a total badass. Still, he, along with my cousins, thought it was funny to terrify me, and while in retrospect it was—at the time I felt it much less so. I miss him a lot.

# ABOUT THE AUTHOR

Purveyor of dread, bon vivant, and scribe of middling import, Patrick Kitson has been a lifelong student of the macabre, the satirical, and the intellectually dubious. Born and raised in The Roaring Fork Valley, he's coined the term, "Valley Horror" in reference to his particular brand of homebrewed speculative fiction which largely takes place in and around the snowy climes of Colorado.

www.ingramcontent.com/pod-product-compliance
Lightning Source LLC
Chambersburg PA
CBHW032021310726
48972CB00002B/489